Walking on Water

GRAHAM HAMER

MAY YOUR SAUSAGE SANDWICH NEVER GO COLD AND MAY YOUR CALVADOS NEVER GROW WARM,

THANKS FOR YOUR HELP!

GRAHAM

ISBN: 1530126738
ISBN-13: 978-1530126736

DEDICATION

This book is dedicated to Ian

I closed my eyes for a moment and suddenly a man stood where a boy used to be. I may not carry you now in my arms, but I will forever carry you in my heart. You have given me so many reasons to be proud of the man you have become, but the proudest moment for me is telling others that you are my son.

CONTENTS

ACKNOWLEDGMENTS

Thank you once more to my old buddy Oliver, for helping shape the skeleton, then mercilessly applying the scalpel. And thanks, too, to my friend and neighbour, Terry, who spent countless hours attached to a bottle of Calvados and a sausage sandwich, correcting my grammar and bad writing. I owe you both!

But where would I have been without Nadine Sgoura who went on the hunt for my typos, errors, omissions and plain bad writing. Nadine does this stuff for a living - and it shows. Her attention to detail deserves a special mention in dispatches and a commemorative medal.

CHAPTER ONE

Nick Ferris forced a smile onto his face. What he really wanted to do was to smack his customers' heads together, but that would have meant touching them and Nick's customers were largely untouchable - except for the girl in the shadows of the far corner who looked like she didn't want to be there either. No smile broke the straight lips of her red-painted mouth, which perched between eyes as blue as a Caribbean shoreline and breasts like plump aubergines in a vegetable market. Nick normally wouldn't have minded touching her at all, but he sensed that she was bad news for other reasons. And Brigitte, who knew everything that went on in the town, or at least everything illegal, had confirmed it to him earlier.

As for the rest of the customers, Nick wouldn't even want to get within spitting distance of them, given the choice. The fair-haired twenty-something perched on a barstool with his legs bent under him like ice tongs, who'd spent the evening spying on him without making eye contact. The heavy-shouldered man with a nose full of veins and a mouth full of sneers, whose Rottweiler dozed on the floor amongst the cigarette ash. It occupied the bar space of at least two grown men, but nobody was asking it to move. And Nick's least favourite, the heavily tattooed punk whose bottom lip was tormented by a wealth of ironmongery. He was a regular whose evenings habitually involved supping too much beer and offering packets of white powder to equally picturesque acquaintances. De Hardin's was a popular watering hole that assaulted your nose with hops and marijuana and disreputable low-lifes.

"Pardon?" Nick yelled, through the boom and thud of the speakers that shook the fabric of the building. As often happened when the volume was up, he was struggling to understand the shouted drinks orders with their strangled consonants and guttural 'g's. Strange words that a foreigner still found confusing. This evening, like so many others in the last six months, Nick had found it necessary to revert to English, the second language in The Netherlands, understood by everyone, even the stray dogs.

The fair-haired spy who lacked the art of surreptitious observation drained his beer, unwound his legs, and stood to leave, taking care not to disturb the Rottweiler. He reached into his hip pocket, pulled out a business card, and spun it across the bar to Nick. "Check out the Anglican church services in Rotterdam," he said, in near-perfect English, then turned towards the door.

From the darkened periphery of the room, Miss Red Lips' brow furrowed. She stood and zipped up her leather jacket, stopping to ease an overflowing morsel of plump aubergine into place before finishing the zipping process. One quick side step and she was out from behind the table.

Nick's attention was drawn by the card, which he struggled to decipher under the dim light. In italic script he could make out http://www.joinmychurch.com. No name, no title. He turned it over, instinctively expecting more. On the back, a handwritten jumble of letters and numbers that meant nothing to him.

He glanced towards the door that led directly onto the market place, but it swung emptily on its hinges. The young man had gone. With a shrug, Nick tucked the card into the pocket of his jeans and checked his watch. Just after midnight. Another two or three hours before he could clear up and go home to bed.

He looked up to see the heavy-breasted young lady leaving the bar, soft dark wig swaying across her leather-clad shoulders. When you're an experienced law-avoider, a clandestine cop is easy to spot. She acknowledged Nick with an almost imperceptible nod of the head. She'd caught him watching her, and the red-painted mouth smiled but the blue eyes didn't. He checked quickly to make sure she'd settled her tab. Police were an untrustworthy breed.

As she disappeared from sight, Nick eased open the door behind him just a few inches and slipped through the gap. It was done quickly, like he had turned himself into smoke and poured himself through the keyhole. Nick Ferris had the physique of an anorexic spider – ideal qualifications for slipping unobserved through narrow openings; usually into houses that didn't belong to him. He had what his lawyer had once described to the judge as a 'colourful' personality, though Nick could turn colours into shadows when he chose.

The door behind the bar led into a brick passage between De Hardin's and the adjacent shop that sold cheap jeans to cheap youths. The alleyway had long since absorbed the smells of rotting vegetables and urine. Followed by Faggot, his friend's dog, Nick walked quickly the few steps to where the murky side access met the hubbub of Grote Markt - the old market place that would throb with nocturnal activity for a few more hours yet before the beer-swilling, table-thumping, song-singing hoards decided to call it a night and stagger home to bed. The sky was dark and clear. Nick stopped, keeping his pale body in the shadows, and peered around the corner of the building. Faggot cocked his leg against a trashcan behind him.

The young man had gone, though the girl's back was still visible. She walked briskly along Vlamingstraat, her callipygous shadow waxing and waning under the neon streetlights that kept vigil over the locked shops. Nick glued his eyes to her rear until her swaying hips disappeared into the distant gloom, then he watched a few minutes longer before turning and stumbling back through the overflowing trash to the rear entrance of the bar. He had the unpleasant sensation, like a thousand sparrow wings in his gut that it was time to move on. He'd had fifty years practice in moving on.

As he eased open the door, the light of the bar spread into the dim night like a pie wedge, fading as it reached the opposite wall. A movement behind him caught his eye and he turned his head, straining to look into the deeply shadowed dead end of the alleyway. As his vision adjusted, he could make out a tall man with ponytail hair, leaning against one of the dustbins, his face contorted into a smiling grimace. Crouched in front of him was an off-white fur coat that contained Faggot's owner.

"Evening Brigitte." Nick called.

The coat grunted, while its client opened his eyes and stared at Nick through rimless glasses.

Nick closed the door behind him, leaving Brigitte and the punter in peace. It was going to be another busy night.

Half-an-hour later, Miss Red Lips stepped out from the shop doorway in Geleenstraat and checked her watch. Anthrax now appeared to be safely tucked in bed. It was too late to go and disturb the boss. She could bring him up to speed tomorrow. For now, she had two options. She could go back to De Hardin's and retrieve the card off the English barman, or she could go home, get some sleep, and leave things to develop further. Probably best to let events move on, she thought. After all, if there was no crime there could be no confrontation. And after previous warnings it seemed that only confrontation would stop Anthrax now.

* * *

The quay was deserted. Its floodlit ramparts sulked silently as the car ferry manoeuvred alongside. Despite its morose appearance and his own depression, George Riley deemed it to be considerably more inviting than the docks at Dover where he had spent the earlier part of the evening avoiding one of Big Jack's thugs. George hadn't planned to arrive in Calais at such an ungodly hour - in fact, he hadn't planned to arrive in France at all. He had tried to reason with Big Jack about his debts; restructuring, George had called it; Jack had called it bloody theft and, like Shylock, he wanted his pound of flesh.

Though George's girth held a considerable surfeit of

flesh, much of which he could afford to lose, he had become rather attached to it and had every intention of keeping it that way. He leaned his bulk on the ferry rail.

A cloud of diesel fumes hung heavy in the night as the ship's engines beat in reverse to bring the vessel to a halt. Momentarily, the cool wind changed direction and the smell of grease and hamburgers floated on the breeze from the galley below. George sniffed. He could have sworn they were doing it to annoy him. It felt like he hadn't eaten for days.

But his concern now was to avoid whatever brother Jack had in store for him. France, Germany, or even sheep-shagging Australia was preferable to staying in Britain with his brother on the rampage. Big Jack had made that abundantly clear to him when, twenty-four hours earlier, George's sleep had been rudely interrupted by the sound of a pair of size fifty boots kicking down his front door.

Not without some enlightened forethought, George's bedroom door had been locked and bolted. It was a habit he had acquired during his teenage years in the tough East End of London, and which he'd reacquired as soon as Jack had insisted on immediate settlement of the debt. The strengthened steel bolts gave George just enough time to grab his clothes, hurl the window open, and have it away through the undergrowth, his fleshy extremities struggling desperately to keep up. As he charged through his neighbour's vegetable patch, he heard the smash and crash of his bedroom door being demolished.

George Riley was built like a bathyscaphe, with a stomach that touched his thighs and a backside that surrounded his knees. In addition, his legs were not aerodynamically designed for the somewhat athletic activity of toeing it. It was fortunate, therefore, that his would-be-assailant chose to search the house before looking outside, otherwise the outcome might have proved more final. George stopped to dress only when he found himself in a small wood a mile from his home, but not before a surge of angry nettles had swiped his legs and feet into a rash of puffy flesh.

The ensuing daylight hours turned into a high-adrenalin game of hide and seek, making his escape from a tenacious bruiser who was never far from his heels. Using the protection of the crowd, George managed to catch an early morning flight from his island home and, sweating like a prize-fighter, he found his way to Dover on England's south coast where he succeeded in stowing his torso onto the cross-channel ferry to France. Always too close for comfort was the man with a knife; intent on removing his liver and delivering it in person to Big Jack. The only thing that had stopped him was finding the opportunity to fillet George in private with nobody else around.

It had been a close call at Dover. At one point, the guy was just a few yards behind, waiting for the right opportunity, next minute he had disappeared and George, wearing a 'borrowed' high visibility vest with 'Port of Dover' printed on the back, had siphoned himself into the ferry's cargo bay while no one was looking.

Now, as the ship docked, he was ready to set foot on foreign soil. He sucked in a deep breath to clear his head, and stared sadly down a flight of double chins to his grumbling stomach. George Riley was never the best-dressed beau in town, but tonight he looked as though he had declared war even on average tailoring. Buttons were ready to explode and his fly zip was several notches short of home. George and his shiny suit had creases in places where other people didn't even have places.

He was a mess.

All thanks to Big Jack.

George hated his brother Jack.

He had hated his brother Jack for as long as he could remember.

He hated Jack more now than he ever had in his life.

"Big Fat Bastard" he mouthed to the empty quay.

Jack had given him good reason to hate him. Jack was two minutes older than George and had never let him forget it. If there was any bossing to do, Jack had done it. Suffering had been George's speciality – from which he had found sanctuary in gambling. And losing had been a weakness that had led to him being on this boat in the early hours trying to avoid a man with a knife.

George felt in his pocket to see if a stray sweet had found its way into the fluff at the bottom. He was disappointed. But nowhere near as disappointed as Jack was going to be when he got the news that George had escaped. Big Jack had long arms though, and an even longer memory, particularly where money was concerned. There would never be a time when George would feel safe again.

The hired thug had given George little chance to gather many of his belongings and now his only assets were the clothes he stood in, his passport, driving licence, a few bits of loose change, and a tiny red note-book that might yet save his life.

It had been a long time since he'd been involved in petty theft, preferring the less personal and slightly more lucrative world of illegal substances and misplaced credit cards. But now it seemed he would need to brush up on some of his former skills in order to survive. He'd manage. Low budget survival wasn't new to him. On the other hand, running for his life was, and the concern was evident on his face.

The boat's engines stopped. George coughed as his nostrils registered a different smell. With the vaporisation of the diesel and ship's food into the night air, there was nothing left to mask the sour bouquet of his own sweat.

Unable to shake off the feeling that he was still being watched, he glanced over his shoulder at the commercial vehicle drivers who were descending to the lower decks to be reunited with their lorries. He turned away from the handrail. Adopting the heavy Irish blarney that he reserved for anonymous situations, it would take only a few minutes to find a driver who wanted a bit of company during the early morning hours – as long as the driver didn't have a sense of smell. When the sun rose, it would be the first day of May. Hopefully an early summer would bring warmer weather, it would make the next few weeks a little more tolerable.

CHAPTER TWO

Polite silence was Sandy Ferris' only weapon as Theo Padmos lectured her on the bright future she was throwing away. As he spoke, she tried to upside-down read the printout of her account, which Theo had been studying when she had entered the interview room. Not that it caused her any concern; she knew exactly what was on it. She stifled a yawn, stared at the silhouettes of the shoppers passing by the window that overlooked Wagenstraat, and wondered when he would arrive at the predictable part of the speech. With Theo, it was only a matter of time.

"What will you do for an income?" he asked.

"I'll find something," she replied, in a croaky, broken voice. "Once I've got over this depression."

"Are you sure the bank can't do something to help? A few days leave of absence is quite in order in situations like this."

Sandy examined her cherry red fingernails and exhaled noisily. "I think it will take more than a few days," she said, with the long-practised skill of an expert worrier. "I just have to get away from the routine and the pressure. I know it's short notice, but I really can't handle the tension of working here any longer."

Theo sighed in sympathy, flicking back a wispy hank of custard-yellow hair that had fallen like the finger of a neglected glove over his rimless glasses. "I'll hold vigil for you," he said. "We'll all hold vigil for you. The Great Mother works in…"

A smile flickered across Sandy's face and was gone, like a rustle of wind in a cornfield. The predictable Theo had arrived and she struggled to keep her lips pursed as he expanded his theories on the mysterious ways of his sect's mystic-guide. Sandy was relieved that today was a spectacle day, not a monocle day. If it had been a monocle day, she would probably have surrendered to one of her renowned giggling fits.

To occupy her mind until she could politely leave, Sandy tried to imagine bedding the chief cashier. That kept the smile off her face. Theo was embarrassingly tall, short-sighted in one eye, and had a permanently moist chin where excitable spittle found a home until he wiped it off with his handkerchief. He didn't really have a proper face. People had trouble recognising him without his monocle or his silly hat.

Theo had not yet reached thirty; an age when most upwardly-mobile chief cashiers would have jumped at the opportunity to offer close physical comfort to a nubile twenty-seven year old bank clerk with long, black hair and café au lait complexion, who was seemingly on the verge of a nervous breakdown. But Theo blushed easily and was an eager servant of

The Lord. Or at least his version of The Lord. Theo was also so besotted with his fiancée, Joska, that he fervently averted his eyes from any other hormonal temptation. Or tried to.

"... so when you commit your life to The Great Mother..."

Sandy stood to cut him short and end the interview. Game over. She had better things to do. "Thank you for your prayers," she said in an intentional monotone. "I'm sure they'll be of great comfort to me in the weeks ahead," She bent to pick up her handbag and give Theo one last chance to secretly examine the parts of her anatomy that were not normally revealed in public. She had a firm, rounded bottom, like grown-up billiard balls in a velvet bag, but she was beginning to wonder whether Theo would recognise an erection if he sat on it. It was an entertaining diversion trying to give him one, though. Her own worldview was that if you didn't die from it, it was healthy - and she'd lived a very healthy life.

Ex-employee Ferris straightened again and caught Theo eyeing up the space that the tops of her stockings had just occupied. The bank's chief cashier had been watching her from the corner of his eye for weeks. There was nothing unusual about that since, dressed in her normal short skirt, she would often bend double like a pocket knife to reach into the bottom drawer of a filing cabinet just for the fun of hooking him into a forbidden thought as he peered at her through his rimless spectacles or monocle.

Poor Theo, she thought. Like a worm-infested apple, he was riddled with the sexual turmoil that comes free with every Calvinist upbringing, and membership of his religious cult didn't seem to improve the situation any. He was a nearly man, a certified supporter of living today for tomorrow, and he didn't stand a chance in the real world. Sandy knew that looking was as bad as thinking was as bad as doing in his book.

Recently, though, the look had changed. Not enough to be noticed by other members of the staff, but enough for Sandy to know that it was time to leave before she was caught. Her instincts had seldom let her down in the past and now she knew that it would be prudent to evaporate silently into the shadows before he called her integrity into question and delved too deeply into her activities. Apart from that, her father also suspected that they were being watched, and her father's hunches were usually as good as her own.

After six months working for Alliance Bank, her secret account at a rival bank showed a very healthy balance whilst her account printout at Alliance reflected exactly the normal lifestyle of a humble bank clerk.

Sandy bade him farewell, her employment terminated.

"God speed," Theo said, wiping the spittle off his chin. "Get well soon."

She was sure that she would.

* * *

Over sixty percent of The Netherlands lay below sea level. Many centuries ago when all the high ground was cultivated, men grew food for their families on small pieces of swampland by draining away the water with ditches that led to a river or the sea. Unfortunately, on Spring and Autumn tides, the land flooded again and they had to start all over. In the eleventh century the resourceful Dutch began to construct earth banks to hold back the water and protect their cultivated ground. Over time they improved their dike-building techniques and methods of drawing away the water, and The Netherlands was now as dry as the constant rain allowed.

The big sloop-shouldered Dutchman pulled his tractor and trailer to a halt at the end of the track where a hand-painted sign said Welcome to Hans Brinker in four languages, though reading it was becoming progressively more difficult as the nails that held the sign together left trails of rust over the flaking paint. Beyond the sign, the Hans Brinker Campsite occupied an artificial polder – reclaimed land that had once been drained by nineteen windmills, lifting water through stepped channels into the River Lek. The remaining windmills were tourist attractions now, as mega-voltage electric pumps had long since taken over the task.

The owner of the Hans Brinker campsite, who looked like the frayed and faded work denims that he wore had forty years previously bet on the fact that the economic advantages of tents and touring caravans would outweigh the smell of cow dung and wet hay. He had been right. After planting a few fast-growing cypresses and erecting a primitive toilet block that still housed their 1970's sanitary fittings, he had named the camping site after himself and opened for business. He told anybody who cared enough to enquire that the site was named after the

Hero of Haarlem, an eight-year-old boy who, according to folklore, had saved the entire country from flooding by sticking his finger into a leaky dike until help arrived.

Good job too because, from his perch on his tractor at the entrance to the site, the real Hans Brinker could only look upwards over his nailbrush moustache at the ships and tugs and barges that plied the huge river twenty feet above his head. This was no clear country stream meandering its way slowly across a marshy pasture; this was a wide, dirty, working river that took the water drained from the flatlands of the huge isthmus and discharged it harmlessly into the North Sea. Billions of tons of water held back by an earth bank no more than a hundred feet wide at the base. He knew it was only a hundred feet – he'd calculated it.

By his own estimate, The Netherlands would be ten percent smaller if the mighty Lek were allowed to obey the natural rules of gravity. But he never voiced this opinion to his neighbours; the fragility of their existence was something about which the antlophobic Dutch did not like to be reminded. Anyway, his neighbours never spoke to him.

Phthook.

With uncanny accuracy, he ejected a glob of spit onto an adjacent cowpat as he leaned down and took fifty euros in small change off the fat Englishman who had arrived on foot with a rolled-up tent under his arm. Hans pointed him to the far corner of the site where he hoped he wouldn't see him again until the following week when he could charge him another fifty euros. He left the Englishman to his own devices, parked his tractor next to the barn and strode away. He had things to do and only a few weeks to do them in.

George Riley was pleased to get rid of some of the coins. Notes were easier to hide. He had borrowed the money from a lady's purse in the supermarket in Kinderdijk, along with some personal papers and credit cards it had contained.

The Hans Brinker polder looked like just the right place to pitch his new tent, which he had just dismantled from another campsite taking care to ensure that it wasn't occupied at the time. It looked like the sort of place where, if a sparrow fell out of a tree, everybody would stop what they were doing to take a look and hold a post mortem discussion. The sort of place that made George's quiet island home look like an urban Mecca. But, in its favour, it was just the sort of anonymous backwater where he could rest his aching bones until the heat died down.

Not that George was under any illusion that the heat would ever die down. The only sort of dying his brother understood was the terminal variety. It had nothing to do with forgiving or forgetting. Big Jack wouldn't give you the steam off his porridge, the bastard.

George hammered home the last tent peg with a wet stone and, with difficulty, straightened up and wiped the perspiration from his forehead with the back of his hand. Hypocritical to think of Jack as a bastard. They were both the illegitimate sons of some testosterone-rich father whom they'd never known. And they were as alike as peas in a pod. "You're just like a pair of light bulbs." their mother would chuckle. "Different power output, but you've got to read the label to spot the difference."

After their mother's premature death they'd discovered papa's name, but papa claimed to have an alibi on the night of their conception so Big Jack exercised his usual charm and had him neutered without an anaesthetic, just so he couldn't do it again. Nice guy, Jack.

If only papa hadn't been in such a hurry to find a nice little Jack egg to fertilise. If only Jack and he had been born a few years apart. But no such luck. George had long endured the mistaken identity that frequents identical twins. For normal twins, such mistakes were of little consequence but, with a twin brother like Big Jack Riley, mistaken identity carried a government health warning. At best it could prove painful: at worst, life-threatening.

The last five years had been the most carefree of George's unproductive life. At the age of thirty-two, he had relinquished his God-given duty to take beatings that had been meant for his brother and had escaped the grimy streets of East London. Ever since then, he had led a near blameless existence - for a fat, Irish scallywag with a penchant for borrowing things. But now there was no refuge, not even on his island home. Now he was on the move again and suddenly the world was full of tiny flakes of whispery snow, dancing about in the wind like a plague of white insects. He shivered and glanced up at the clouds that looked as though they might descend on his head at any moment.

Thanks Jack.

* * *

Rolien van der Laan rested her fingers on her boyfriend's shoulders and watched blocks of numeric code squirm across the computer screen. As each line appeared, the screen scrolled down another row like regimented lines of white figures marching double-time before melting into a tangle of jagged edges.

Anthrax shook his head and tutted. "Pity; with his daughter's job, that barman at De Hardin's should have access to some juicy accounts."

Rolien massaged his shoulders in a circular motion. "Never mind, it's only been three days. Why don't I see what I can do to compensate."

"Like another little siesta?" he muttered, leaning forwards to examine some code he had written earlier.

"Well, if you don't want to…" she said, letting her hands drop to her sides.

Anthrax tucked his legs under him on the chair, tabbed to his e-mail programme and scanned through the note that had just arrived.

"What is it?" Rolien asked. "Another message from your friend, The Redeemer?"

Anthrax – Hjalmar Linnekar in public – ignored her. "Looks like he's getting closer to resolving it."

"Resolving what?"

"Proving the existence of one-way functions."

Rolien tutted. He could have been talking about

time worms in space for all she knew.

"It makes Graph Isomorphism look like a kindergarten question," Hjalmar said, face absorbed into the screen. "He's bright, The Redeemer. If we pooled our resources, we could probably sort it out. "

"So why don't you?"

Hjalmar shrugged, uncurled his legs, and headed for the kitchen. "You want a beer?" he called.

Rolien deliberately ignored him - he knew she only drank Martinis. She stuck out her tongue at the computer, which, along with its associated wires, modems and god-knows-what gadgetry, occupied one whole corner of the living room. She hated the computer community's use of silly pseudonyms and she hated his computer. Not because she didn't understand what he did on it all day, but because it apparently needed all his time and all his attention.

Computers were Anthrax's thing. They were his vehicle, his weapon, his agent, his whole world, the ecosystem within which he thrived – and from which Rolien was excluded. To her boyfriend, his computer was the tool for creating his JoinMyChurch programme and for writing nasty little viruses that he linked to it, so that they would lodge into the networks of the big banks and financial institutions and cause a bit of unnecessary disruption.

She had no issue with the moral aspect of Hjalmar's activities, just the amount of time he spent glued to the screen. Time that could have been more pleasurably spent in her bed.

Rolien stared out of the window at the monotonous sky that reflected her monotonous life. Mostly, it rained in The Netherlands. When it didn't, it was just a tedious land without shadows. Like living inside a Tupperware box. Below her upper floor window, the glazed cobbles of Geleenstraat were impatient for their evening transformation when they reflected the pink fluorescent lights of working girls' windows and the green and brown banknotes of pimps' wallets.

During the day, Geleenstraat was as quiet as a dose of Valium. It was only about seventy-five metres long, but every centimetre of it belonged to Rolien – along with numerous other assorted houses and apartments that she had inherited four years earlier at the age of twenty-two. In addition to property, Rolien was heir to her mother's stunning good looks and her father's nose for a sound business deal, and she wasn't averse to using either asset to increase the financial stability that had been dropped into her lap when an untimely road accident had left her alone in the world. Financial stability was the only kind of stability she had known apart from Hjalmar, and she had guarded it well. The forty-odd houses and apartments left to her by her parents had increased to sixty-eight in only four years, and, in a country the size of a shoebox, where seventeen million people were causing the sides to bulge under the strain, property was a highly prized commodity.

Her maudlin thoughts were disturbed as Hjalmar stepped back through the kitchen door.

"Just going out a minute," he said, "then we'll see what we can do about those tax assessments."

Rolien nodded. If he wasn't in her bed, she didn't

much care what he did. The outer door banged closed and Rolien peered through the window again. Her boyfriend marched to the end of the street, head down against the wind. Rolien's own head lowered in unison as she wondered whether Hjalmar's computer skills could save her from the wrath of the Internal Revenue this time.

During the two years that Rolien and Hjalmar had been together, she had never seen a telephone bill, an electricity bill, a gas bill, or indeed any other kind of bill for any of her properties. Her boyfriend's ability to plunder and amend the electronic records of the various authorities had seen to that. If only he could do the same for the income tax. Apart from her lover's obsession with his computer, the only burdensome cloud on Rolien's horizon was the constant threat of finding a bailiff standing on her doorstep wielding a warrant for her arrest.

The tax authorities had been sceptical about the low declared income from such a large portfolio of property and had sent a strongly worded suggestion that she might like to reassess the situation before filing her next tax return. Rolien had no intention of reassessing the situation. In fact, since Hjalmar had so far been unable to alter the figures for her, she had no intention of being in The Netherlands by the end of the year when the next tax return was due. It was time to sell up and move on.

Though she had been brought up amongst the gabled architecture and watery landscape, she would be just as much at home on Curaçao or Bonaire or St. Maarten in the Dutch Antilles. They, too, had adopted the gingerbread houses, the canals, the Lego roads, traffic lights and prostitution. But, to a wealthy, sun-loving, sexually active twenty-six year old, the tax advantages and year-round topless bathing seemed infinitely more attractive than the rain, high fiscal burdens and puritanical undertow of The Netherlands.

Rolien reached down, picked up Marcus Foyer's business card, and twirled it around in her fingers. She breathed out. Almost another sigh. Somewhere between resignation and relief, but neither one nor the other. She watched with detached fascination as the card whirled around her fingers. It was a card that her favourite lawyer had given her, with the promise that the estate agent could be trusted to carry out her wishes. Her lawyer was good at these things. She'd warned Rolien that it wasn't going to be easy selling so many properties without attracting the unwanted attention of the government, but that she'd used this particular real estate agent before and found him to be reliable and discreet. As attractive a legal mind as one could possibly hope to stumble across, her lawyer had winked when she'd told Rolien that she might also appreciate some of Marcus Foyer's other talents. She was not, it seemed, restricted to mental agility. The physical side obviously acquitted itself with the same enthusiasm.

Rolien took charge of her fingers, and dropped the card back onto the coffee table. She examined a chipped fingernail on her left hand. After her introductory phone call earlier in the week, the estate agent had called round and discussed tactics and, judging by his none-too-subtle flirting, it would probably be a good idea to do a bit of primping and preening before she met him again. Anyway, Hjalmar had complained that her broken nail had scratched his back last night and she certainly wanted to keep him happy. Despite his love affair with computers, he provided the only bit of equilibrium in her sometimes haphazard life. She'd not approached him yet about disappearing to the Dutch Antilles with her. As long as there was plenty of electronic gadgetry there, she was sure he wouldn't mind.

* * *

So this one's recently become available?" Sandy asked stepping onto the fourth floor balcony.

"Just got instructions yesterday," replied Marcus Foyer, the real estate agent. "The whole building, six apartments, is up for sale though, so the lease is only short term. Three months maximum."

"Suits me fine," Sandy said, looking across the rooftops of the shops opposite. The old town centre had grown haphazardly two centuries earlier, and the buildings were imperfectly vertical and impossibly misaligned. Some of the older ones were held together only by force of habit, tottering so far over that the only thing keeping them from crashing into the shopping street below was that the street wasn't big enough for them to crash into. Sandy knew the neighbourhood well. It was like a village within a city; cobbled alleyways and ancient real estate stretching erratically as far as the Binnenhof parliament buildings half a mile away.

Ten turns of a bicycle wheel to Sandy's left, the paving stones of Vlamingstraat led into Grote Markt, the old market square filled with wicker tables and chairs. At the first sign of any blue sky the locals would chain their bikes together, ten deep, and sit and drink coffee or beer in the open, even when temperatures demanded snow boots, ski hats and thermal knickers. They were hardy folk, the Dutch, and God help anyone who wanted to unlock their bike and leave early.

"You'll take it then?" Marcus Foyer asked, disturbing her thoughts.

Sandy looked him up and down quickly. His skin was attractively weathered rather than tanned and, though far from overtly muscular, his body had that sinewy, taut look of fitness that suggested someone who was content with his physical home. His eyes told her more. Here was a man she could do business with.

"How much for cash?"

"You know we can't do that. There are laws against it."

"And you're telling me you're not prepared to bend a law or two to help the landlord?"

"Landlady," he corrected. "You're English aren't you?"

Sandy nodded.

"So you probably don't work for the Internal Revenue then."

She laughed and patted him good-humouredly on the shoulder. "Do I look like a tax inspector?"

"Dunno. What does a tax inspector look like?"

"Short-sighted, bald, wobbly belly."

"Then I can assure you that you look nothing like a tax inspector. Or if you are, you're the best looking one I've ever had the good fortune to stumble across."

"Tell you what," Sandy said, still smiling, "why don't you take me for a drink and we'll talk about how much discount you're going to give me if I give your client three months cash in advance? I'm sure you'll be able to claim it on expenses."

"Sounds good to me," said Marcus Foyer, reaching for his wallet.

CHAPTER THREE

With his left hand, Theo furtively made the sign to ward off evil as the senior bank inspector dropped into the manager's chair, his unsmiling colleague sitting next to him in a chair meant for visitors. The inspector stared at Theo's monocle. "Why did you call us here?"

The bank manager, standing next to Theo, on the other side of the desk intervened. "Mijnheer Padmos, explain your suspicions please."

Theo took a deep breath. He'd known for a few days that they would have to call in the bank's inspectors, but knowing that didn't make it any easier now he was face to face with them across the desk in the manager's office. A strand of yellow hair began to weld itself to his forehead, and a bead of perspiration trickled onto his eyebrow. Theo's voice was faltering "One of our staff, an English woman called Sandy Ferris, has gone missing. We suspect that she may have been doing something dishonest but we can't prove it. A week ago she left the bank without giving notice. She said she was on the verge of a nervous breakdown."

"But you don't think she was?"

"Was what?"

"Having a nervous breakdown."

Theo hesitated. "I did at the time."

"But not now?"

"No, not now."

The bank inspector waited for him to continue. Theo didn't realise until the manager prompted him. "Perhaps you'd like to share with us why you've become suspicious," he suggested.

Theo peeked round his monocle at him as though the answer was obvious; after all, he'd explicated it all to his manager the day before. "Her home phone has been disconnected. I tried to telephone her to see if her health was improving but the phone seems to have been cut off, so I called round to her apartment but there was no reply." He didn't like to admit that he had called to see her because he rather missed having her around. He hadn't even admitted it to himself yet. "One of the neighbours said she thought Miss Ferris had moved out. She saw her and her father leave their apartment carrying suitcases."

"And you say that you only suspect that she may have been doing something wrong?"

"We have no firm evidence," Theo replied. "That's why we waited. We were watching her to see what we could find out."

"Who's we?"

Theo looked at his manager to lend a hand. The manager kept his arms folded across his chest, his hands tucked into his armpits. "Me," Theo said eventually. "I was watching her."

"For how long?"

"About two months," he muttered to the shine on his shoes.

"How long?"

"About two months."

The inspector made a note on his pad; stabbing his pencil on the paper to make sure the 'I' was dotted and the 't' was crossed. "And when did you make your manager aware of the situation?"

Theo looked again at his manager who answered for him in a voice like grated lemon. "I was appraised of the situation yesterday," he said. "I called you immediately."

"Well at least somebody knows how to read a rule book," the inspector said. "Tell me, Mijnheer Padmos, what do you suspect this Sandy Ferris might have been up to?"

"I really don't know."

"But you must have had reason to be suspicious."

"Yes. It was something that a client of the bank said – a client who is also a friend of mine. He and I worship together."

A pause.

"Go on."

"He told me that the English woman who worked here had bought five rather expensive watches at his shop."

"Five?"

"Five. Expensive. That's what made me suspicious."

"And how did Miss Ferris pay for these watches?"

"Er… I didn't ask him," Theo mumbled. "I just assumed it was cash because I checked Miss Ferris's account and there was no sign that she had used her card or paid with a cheque." Theo was beginning to wish he'd never said anything to his manager. It would have been easier to forget the whole business, but things weren't that simple once you'd let The Great Mother into your life. The Great Mother had truth rules and honesty rules and don't look at women rules and lots of other rules, and they all had to be observed. There were times when Theo would gladly have disobeyed them. And now he was beginning to wish that he had.

"So you just assumed she was stealing cash?"

Theo reached for his handkerchief and wiped his chin. "I suppose I did. Yes."

"And did it ever cross your mind, Mijnheer Padmos, that we balance cash receipts and withdrawals to the exact cent every day?"

"Of course, that's why I was puzzled," His chin was

wet again.

"So did it not dawn on you that stealing cash was probably not her Modus Operandi?"

"But how else could she have done it?"

"That, sir, is what we are employed to find out. Now, thanks to your amateurish attempts to play Sherlock Holmes, we shall probably never know." The inspector addressed himself to the manager. "When was the last time you had a full internal audit?"

"About three years ago."

"Another one has just begun. Please vacate your office until it is over. Advise your staff that the audit is routine." He turned his attention back to Theo. "Do not tell anybody the real reason for us being here, enough damage has already been done."

Theo nodded, shifted uncomfortably and bowed his head, concentrating on the design on the carpet, while his manager dry-washed his hands in a manner that suggested to Theo that he was not a happy bank manager. Not a happy bank manager at all.

"First of all," said the inspector, "we shall want a print out of Miss Ferris's bank account. How long has she worked here?"

"Almost six months."

"Okay, bring me the whole six month's details."

Theo looked up. "There's nothing in it that will give

you any clues. I've already looked. It's just an ordinary account for someone on her range of salary."

The inspector thumped the desk with a beefy fist, causing Theo to stand bolt upright like a newly-erected fence post. "Mijnheer Padmos, it is due to your negligence that we may be too late to stop theft from happening. It is due to your crass incompetence that the suspect appears to have flown before we could get a chance to talk to her. It is due to your simple-mindedness that, if there is a loophole in the bank's procedures, it remains undiscovered and unplugged." He paused for breath. He didn't pause long. "I give you warning, sir, that your own position as chief cashier at the bank is precarious to say the least. You would do yourself a great service if you stopped playing detective and got on with the job for which we pay you."

In the silence that followed, the hostile atmosphere crackled like summer lightning. Theo's monocle fell to his chest where it dangled forlornly at the end of its cord, and the bead of sweat that had perched on his eyebrow finally abandoned ship. His legs were shaking and his hands clenched into fists as he fought the tremble in his voice. "I'll get you the print-outs," he said, hurrying from the room with the air of someone ducking bullets.

"Damn her," he muttered under his breath. It was as near as he'd ever come to swearing. He slammed the door behind him, and stomped across the banking hall to his own desk.

Damn Sandy Ferris. Damn and damn. He'd worked for Alliance Bank since leaving school and he'd never been spoken to in such a manner. Damn her and damn the bank inspectors too. He'd only done his job. He'd worked and studied hard to get the chief cashier post and he had a managerial position in his sights. What sort of reward was this?

Suddenly, in the space of time that it took him to brush his teeth before going to bed, his career progression had fallen under threat. Theo understood enough about bank philosophy to know that only serious breaches of conduct were punishable by a verbal admonishment such as the one he'd just suffered. He also knew that such a strong scolding could, and almost certainly would, lead to a written caution.

If he didn't sort things out quickly, he would receive a letter one day soon, his file would be marked and graded by the inspectors, and he'd have no further promotions to aim for. He remembered his friend, Ronnie, who had mislaid a batch of internal memos and had been moved to one of the quiet country branches where the day's most exciting event was farmer Bob banking the proceeds from selling a cow. He didn't want to consider the consequences when Joska found out about it. She'd often told him how she dreamed of being the wife of someone important in the community, and now it was all going pear-shaped. And the whole thing was Sandy Ferris's fault.

Theo sat despondently with his head in his hands. His throat was dry and burned like sandpaper. A bespectacled middle-aged lady with a puppy face and Barbie Doll eyelashes placed a coffee in front of him. She touched him lightly on the shoulder then floated away again to re-sort the papers she'd already sorted twice. Theo was grateful for her concern. Clearly the whole bank had heard the uproar from the manager's office. A younger lady, one who wore sensible dresses, gave him an embarrassed smile before staring intently at her finger nails and humming a little tune to herself. But Theo didn't want their pity; he just wanted to redeem himself in the bank's eyes.

In his own way, Theo had always considered himself to be a man of action, and action was what was needed now. He would find Sandy Ferris and turn her over to the authorities; redeem himself, career unchecked. He glanced at the face of the big white clock that told the time in six different countries. He'd take an early lunch and track her down. Now wasn't the time for prudence. Now was the time for measures. He wiped his chin, even though it was only his thoughts that were excited.

Had he known the effect that his quest would have on his sheltered world, he might have been a little less impulsive, but he shook off all thoughts of caution like water from a wet dog. Theo was not renowned for over-meditating on such issues. Make a decision – get on with it. Even if it was a bad decision.

As he twiddled with the silver medallion that hung round his neck, he knew that success would be his. After all, he had a secret weapon. He had The Great Mother on his side.

But maybe he should have reminded The Great Mother whose side she was on first. Because, six hours after his reprimand and his decision to take action, Theo's spiritual guide still appeared not to have noticed that she was Theo's secret weapon. The chief cashier watched the clock tick at snail's pace towards the hour when the big hand and the little hand would be in a vertical line; then he could go home and close his eyes and ease his headache.

Sandy Ferris was proving more elusive than he had at first imagined. Maybe he should have planned it better. Maybe he had been a little impulsive. But who could blame him when the bank inspector had raised his voice and been rude to him in front of his manager?

As he massaged his temples, the day's activities played back through Theo's head. During an extended lunch break, which his manager had quite unnecessarily commented on when he had finally returned, Theo had stretched his friendship with a civil servant in the Stadhuis - the Town Hall – who checked the records for any trace of his missing cashier, only to tell him that she'd probably left The Netherlands. Then he visited the Justice Department claiming to be Sandy's long lost brother. There, the police officer, who never bothered to ask Theo for his credentials, was unable to give him anything other than the address at which she'd been registered - the address that he already knew.

Maybe it was The Great Mother's way of letting Theo know that he should stop telling untruths. Maybe The Great Mother could see his crossed fingers. Of course she could. The Great Mother saw everything. The Great Mother was listening to his thoughts like a radio ham scanning the airwaves. But surely The Great Mother would understand, because Theo was a good believer really and he knew that The Great Mother loved him. The Reverend van Aanroy had told him so.

As the clock shambled towards the hour, Theo suddenly felt very alone. How could he tell his fiancée, Joska, about the events of the day? He couldn't, that's how. He couldn't tell Joska lest she, too, reprimanded him for not having reported the matter sooner. One castigation a day was more than enough, and he knew that Joska could be even more plain-spoken than the bank inspector had been. His only allies now were The Great Mother and the Reverend van Aanroy. Since The Great Mother seemed to be annoyed with him for not respecting the truth, it probably wasn't the best time to be bothering her with his Sandy Ferris problem. Maybe Reverend van Aanroy could help.

To hell with waiting for six o'clock to arrive. Twenty minutes early, Theo shut down his computer monitor, screwed his monocle in place, and left the bank.

An hour later, with one eye on his watch, Reverend van Aanroy bade Theo a curt goodbye and closed the door. Probably a little too abruptly. His mouth was tight as he crossed the lounge towards his modest study. It tightened even more when he discovered that the television documentary he had been watching had finished and been replaced by a weather chart covered in rain icons. How unusual.

Ignoring normal Dutch tradition, which dictated that curtains should never be drawn lest the building's occupants were tempted towards wickedness, and even though it was still light outside, the Reverend pulled his window shutters tight and swung the heavy iron bar into the locking cradles. Taking care not to damage the precision curve of his fingernails, he untied the white tasselled cord around his waist and slipped his royal blue gown over his head. Underneath, he wore jeans and a faded yellow T-shirt - not something that was generally known by Theo or the rest of his flock. Preserving image was just one of the necessities of life for an evangelical cult leader.

He threw the gown and cord onto a nearby chair and switched off the television. Thanks to Theo's round-the-houses conversation, he never would find out whether the documentary offered any useful tips as to how to improve his bank balance. What he had seen before his doorbell rang had been interesting, but as depressing as the weather synopsis. Depressing that the American Bible Belt bestowed such wealth on its pulpit-bashing leaders whilst the thrifty Dutch faithful, Theo Padmos included, had to have their euros squeezed out of them like pips from a lemon. The television commentator had been biased of course. He'd been too quick to point out certain apparent discrepancies in the churches' bookkeeping, and had even suggested – strike that from the record and substitute accused - he'd even accused some of the homespun pastors of using offshore banking facilities to launder their money.

Van Aanroy cursed. If only he needed a laundry. But his own followers totalled no more than fifty regular devotees who were hardly likely to provide him with the lifestyle of his televised Yankee counterparts, no matter how much fire and brimstone he poured on their already smouldering heads. It seemed mighty unjust that the American Jesus could kick ass, whilst here in The Hague he had to adopt a different, more-gentle approach to encourage money onto the collecting plate. Fortunately, a large portion of van Aanroy's income came from other sources.

He crossed the room and, from force of habit, secured the door that led to the living room beyond. Though his street door was locked, there were too many secrets in his study to take any chances - secrets that would prove more than embarrassing if ever they were discovered. A large double mortise and three shoot bolts were enough to make sure he wouldn't be disturbed. Stepping to his left, he lifted the abstract oil painting from the wall and stood it next to the television, which had turned itself back on. The painting – post-impressionist, they called it – was one that he had discovered in a yard sale for five euros. It was intended to represent an old woman with a staff. For some reason, the amateur artist had painted a Celtic Cross on the woman's forehead and, for van Aanroy, it had spawned the idea for his sect's motif. It had also, later, spawned the concept that The Great Mother had visionary powers and that she bore the mark for all to see. One of the joys of being sect leader was that you didn't have to remember your own lies; you could just make them up as you went along.

Spinning the dial on the door of the wall safe that had been concealed behind the painting, van Aanroy looked forward to the consolation he would find in counting his cash – just as he did after every busy weekend. This evening he'd been delayed by the voluble Theo Padmos twittering about a missing cashier. God, the things he had to put up with to earn a dishonest crust.

He pushed aside a cardboard box containing silver Celtic Cross medallions and some other tools of his trade, then felt under a pile of buff folders. His hand emerged clutching a leather-bound pocket diary. Flipping the pages, he turned to Monday May 9 and began to write.

He'd checked his Internet site earlier. He'd set it up six months before with great hopes for its financial success, but, after an initial flurry of activity, it had now sunk to new depths. Just one credit card donation this week – twenty-five euros. What a waste of effort. He noted the amount in his diary.

Despite the best efforts of Mevrouw Modderkolk – an elephantine creature with oversized ears and an unfortunate outcrop of top lip hair, who dutifully rattled collecting boxes under people's noses - the week's gospel singing had netted a meagre one hundred and thirty two euros for the missionary work of one Isaiah Sesambokoko.

The good Reverend, in a rare moment of charitable munificence, had once imagined sending a thousand-dollar cheque to Sesambokoko. Naturally, the missionary had gratefully written back in childlike letters (sceptics might have declared it to look like van Aanroy writing with his left hand) thanking The Mission for its most generous donation, and asking for further funds to help The Great Mother's ministry in Uganda. The Mission members had washed their consciences well that week, upping the usually charitable donations to a record high and encouraging van Aanroy to forge himself a few further letters over the months that followed. Judging from this week's poor payoff, it looked as though it might be time to write himself another Sesambokoko epistle.

Van Aanroy double-checked the proceeds from the gospel singing – a sort of easy-on-the-ear medley of Christian hymns, Hare Krishna mantras, and Salvation Army oompah-pah, which his followers performed in the pedestrian shopping area every Thursday evening. He had an edgy feeling that there was a discrepancy of some sort. He'd been out with them last week, setting an example that he didn't particularly enjoy, and had watched with glee as the Modderkolk battleship had hounded money out of late night shoppers in Vlamingstraat. The ageing harridan had even developed a method of making babies cry so that their mothers would pay to get her hideous face out of the pushchair. But her declared takings of one hundred and thirty two euros didn't quite match van Aanroy's mental calculations. Maybe what he'd thought to be two euro coins had only been one euro's. It would have been difficult to have spotted the distinction in the evening glow of the lights from the shop windows.

He shrugged and continued with his arithmetical tally. The day-care centre had taken less than fifty euros, intended for the needs of the poor of the parish. He'd never noticed any poor in his parish to give the money to – but since he didn't even have a parish, he'd never bothered looking. The collections at the Sunday meeting totalled two hundred and twenty five euros.

Van Aanroy arranged the figures one under another, then made a quick computation - a grand total of about five hundred and fifty euros. It hardly seemed worth the effort.

He'd be thirty-five soon. It was maybe time for another change in lifestyle.

He considered the options as he replaced his diary in the safe. Forming a religious group (he didn't like the word sect) had seemed like a good idea a few years ago. The ongoing battle between The Netherland's orthodox Calvinists and fanatical Catholics left people with little choice but Sodom and Gomorrah style atheism. Not that he, personally, had any objection to a Sodom and Gomorrah lifestyle – it suited him well when he wasn't wearing his clerical robe – but he had spotted what he felt to be a gap in the market. Give them something to cling to, but make it different.

And so he had launched The Mission with himself as market leader, though the more conventional title of Reverend was the one he preferred his followers to use. Van Aanroy saw himself as a loud and angry spiritualist, spending a considerable amount of his time conjuring up new sins. He intended for his followers to worry, so spread the good news about eternal damnation and moral correctness with the sort of sententious rhetoric that would have made a Calvinist blush. And, up till now, the returns had been quite good.

Sure, there were some expenses. Like the price of having his book 'The Great Mother in the Future' published, and the price of bumper stickers and Mission medallions and lapel badges. Nonetheless, the margins were pretty sensible. But, though it beat working for a living, it still meant that he had to be around when people like Theo Padmos came banging on his door seeking divine inspiration because they'd cocked-up their miserable lives.

Van Aanroy sighed and flopped into the ageing armchair in front of the television. If he stuck it out for a few more years, he could probably afford himself a quiet corner of some distant sun-drenched beach where he could rest his bones. But he wasn't certain that he could put up with a few more years of Theo Padmos and his life, no matter what the fiscal returns.

* * *

"Why do we need to move on again?" Nick asked. "Now we've relocated to this apartment, we're pretty well untraceable. Anyway, I quite like The Netherlands. I was just beginning to get the hang of the language too. Not as well as you, I'll admit, but I can get the general gist of conversations now."

"It's not that," Sandy replied. "It's a whole load of other stuff."

"Like what?"

Sandy leaned on the balcony railing, four floors above the shopping street. "Look down there, Dad. Tell me what you see."

"People." Nick said, "So what?."

Sandy didn't answer immediately. Something was chewing her up, and she wasn't sure what it was. The bright orange shirts, coats, dresses and hats of the overwhelmingly royalist Dutch seemed to offer hope and comfort, but the comfort was only an illusion, which she knowingly acknowledged. There would be no real comfort until she and her father were back home.

It wasn't that the Dutch were difficult to get on with or xenophobic, in fact, in their enthusiastic push for tolerance, The Dutch had learned to accept other countries' nationals like a pigeon accepts rain. They had learned the art of observation and criticism without eye contact or speech. Their gaze was concealed and cool, but curiously without hostility. It was their way, but it was not what Sandy was used to.

"Be nice to go home, Dad."

Nick turned her by the shoulders and led her into the living room. He closed the glazed doors with his foot.

"You know we can't risk that," he said gently. "We burned that bridge when we robbed Sean Legg. And we also left a couple of bodies behind which the police haven't closed the file on yet." He sat her in a chair. "Come on gal, I'll go and clean up a bit, then take you out for a beer."

As her father left the room, Sandy tried to push the haunting thoughts of their past to the back of her mind. Sean Legg had been her lover, though it hadn't stopped her and her father from relieving his company of its considerable assets. And though she didn't often brood over their past failure, sometimes the memory came back unbidden. Sometimes the forty million dollars that had been within their grasp floated back like a dream that couldn't quite be recalled, but couldn't be forgotten either. And then, as quickly as the money had been theirs, it was gone, and they still didn't know how it had happened.

Now, she had lost her former lover. Now, although sitting on more than a hundred thousand euros in the bank from their latest scam, the life of real luxury they had dreamed of had evaded them. Now, instead of basking under warming rays of Caribbean sunshine, Sandy and her father found themselves in a small, windy, waterlogged, overpopulated country where the rain drove horizontally - every day. The nearest she got to the sun now was when she stood too close to the microwave. Life could be a harsh master sometimes.

But life was for today, not for fretting about ancient history, and Sandy and her father had quickly reverted to old skills.

Sandy often wondered what she might have been if she'd not somehow drifted into banking. She was fairly unaccomplished in practical matters. Unable to type with more than two fingers and never having learned the satanic rites of shorthand, secretarial work had remained an insurmountable mystery. She'd considered becoming an airhostess once, but had decided against having to watch while the rest of the world went on holiday every day. It would have driven her crazy with jealousy. The trouble was, she didn't like working because she had no powers of concentration, at least not for a few measly euros at the end of each month. Concentration was a high cliff, and it only ever occurred to Sandy to scale it if the reward was sufficient to merit the effort.

It was her uncle, dead and rotting now, bless him, who had pushed her into banking. 'It will bring you in contact with the right people.' he had said.

It had.

Sandy and an ageing bank manager made significant contact several times before her uncle used the knowledge to ensure favourable borrowing terms for himself and his business partner.

But her recently terminated job as cashier with the international division of Alliance Bank had not been part of a long-term strategy of making contact with the right people, nor had her father's humble employment behind the bar in De Hardin's. They had just been simple survival techniques by two expert survivors. And, even after the previous failure, luck was never too far away from the raven-haired Sandy Ferris. Within days of signing on to Alliance Bank's payroll, she had accidentally discovered a breach in the bank's otherwise tight security.

It had started innocently enough when one of her own cheques appeared amongst the twenty or so that failed to pass through the bank's automated system each day. Sometimes a minor tear caused this, sometimes a staple in the wrong place, sometimes a pencil mark in the bottom right-hand corner. It was part of Sandy's job each morning to manually process these auto-rejects.

Being a naturally curious person in matters of money, it took her only a few hours to discover that, due to a loophole in the computer software, even if she didn't make the manual entry to debit her own account, and simply dumped her slightly torn cheque in the bin, the recipient's bank had already been credited with the amount. On that first occasion, she had been able to pay her telephone bill without affecting her bank balance. Thus, by means of an accurately placed tear, staple or pencil mark, she could write out cheques as often as she wanted without depleting the funds in her account.

Meanwhile, her father had been busy making contact with the right people – most of them regulars at De Hardin's bar, and all of them of somewhat dubious character. Anything could be supplied to order. Washing machines, televisions, carpets, even home improvements had all been purchased and sold at a fraction of their true value. The suppliers were paid, their contacts were pleased with their purchases, and Sandy and her father had cash in their pockets. The only loser was The Alliance Bank, which had unwittingly funded the whole operation. Now, having quit their jobs and moved apartments, they had to try and find other investment opportunities.

"It's not just the people," Sandy said, hearing her father come back into the living room. "They're kind enough. It's just that it's difficult to get close to anyone whose native language is different to your own."

"You mean you need a nookie-fix?" Nick asked.

Sandy paused. Sex was something they both did but seldom discussed. Her father occasionally brought someone home, but he was discreet about it and his lady friend would be gone before first light.

"I don't think it's just nookie, Dad. There's no shortage of guys who are willing. It's just that I don't feel like obliging."

"You mean you don't fancy the blokes because they're Dutch?"

Sandy shook her head.

"Then what?"

"I think I need something a bit more permanent, that's all." Sandy didn't have to add that her past included an active sex life with non-permanent partners. Her father had been well aware of her activities, behind which had usually been ulterior motives.

"You mean it would be nice to meet someone like

Sean again," Nick suggested.

Sandy didn't know whether to nod or shake her head. She opted to repair her makeup instead.

CHAPTER FOUR

George Riley had only been awake for half an hour but he was having an interesting day already. Since arriving in The Netherlands, his nocturnal activities had resulted in the watery sun being high in the sky before he had stirred from his slumbers. Today though, he awoke at the same time that the rising sun was fighting its daily battle against the early morning mist. He dressed quickly, polished off a packet of chocolate biscuits, grabbed the Swiss Army knife he had found during one of his night-time excursions in somebody else's home, furled back the flap of his tent, tiptoed across the rain-soaked grass, and relieved a French family of their vehicle number plates; one from the rear of their caravan and one from the front of their car.

The caravan was the riskier of the two because the licence plate was only a couple of feet from the head of a snoring Frankie Gauloise and his wife. A slip of George's knife and the Frenchman, whose shoulders were vaulted like an underground sewer, would be breathing garlic down his neck quicker than you could say 'Arc de Triomphe'. But Monsieur Gauloise snored his oblivious way through another snail-biting dream and George tiptoed quietly back to his tent with a set of French plates tucked safely under his anorak.

Until this morning, George had been severely fed up. It seemed that, since he'd been there, he'd had eleven days of endless rain and dreary grey skies. Combined with the wearisome confines of his uninspiring canvas home, his time in The Netherlands had been as depressing as a holiday in a cemetery.

Yesterday, he'd been so fed up that he'd even considered returning to face the music with his brother. If it had been anybody but Big Jack he'd have gladly returned, taken a good kicking and then got on with his life. But George's twin was not a forgiving man. Jack would just as soon bury his own brother in concrete as he would have two helpings of apple pie for lunch. Big Fat Bastard.

Though he still hadn't admitted it openly to himself, George knew deep down that he would never be able to return. He knew that his brother would keep looking for him, no matter how long it took. Not that the amount of money he owed would cause Big Jack any problems, but he'd be looking anyway. Matter of principle. No one owed money to Jack Riley and evaded the consequences. Not even his own brother.

The only remission that George had from his misery was that, so far, his brother hadn't succeeded in tracing him. But then it was unlikely that he would be tracked down to a tiny, neglected campsite with a stupid name somewhere in mid-Holland. The only thing that moved was the surface of the water in the adjacent canal when the wind blew up a strong gust. So, no, it was unlikely that Big Jack would be able to find him here.

Although George had even suffered doubts about that. The day after arriving at the Hans Brinker park, a fit-looking man with grey hair, a powerful motorbike and a bright green tent had shown up and set up camp at the other end of the site. George had suffered an acute attack of déjà vu, convinced that he'd seen the guy before. Trouble was, he just couldn't remember where. But the bloke had happily ignored him and gone about his holiday without even acknowledging George's existence. Eventually, George consoled himself with the fact that the motorbike was big, exclusive and Dutch-registered and he knew that Jack wouldn't go to that sort of expense. Anyway, Jack usually chose impressionable kids to do his dirty work for him and, despite having a strong physique, this guy looked to be well into his fifties.

Maybe George was just getting paranoid about the situation. It was probably all as innocent as a children's nursery, and anyway, as fed up as he had been for several days, this morning George was feeling the breeze of optimism blow through his canvas flaps. First of all he now had a set of French number plates in his possession, and secondly, though the bright green tent was still pitched in the far corner, he had not seen his fellow camper for the last two days, which meant that the said gentleman was certainly not there to do Big Jack's bidding. If the guy had been one of Jack's henchmen, George would have been sinking quietly in the mud at the bottom of the canal by now.

He unzipped his sleeping bag, ready to roll back into a ball and maintain the fine habit of rising late. The sound of a tractor on the far side of the site caught his attention. The site owner, it seemed, was also an early riser.

Hans Brinker, the ageing owner of the camp site, tucked the ancient newspaper clipping that he had been reading back into the top pocket of his overalls. He'd waited patiently inside his wooden barn that backed onto the earth dike while the fat man had unscrewed the number plates of the French combination, not wanting to make it obvious that he'd seen him. Whatever it was that the tourist was up to, he didn't want to know. The last thing he needed right at the moment was the attention of the police. He squelched through the mud, slammed the barn doors shut, remounted his tractor, and moved forward at a gallop. It was three miles to the polder where fresh canal dredging was being deposited and he needed to get there and dump his load of earth before the dredging crew turned up for work at half-past seven. He pulled his denim overalls tight as another coughing spasm racked his chest.

Phthook.

God forsaken bloody country. He didn't have much time left, but he was close now and a bit of coughed-up blood and a few thieving tourists were certainly not going to delay his purpose.

* * *

"He doesn't look anything like me!" shouted Big Jack Riley. "He's shorter than me by at least quarter of an inch, and his sideburns are longer than mine."

"I noticed the sideburns," simpered the lorry driver who had just delivered a trailer of stolen cigarettes to Jack's warehouse. "I fort it was unusual, but I didn't like to say nuffink, finkin' that it was just someone wot looked a lot like you."

"It was someone who looked a lot like me, you dimwit! It was my bloody brother."

"I'm sorry, Jack. I promise you I didn't even know you had a bruvver."

"I don't, I've just disowned him, the big fat git."

"But I thought you said he was your bruvver?"

"He is, Wally, now shut up while I think. Where'd you say you dropped him off?"

There was no answer.

"Wally, where the hell did you drop him off?"

"I fort you said not to say nuffink while you woz finkin'"

"Jesus, Wally, are you going to be a bleedin' moron all your life? Now where did you drop my brother?"

"It was on the A16 just before Dordrecht. No. I lie. It was after Dordrecht, after the river tunnel. Oh wot's it called? Ridderkerk – that's it, Ridderkerk. At the junction with the Gorinchem road. I get a bit confused there now cos they're diggin up the A16 and some of it's finished and some isn't. I was on the way up to Amsterdam for a load of—"

"Shut up."

"Yes Jack."

"So all the time he was in your cab he never said anything about who he was or where he was going?"

"Nuffink. Said his name was Paddy and ate all my cheese sandwiches. Said he was an accountant on a hitchhiking holiday. He was Irish."

The corners of Big Jack's mouth turned up, like he was chewing tin foil. "Irish accountant, my arse. He can't even count the number of legs on a bloody horse, otherwise he wouldn't be in this mess in the first place."

"Wotcher mean Jack?" Wally asked.

The hard-edged smile faded. "Nothin' for you to worry your head about. You've just got to remember one thing."

"Wot's that Jack?"

"You've just got to remember that you never saw this guy and we never had this conversation. Do I make myself perfectly clear, Wal?"

"Perfectly, Jack, perfectly."

"So what did I just say, Wal?"

"That I never saw an Irish accountant called Paddy wot looked a lot like you an' we never talked about him."

"Good."

Jack reached into his back pocket and pulled out a fold of bank notes. He peeled off ten fifty-pound notes and pressed them in the other man's hand.

"Glad we understand each other, Wal," he said, squeezing the driver's fingers like a vice. "I'd hate us to have any sort of misunderstanding."

"Oooh— Ouch— so would I Mister Riley, so would I."

As the door closed, Jack's brows pulled in. His eyes almost disappeared except for small, twin gleams, which studied the road map of Europe that was pinned to the wall. His drivers covered the whole continent, sometimes legally, mostly otherwise, so it wasn't surprising, after the word was put about, that one of them had seen someone who resembled George. It was particularly unsurprising since Jack had announced that he would give five hundred pounds for any reliable information. He believed what Wally had told him. The man was too stupid to dream up the story, and too afraid to lie.

Big Jack's finger traced the A16 through The Netherlands to where it met the A15, the Gorinchem road. He could almost smell George's fear. He knew with absolute certainty that his brother was still in that region. It was a certainty that only twins understood.

Normally Jack sent his minions out to resolve inconveniences like this but, since George had already evaded one of his best men, the matter had now become personal. The law of the jungle said that Jack had to take matters into his own hands and resolve them himself. He knew that, right at this moment, George would be troubled by the sure knowledge that he was coming to get him. That was also going to be a problem - it was like reading each other's thoughts.

Big Jack moved away from the map, eased his mountainous bulk into the leather chair behind the old wooden desk and lit himself a cigar. Along with gambling, it was one of the few habits that he and George didn't share. George didn't smoke and Jack didn't gamble.

He tapped his inflated fingers on the desk. It was time to take a little holiday. The Netherlands sounded like a good country, and Gorinchem sounded like a good town. Once there, he'd soon sniff out his wayward brother, then the debt could be repaid in full. "Big fat bastard," he muttered to his cigar, shrugging his colossal shoulders all the way up to his hairline. 'If I get hold of him, he'll end up with his shoes sticking out of his arse and his feet still inside them.'

He had a phone call to make later. It was all right proving you were king of the jungle, but it was always a good idea to have an insurance policy. If he couldn't find his brother himself, his hired man would. Though they'd never met, and knew each other only as Jack and Andy, previous jobs had been carried out with merciless efficiency. A one hundred percent success rate. They were the only sorts of odds Jack liked.

* * *

George stepped out from the shop doorway and strolled to the Renault that had just been double-parked outside the tobacconists with its hazard lights flashing. A tobacconist was always a good place to get a car – the car owners knew it would only take them a minute or two to purchase their nicotine fix, so it was common for them to leave the keys in the ignition. This one had even left the engine running. George quietly thanked him, put the car in gear and moved gently into the traffic, reminding himself to drive on the right.

Ten minutes later he drew up alongside his tent. This morning, with the Frenchman's number plates safely out of view, he had watched the family pack up and leave just before ten o'clock, then sat back and waited to see if they would return. They would be bound to spot the gaps on the front of the car and the rear of the caravan at some point during the day.

It was safe enough now to assume they weren't coming back.

A further ten minutes and the Renault's Dutch licence plates had been buried deep in the bushes that lined the campsite. Now, the car spoke French. George delved into his pocket for the tourist sticker that the newsagent in Kinderdijk had been careless enough to leave unguarded. He peeled off the backing paper and stuck it to the windscreen. I (big red heart) Holland, it said. Of course he hearted Holland. Now that he was mobile, if his brother came looking for him he stood a chance of escaping with his skin still attached to his body. Of course he bloody-well hearted Holland.

He glanced across the site to make sure nobody had been watching. Nobody had. Not only had the guy with the motorbike temporarily left, George had also solved his transport problem. Now he could pick and choose where he did his nocturnal shopping. Maybe even play at being the innocent tourist for a while.

* * *

Martijn Boermans, the owner of De Hardin's bar, was used to visits from the police. Usually it was to register complaints from the neighbours about the noise levels, or to check that the Dutch laws on the use of soft drugs weren't being flaunted on his premises, or to ask questions about one of his regulars who had been caught crossing the boundaries of legality. He was less used to being questioned about one of his staff.

He'd seen the well-built young lady with the bright red lips in the bar a couple of times, but hadn't taken too much notice of her so hadn't twigged her as police. And now she was back, asking him about Nick Ferris. He led her outside into the market place to avoid the early evening noise of the bar. It also protected his establishment's reputation. "I tell you," he said, "Nick came in one evening about ten days ago and told me he'd got himself another job."

"But he didn't give you any idea where?" Red Lips asked.

"No."

"And no forwarding address for his wages?"

"Oh come on, love, you know the score. Late night bars don't normally attract salaried staff. We have to employ whoever we can get, and that usually means cash at the end of the evening."

"Did you ever know his address?"

Martijn shrugged. "I probably scribbled it on the back of a cigarette packet or something."

"You know you're meant to keep proper records,

don't you."

He shrugged again. "I could tell you that he never worked here, and that he just helped me out a couple of times as a favour. As it is, I'm trying to help you, so I'd appreciate a bit of co-operation in return."

Red Lips was well used to maintaining the status quo. She also recognised a stone wall when she saw it. She handed Martijn a small card. "Ever seen one of these before?"

He flicked it over in his hand. "Can't say I have, but it's unusual. That's a web site address isn't it?"

She nodded and took back the business card. "You'll let me know then if you see Nick Ferris?"

"Sure, where can I get you?"

She inclined her head towards the concrete police station with the get-stuffed architecture less than a hundred yards away. "Just describe me," she said. "They all know who I am."

Martijn watched as her well-formed hips swayed across the square. She was far too good-looking to be a policewoman, but that didn't make him feel any more co-operative. Tell them nothing but let them think you might, was the order of the day. He turned and went back to tend to his flock.

Red Lips was aware of being watched, and it wasn't by the bar owner. She was used to having her body caressed by anonymous eyes. Heavy-busted women often attracted the unwanted attentions of various males, particularly heavy-busted thirty year olds who still looked like they were in their early twenties. It must be a hormone thing, she thought.

High above the market place, Nick Ferris rolled up the cuff of his yellow fluorescent shirt. "What do you think it means?" he asked.

"Dunno" Sandy said, as she read the card. "http://www.joinmychurch.com. It's obviously a web site of some sort. Who'd you say gave it to you?"

"Some bloke in the bar about a two weeks ago, just before I left. I forgot about it till I was about to put my jeans in the wash. He said something about checking the Anglican church services somewhere. Rotterdam, I think."

Sandy turned her attention to her laptop where she had been surfing the web for any signs of a site that smelt of profit. "Might as well see what it's about."

"I'll do it," her father said.

Sandy noticed that her father's tongue stuck out slightly as he concentrated, like a child writing the alphabet. They both watched as the screen rebuilt to show what looked like a directory of churches.

"Now what?" Sandy asked. "Looks like some religious thing."

"Don't know. Let me just mess around for a minute."

She floated on to the balcony, peeled back the wrapper on a candy bar, and stared over the rooftops towards Grote Kerk, the imposing brick-built church whose tower dominated the central shopping area of The Hague. The bloodshot sun was slotting behind the church roof, like a coin sliding into a piggy bank, but Vlamingstraat, the narrow street four floors below, bustled with residents doing their evening shopping.

The mumble of good-natured conversation cut through the bluster of humanity. Snippets of words like splashes of colour on pieces of a jigsaw. A band of revivalist gospel singers competed with the blaring pop music of the puerile clothes shop opposite; the Old Wooden Cross versus Head Bangabang. While the guitars strummed and the tambourines rattled, a huge woman with bloated ankles and too many breasts intimidated lady shoppers with children into releasing their small change, and young men into emptying their wallets. And all for Jesus. Hallelujah.

From her fourth floor balcony, Sandy could see the entrance to De Hardin's. A few minutes earlier, she had noticed Martijn, the owner, standing in the square, talking to a young lady with bright red lipstick and a porcelain doll figure. Sandy spent a lot of time on the balcony. Here, from her crow's nest on the top floor, she could study the leaning chimneys, twisted roofs and curving gables that nobody else could see. She could watch the world without the world watching her; like taking a train that passes through the back of a city and you get to see the place with its pants down.

For a change, it wasn't raining, though that probably wouldn't last for long as the blustery weather whipped the red, white and blue stripes of the flag on the church tower into a tangled mass of colour, and spun the gold-plated weather vane in all directions. The air smelt as sharp as a freshly laundered towel, with occasional undertones of burgers and shoarma from the eat-all-day shops below. Gusts of wind sliced low and sly round the angles of the buildings and women didn't know whether to hold down the hems of their skirts or arrest the imminent launch of their hats. A typically Dutch ball-shrinker, as her father called it.

"Do we have a code?" he called from inside the apartment.

"What's that on the back of the card?" she called back.

"Clever cow."

Sandy smiled to herself and watched a group of sit-up-and-beg cyclists fight their way past the gospel singers in the narrow street below. She bit into her candy bar and gazed westward over a jumble of steep roofs. This new apartment had a secure feel to it: close enough to be in touch with the world but far enough away to be anonymous – and served by a small communal entrance door adjacent to De Engel café in Grote Markt, just round the corner. A couple of beers with Marcus Foyer, the real estate agent, had persuaded him to talk their landlady, a woman of about Sandy's age, into accepting cash in advance and forgetting the legal paperwork.

Inside, the layout was the reverse of normal - an upside-down-apartment, as they called it. The entrance and two bedrooms were on the third floor; the living room, kitchen and balcony on the fourth floor above. From the balcony, it was possible to clamber over the rooftops to arrive at the head of a steel fire exit belonging to a gay bar in Raam Straat, a narrow lane fifty metres to the north. To Sandy's way of thinking, an escape route was as essential as a pot of strong coffee when she got out of bed in the mornings. More so, perhaps.

She had an apartment that suited her lifestyle, though home still seemed a long way away.

"How are you getting on?" she called to her father.

"Come and look."

She screwed up her candy bar wrapper and launched it at the gospel choir below. It bounced off the brick-built lady with the collecting box though she seemed not to notice as she interrogated a scared-looking youth who was holding out for his beer money.

"Where did that guy tell you to look?" Sandy asked, returning to the living room and closing the glazed door to smother the singing.

"Anglican churches in Rotterdam," Nick said. "But I'm well past that stage."

She looked over his bony shoulder. Her father was as thin as a filleted anchovy despite the plate-swamping meals that she prepared for him. He was the cartoonist's dream, scrawny and lupine with so much in the face to distort and exaggerate; the deep trenches in the cheeks, the sharpness of the nose, the sweeping hair that tried vainly to disguise the pale scalp below.

She focused on the computer screen - clean text on a pale grey background. It certainly looked professional. "What's all that then?" she asked.

"You want a quick summary?"

She nodded.

"Well, as you might have guessed, the site's got naff-all to do with religion. Quite the opposite. According to the spiel after I entered the code, we get just one chance to transfer the balance of someone else's bank account into ours."

"You're joking."

"I jest not, Sandy. If it's true, we could make a killing... If it's true!"

"Sounds extremely dodgy to me."

"That's what I thought, but the guy who gave me the card was certainly no saint, and the instructions seem as though it could be worth a try"

"How do you mean?"

"I mean – like they're plausible."

"Why, what do they say?"

As he spoke, her father followed the words across the screen with his finger. "We've got to click here so our connection goes through a proxy IP Address. Then we enter in the bank and account details that we want to hit - up to three accounts but all at the same bank. Then we enter our own bank account IBAN code and press the button. Dead simple really."

"If it works."

"Yeah, if it works. It looks too good to be true."

"And normally, if it looks too good to be true then it is too good to be true," added Sandy, knowing that this was a mantra her father had drummed into her from an early age.

Nick continued, "It says here that the author of the programme, probably the guy who gave me the card, gets ten percent of the deal transferred straight to his own bank."

"So what do you think?"

"Couldn't say. Could be a wind-up. Could be a set-up. Could be just a load of bollocks."

"Could be the guy just wants to get hold of our bank details." Sandy said. "Who was he, Dad? Did he look like a cop or something?"

"No, but I'm fairly sure someone was following him. He just looked like an ordinary De Hardin's punter."

"A bit dishonest then!"

"Yeah! He seemed to be sizing me up. Drank a few beers then left. Anyway, if there's not much chance of tracing the transaction back to us, what have we got to lose?"

"We're fairly anonymous here," Sandy said, airing her thoughts. "The rent's pre-paid and our new landlady didn't bother to write down our names. She was just keen to take the cash. If the proxy server thing works, then there's no trace back to us. Like you say, what have we got to lose?" She turned back to the screen, then stopped. "Whose account are we going to hit?" she asked, as if surprised by her own question.

"What about some big accounts at Alliance Bank?"

A frown creased Sandy's brow and she plucked her bottom lip like a harp string. "Don't know the account numbers," she said. "If I'd known about the card a bit earlier I could have got them easily enough, but it's too late now."

Her father humphed. "I suppose you're going to tell me I should put my jeans in the wash more often."

"Well it would have been more…" Sandy stopped as she noticed a slow grin light her father's face.

"Still got Sean Legg's bank details?" he asked.

"You wicked sod, Dad. Do you reckon he's still got the same bank accounts?"

"What have we got to lose? He's the only bloke I know who's got, or at least who had, loads of money."

"Yeah but we helped ourselves to that heap six months ago."

"Jesus H., Sandy, don't you think a guy like Sean would have rebuilt the Company? Don't you think he'd have had insurance or something? Let's go for it. We don't know anyone else do we?"

She paused, silently shaking her head. "Do you think it'll work outside The Netherlands?" she asked.

"Don't know."

"And what about the money? Sean's accounts are in sterling and ours are in euros."

"Listen, love, I know as much as you. Let's just do it, eh? Nothing ventured, nothing gained, as they say."

Sandy picked up a leather-bound personal organiser from the table, flicked through the memo pages and gave a satisfied murmur as she found what she was looking for. "You're right, Dad. We might get a dumb message at the end telling us it's all a joke, but who cares. At worst it's a bit of fun, at best we could gain a few bucks. The only thing that worries me is that we are giving away our own bank details."

Her father nodded but vacated the chair anyway.

Sandy settled on the still warm cushion and pressed the Tab key. They watched the screen change to single line commands with a space to type the responses. Sandy read aloud. "Your internet is connected by telephone landline. To re-route the connection, enter a phone number that's not currently in use. Oh hell, I forgot about that. What number are we going to use?"

Her father checked his watch – one of five that Sandy had bought him. "What about the bank?"

"What bank?"

"Alliance."

"Why them?"

"'Cos they're closed. Jesus H., Sand, it's almost eight o'clock and they close at six. They'd have all gone home at least an hour ago."

Sandy pondered for a moment. "I'll use Theo Padmos' number, he's probably busy putting a paper bag over his girlfriend's head right now!"

Her father displayed his vandalised teeth again as Sandy typed.

"Now for Sean Legg's bank details," she muttered, flipping the page in her organiser. "I can go for the pension fund, the deposit account and the trading account." She continued typing, entering her own IBAN number at the local branch of Avrobank - the place where they had already deposited the proceeds of the previous six months. "What now?" she asked. "What about if Sean's accounts are overdrawn? Will we be paying off his overdraft?"

"I really don't know, love. Anyway I'm willing to take a little risk. Nothing ventured eh?"

Sandy still looked uncertain.

"What's holding you back?" asked her father.

She shrugged. "I guess maybe I don't like the idea of hitting Sean again."

"You've never let sentiment get in the way of profit before."

"I know, Dad, but don't you feel ashamed sometimes when you look at yourself in the mirror?"

"Sure," he smiled, "but it passes before I've really noticed it." He leaned in front of her and pressed the Enter key. The screen changed to a swirling tornado of dollar signs gyrating upwards into a sky of gold bars. "Good effects," he said.

After a few seconds they looked at each other with eyebrows raised.

"Reckon we've been had," from Sandy.

"Reckon."

As they spoke, the screen rebuilt again - this time red text on a yellow background. It was as subtle as ketchup on an egg yolk. Congratulations. Your Avrobank account 850.93.94.099 has been credited with EUR 752 422,88 Please destroy the card you were given. The access code is no longer useable.

They read and re-read the message. Only the Hallelujahs of the gospel choir outside broke the silence.

Finally, Nick whistled. "Jesus H. Seven hundred and fifty thousand euros. That's about half a million quid." He still counted in English.

"And all in the time it takes for the average Dutchman to clear his throat."

"Do you think it's for real, or just a big wind-up?"

"Only one way to find out, Dad."

"How?"

"Let's go for a beer! We'll stop by at Avrobank and

check it out."

"Banks are closed."

"I know, but I can still ask the automatic teller for the balance of my account!"

"Jesus H. Come on, lady, what the hell are we waiting for? Let's do it."

Sandy grabbed her coat and handbag while her father waited impatiently for her at the door in the entrance hall below.

"You realise," she said, checking that she had her keys, "that I'm supposed to be meeting with Marcus Foyer for a beer this evening, and also that if this thing has worked, you're going to have to thank the guy who gave you the card."

"Don't worry about either of them," Nick said, diving through the door and descending the communal staircase two at a time. "You can call your real estate friend after we've checked the bank and, if this has worked, the guy who gave me the card will have just earned himself about seventy-five thousand euros."

A mile away, in Geleenstraat, Hjalmar pushed himself away and eased from the bed.

"Where are you going, lover?" asked Rolien, raising herself on one elbow. "It was just getting interesting."

"Yeah well it'll have to wait a few minutes. I need to go to the little boy's room, and I just remembered that I've not checked the JoinMyChurch programme today."

Rolien allowed her silk blouse to part, exposing her firm, rounded breasts. They were the twin parts of her anatomy that most interested and aroused him, and the evidence was clear in his boxer shorts as he tried to look inconspicuous.

"Hjalmar, come back… please?"

"I can't sweetheart, you know I need to check JoinMyChurch to see if I've got a hit. Anyway, the evening is young yet."

She pouted like a spoilt child and flopped back onto the pillow. "You and that damn computer of yours. It's all you ever think about."

"Not quite." he said, gazing at her body. "But you know I've got to check it at least twice a day so I can deprive the lucky recipient of his ill-gotten gains before he has a chance to spend or withdraw anything."

"But you've been waiting nearly two weeks for this one. Isn't it obvious it's not going to happen?"

He shrugged. "You might be right. It's probably time to change the code and find another punter."

Rolien eased the blouse open some more. "Hjalmar, please? For me?"

He paused for a moment before stepping into the bathroom. "Sorry, love, I can't," he said, closing the door behind him. "You might be filthy rich, but I need the money."

Rolien thumped the pillow in frustration. Men could be pretty dumb when it came to working women out. Didn't Hjalmar realise that she needed as much attention as the next person? Couldn't he understand that? Him and his damn computer.

Her eye caught on the long-handled nail file that she'd been using before she'd managed to attract Hjalmar's attention and relieve him of some of his clothes. A wicked gleam lit her face. Without a second thought, she grabbed the file, leaped from the bed, and dodged down the hallway into the lounge.

Like many computer geeks, Hjalmar's computer was built of the best bits from various sources. And like many computer geeks, Hjalmar didn't care what it looked like, only how it performed, so the working parts lay exposed. Rolien poked her nail file into the depths of the gadgetry as far as it would go and wiggled it madly from side to side. Whatever circuitry was hidden down there, she was making serious contact with it.

She heard the flush of water and rushed back to the bedroom, jumping onto the bed just as the bathroom door opened.

Hjalmar tipped her a wink. "Be back in about five minutes," he said. "Keep it warm for me."

She started to feel guilty straight away. Surely she could have waited five minutes? But that wasn't the point, was it. The point was that Hjalmar was putting his damn fool computer before their relationship. His priorities were all screwed up.

She lay back and waited. She didn't have to wait

long.

'Ah bollocks.' she heard from the living room.

She closed her eyes and smiled. A few more minutes and Hjalmar would be back where he belonged.

Five minutes passed, and then ten, so she opened her eyes, rolled off the bed, and stepped into the lounge. She didn't need to ask what was keeping her boyfriend. He had started dismantling the computer and was peering at the circuit boards with a puzzled expression.

"What's up, Hjalmar. I thought you were coming back to bed."

His attention remained focussed on the convoluted circumbendibus of soldered circuits. "I can't come now," he muttered. The damn computer's on the blink and I've got to try and fix it."

"But Hjalmar, you promised."

"Yeah, well later."

In a passion of pent up anger, Rolien stomped back to the bedroom, slammed the door, and flung herself onto the bed. As she fumed, all she could hear was the excited chatter and giggles of the working girls in the street below.

The Hague often caught the new visitor unawares. One minute you would be walking through a quiet, respectable, residential area, the next you would be surrounded by stunning young ladies in skimpy underwear beckoning you from behind bright, fluorescent windows. It would make no difference whether you were male, female or eunuch; black, white or green; AC, DC or XYZ: they catered for all tastes and would barter with a three-headed Martian if he had banknotes in his pocket.

Streets like Geleenstraat weren't on a scale of the red light district of Amsterdam, which had become little more than a seedy tourist attraction, but serious money changed hands nonetheless. Innocent visitors would scamper quickly past the ladies of the night, hiding their embarrassment until they found themselves comfortably back in what they believed to be authentic Holland again.

First time visitors generally imagined The Hague to be an austere place hovering around the International Court of Justice - a civilised city with canals down the middle of the roads. Their heads are filled with pictures of bright-eyed parents trundling over the cobbles on their bikes with their fine-mannered children sitting behind, shopkeepers like well-dressed marionettes, and street sweepers working in symmetrical groups like marching bands – a candy-box city. That's how they imagined it.

The reality was a less-than-respectable, anonymous city that catered to all tastes, so long as there was money in your pocket. And even the ornate brick and carved timber warehouses, the picture postcard gables, the unassuming van Gough bridges, all held their own secrets, hiding contract killers like Andy Nottley behind the dark windows, the closed doorways, the cornices, and the exuberance of crooked alleys.

Andy Nottley wasn't his real name, it was one he'd spotted in an English telephone directory and took a liking to. In fact, Andy Nottley was about as authentic as a Rolex watch on the beach in Acapulco. Nothing about him stayed the same for long – even his bank account kept getting bigger. His long, dark hair, pulled back into a ponytail, had been purchased at an exclusive wig shop to make sure it fitted snugly over his army-style crew cut. It was one of several wigs he used, depending on the character he needed to metamorphose into. When venturing out in public, a grey, silk Armani suit replaced the faded denims that he now wore, and his Nike trainers were exchanged for crocodile skin shoes imported direct from Italy. When he displayed a false face to the world, even his own mother couldn't recognise him. He knew – he'd once knocked on her door and asked for directions.

Andy Nottley was a man with a little-known but well deserved reputation for secrecy, and ruthless efficiency. A contract killer with an alternate lifestyle that was so normal, nobody would ever imagine that he could be connected to a trail of dead bodies that spanned three continents.

After the second ring of his mobile phone, he muted the stereo system, even though it was no more than quiet background listening. For over a minute he said nothing, just listening and making a few mental notes. With the word "Agreed." He closed the connection, crossed the room to the mirrored bar and poured himself a generous measure of Talisker Whisky. As he savoured the peaty aroma, he allowed a satisfied smile to turn the corners of his mouth. It was good to be back in business after a few week's break, particularly since he had worked for this English client before and knew he could rely on quick settlement of his bill. His only doubt came from the fact that this particular contract was local. Though he'd done it before, he preferred not to kill on his own doorstep.

He reached for a notepad and jotted a quick summary of the phone call, using his own private code to render it unintelligible to anybody else. His secret lifestyle hid his secret affliction - a severe form of Narcolepsy - which meant that he had suffered all his adult life from temporary blackouts and sometimes even memory-loss, so it was a long-acquired habit to write things down. Ever since he could remember, he had been prone to these blackouts if the order of his brain was disturbed. When everything went to plan, his mind remained calm, composed and objective, but an unexpected event often release a cacophony of noise in his head from which his only escape was to move into the darkness of his mind for a few moments. But it wouldn't do to forget that he had a contract to fulfil. It wasn't professional and, blackouts or not, Andy Nottley was nothing if not a professional.

Less than ten minutes walk from Andy's house, Theo Padmos strode through the town centre with the uncoordinated stalk of an unnaturally elongated person – his feet appearing to go in two different directions at the same time. Theo had been faced with such a choice of difficulties that it seemed as if even The Great Mother had deserted him. It had been almost two weeks since Sandy Ferris had left Alliance Bank, and the trail was cold. This was his last shot. His visit now to the smoke-filled bar of De Hardin's was the end of the line. He didn't know what he was going to find there, but anything was better than nothing. Even the Reverend van Aanroy seemed disinterested in his problems. Theo called to see him most evenings to ask for his advice, but his spiritual guide seemed unable or unwilling to offer any ideas. Puzzlingly, he had even suggested that

Sandy Ferris was unimportant and that Theo should abandon his search.

Theo had been told about the bar by one of the other bank cashiers, the one with the sensible dress, who had told him that Sandy had mentioned it once or twice during coffee breaks. The staff had taken pity on their chief cashier, who was being given a particularly hard time by the internal auditors and by the manager who was temporarily without his office. But Theo didn't want their pity; he just wanted to redeem himself in the bank's eyes. And, with The Great Mother's help, he would

As he entered the bar he adjusted the peak of the blue tartan deerstalker hat that Joska had given him – to prevent head colds, she had told him. He rearranged his monocle and ordered an orange juice from the hairy-armed man behind the bar, who proceeded to blatantly overcharge him. It wasn't in the nature of a thrifty Dutchman to accept an overcharge without comment, but accept it Theo did. What he wanted today was information, not an argument

He sniffed and peered around the room. The bar was dirty and dark and, since no-one seemed to have heard of the laws that banned smoking in public places, smelt of sweet tobacco and other substances. There were few customers at this early evening hour, but nonetheless the music bounced off the walls from the big bass speakers mounted on brackets high over his head. In a remote corner, two unshaved youngsters shared a beer and a joint. Even from the distance of the bar, Theo could see the faraway looks in their eyes that told him they were more than just cannabis smokers; these guys were serious smack-heads.

Theo resented his government's legalisation of so-called soft drugs. The politicians liked to consider themselves liberal thinkers. But Theo was not a liberal thinker. Theo wanted to tell these people how they were wasting their lives, how The Great Mother would forgive them and help them if they turned their backs on this evil. But that would have to wait for another day. Perhaps he could persuade The Mission to start visiting bars instead of just singing in the street on late shopping nights.

Tonight he'd excused himself from the hymn singing and told them that he had to work late. Another lie. Tonight he just wanted to know about Sandy Ferris. Where was she? Why had she done this to him? His instincts told him that she was still nearby. Only two days ago, she'd drawn cash from her account using the automatic dispenser outside the bank. The internal auditors had found nothing so far, so there was no reason to suspend the use of her card. All she was guilty of was leaving the bank's employ without giving notice. It was hardly a hanging offence, though Theo was beginning to wish that it were.

The only customer other than the two junkies was a lone woman wearing a white fur coat and a scruffy off-white poodle. The poodle looked as though it could have been cut out of the coat: or had the coat been fashioned out of poodle pelt? Maybe she'll know something, Theo thought. He moved to one side and sat on the adjacent barstool, facing her. "Hello," he shouted, "my name's Theo. I wonder if you can help me."

"I'm sure I can," she said in a deep, husky voice that was only just audible over the booming bass. "What's your pleasure?"

"I don't understand," he said. "I'm looking for someone."

"We're all looking for someone, Theo, and you just found me, you lucky man. Now, what would you like to do with me?" She bent down and carefully positioned the poodle on the floor at her feet, letting her coat fall open to display the near naked body beneath.

Theo gulped and spilled his orange juice down his shirt. She had small, unfettered breasts and, above her stocking tops, a very masculine bulge inside a pair of men's briefs.

The blood drained from Theo's face and neck. His monocle hung loosely on his chest just fractionally below his jaw, which had fallen totally off its hinges.

Then the full ancestral wrath of Johannes Calvijn kicked in. "You abomination!" he shouted, jumping down from the stool and standing to attention like a sergeant major on a parade ground. "You detestable, despicable, lewd creature. What sort of person are you? Have you no shame? Have you no humility?"

Apparently not! The shameless creature looked at him from behind cow-sized eyelashes with a puzzled expression. But she said nothing.

Theo's chin had collected a sizeable pool of spittle, which he ignored. "You devil-worshipper!" he continued in full rant, drowning out the music. "You child of Satan. Repent or be damned!" The words of the Reverend Van Aanroy sprang into his head like a coiled Jack-in-the-box. "You can find The Great Mother. You can be saved. Forsake this wickedness, follow ye the ways of—"

A large hairy hand, attached to a large hairy arm, slid between his legs and grasped him tight by the testicles, choking his words. As the fingers of the hand squeezed like a vice, sick pain bellowed its way from Theo's crotch up into his stomach and down into his thighs. The matching hand closed tight on the back of his neck and he was half dragged, half marched, to the door, hauled bodily outside and dumped unceremoniously in the market square. Red hot slivers of pain shot down both legs, which buckled underneath him, landing him on a greasy polystyrene tray of mayonnaise – the remnants of a discarded take-away.

"If you want to preach, go do in church, not here." Martijn Boermans shouted in his face.

Theo clutched his crotch and groaned. "I just wanted to find someone," he spluttered, gasping for air.

"Well you just found me!" shouted the bar owner, taking a step away from the crumpled body. "If you've lost someone, go tell the cops."

"I did, I've been there, I've been to the Stadhuis, I've tried everything."

"What makes you think you'll find him here?"

"Her," Theo corrected, after a large gulp of air. "I'm looking for a woman."

"Aren't we all?"

"I don't mean like that. It's a young lady who used to work for me. I was told that she used to come to this bar."

"What's her name?" Boermans responded, marginally more sympathetically.

"Sandy." Theo croaked. "Sandy Ferris." The name stuck in his throat, like the air that he was still gasping for. "She's English. Do you know her?"

"Why do you want to find her?" Martijn asked, staring at Theo's monocle, which swayed like a pendulum on its bright red cord. "You're obviously not the police."

"No, I'm just a messenger. A friend of hers left a parcel with me and I just wanted to pass it on to her." Another lie. Excuse me, Great Mother.

"Well you've got a funny way of asking." the barman said. "You come in my bar, you drown one of my regulars in a religious tidal-wave, and you expect me to help you find her." He reached out and helped the chief cashier to his feet. "Her father used to work here," he continued, "but he finished about two weeks ago and I've not seen either of them since."

Theo picked up the blue tartan hat and dumped it on his swathe of bright yellow hair. It was probably back-to-front, but who cares. "I'm sorry," he said, straightening unsteadily through the pain in his groin. He tried to brush the mayonnaise off his suit and succeeded only in spreading it further. "I'm just not used to seeing these sorts of people. It came as something of a shock to me."

Martijn allowed the corners of his mouth to turn up. "Yeah, I've seen that reaction from tourists sometimes." His lips straightened again and the smile hardened. "Don't forget, my friend, it takes all sorts to make a world. Brigitte, the bloke you just tongue-lashed, may seem a little strange to you, but if ever you were in trouble she'd be the first guy to come to your aid." He turned on his heel and went back inside leaving the chief cashier nursing his bruised manhood and trying to puzzle out the gender conundrum.

Theo closed his eyes, bent forward again with his hands on his knees, and took a few more deep breaths to try to relieve the hot ache in his groin. The hair that protruded from his lopsided deerstalker was sweaty, lying on his brow like wet straw. A fresh wave of nausea passed over him.

The rattle of a tambourine and Joska's voice asking him what on earth was going on, brought him back to reality. What did he think he was doing showing her up in front of the other members of The Mission, and why did he have grease and mayonnaise all over his nice new suit, and why was his nice sensible hat back-to-front, and why was he holding himself in that place?

Theo deferred the eye-opening process and groaned. Mevrouw Modderkolk, the ageing despot who would have blended well in the galactic-speakeasy scene in Star Wars, pushed her triangular bulk past Joska, stared at Theo like she was assessing a particularly truculent item of stock at an agricultural auction, and shook her collecting box in his face.

Theo cowered. It was going to be a long night of explanations and he still hadn't found out about the person who'd caused him all the trouble. Suddenly Sandy Ferris had grown horns and The Great Mother seemed a long, long way away.

* * *

George Riley reached into his meagre belongings and removed his red notebook. It would be safer if he hid it somewhere, buried it in the bushes or something, like he had the old car number plates. He didn't want to get caught doing another runner and leaving it where Jack could find it. Whilst the contents of the book were the real reason why Big Jack had sent his thugs to get him, they might also be responsible for saving George's life. Brushing a dusting of biscuit crumbs off his legs with one hand, he allowed the podgy fingers of his other hand to flick through the pages. Details, so many details, copied quietly while Jack had been away on holiday.

Jack hadn't meant to leave his own little red book lying around where George could find it. In fact, he hadn't. Five years earlier, in Jack's temporary absence, George had simply been examining the contents of the locked drawers in his brother's desk when he accidentally sprung the release catch to a concealed compartment. It was like discovering an ancient Egyptian tomb, full of hidden secrets that were never meant to be shared. Offshore bank accounts, favours owed, illegal gambling rackets, shady contacts, warehouses full of stolen booty, companies within companies within companies, money laundering, prostitution. There wasn't much that his brother Jack wasn't involved in, and it was all meticulously noted in his little red book – and meticulously copied by George into his. Not that George ever intended using the information to rob or blackmail Jack: that sort of mistake would certainly be his last. It was more like having an insurance policy in case Jack accidentally passed away and forgot to tell him where the family silver was.

After replacing Jack's book and re-securing the hidden compartment, George used his brother's absence as an opportunity to leave the grimy river and wharves of London. Leaving behind, too, his brother's influence that he'd loathed for so long.

A while later, George had emerged with a clean sheet and a little red notebook of his own amongst the heather-covered hills of the Isle of Man, a small independent community slap in the middle of the Irish Sea. Within days of his return from holiday, his brother had, of course, tracked him down, and had offered some considerable verbal encouragement to George to return to the fold – his fold. Jack was a shepherd who didn't like to lose any sheep; even those that didn't belong to him. He even sent a pair of Italian-looking types with greasy hair and plastic sunglasses to encourage George to return.

George got the message but stood firm for once, and Jack eventually gave up and left him to his own devices. Had his brother applied more pressure than he did, George might have been tempted to use his notebook to warn his brother off. As it was, he'd been able to keep his insurance policy intact for a rainy day.

It was five peaceful, Jack-free years later, after his brother called in his gambling debts, that George considered how best to use the little red book. Whilst his brother's empire had undoubtedly grown in the intervening years, and whilst some of the information in the notebook had undoubtedly become out-of-date, George knew that much of the information would still have been current. George had kept it in reserve for an emergency and, when his brother gave him twenty-four hours to settle his debts in full or face the consequences, he cashed in the policy.

Big Jack was furious.

Understatement. Big Jack went absolutely ape shit, demanding to know how George had found the secret compartment in his desk, demanding that George deliver his copy of the information to him – in person – immediately.

That had been on the Friday afternoon, and had led to the events in the early hours of Saturday morning, when George had found himself standing bollock-naked in knee-high nettles trying to avoid a man with a knife.

But, though the contents of the little red book were the real reason why George's life was at risk, they might also at some point turn the situation around. If Jack thought that the notebook was in the hands of a third party and that it would not be revealed as long as George's health stayed good, he might have to call a suspension to hostilities.

The trouble was that George didn't know any third parties. Best to hide the notebook and bluff it out, he thought. He dropped the book onto his bedroll and popped another chocolate biscuit into his mouth. He noticed it was the last one. As soon as it was dark he'd bury the notebook behind the tent. Then he'd go 'night shopping' again.

So far he'd been fortunate enough to pick up a few euros on his evening travels and, a few nights ago, a clandestine visit to a nearby clothes shop had netted him enough to live on for several weeks. The owner would probably take more care to lock his cash away in future.

George pulled his bell-tent sweater over his head, slid his feet into his new shoes – one of the pairs provided by the owner of the clothes shop - and finger-combed his sideburns. Time to try out his new car and take a little drive to the café - get himself a good plateful of something. It had been hours since he'd eaten anything.

Forty miles away in The Hague, Sandy and her father weren't interested in eating, but a magnum of Dom Perignon sat on the table between them. Sandy glanced at her watch.

"Your friend will be here soon," Nick said. "Meanwhile don't get all carried away and forget to get that money out of the bank tomorrow morning."

"First thing!" Sandy agreed, as she raised her glass again and saluted her father. "As soon as the bank opens, I'll empty the account and close it."

"First thing." Nick repeated. "Jesus H., I'd hate for a repeat of last time when we got so close, then lost it all."

"Don't worry, Dad, no slip-ups this time. Cash into a big carrier bag, take it home, hide it where only the two of us will ever find it."

Their favourite French Restaurant, Le Bistro de la Place, was quiet tonight and only one other table was occupied. Sandy watched the hurried arrival of Marcus Foyer. "Over here," she called. "Come and join us for a glass."

"Can't stop long, I'm afraid," the estate agent said, "Something unexpected cropped up." He parked himself into the adjacent chair and helped himself to champagne. "What are you celebrating?"

"We just discovered that there's a good Anglican church in Rotterdam!" Sandy said.

Marcus raised his eyebrows along with his glass. He'd always known that the English were strange but the attractive Sandy Ferris and her oddball father were a real irregular couple. There were as many Anglican Churches in Rotterdam as there were massage parlours in The Vatican.

CHAPTER FIVE

Sean Legg was a big man, so he shook his visitor's hand with care, knowing that his handshake could hurt people. "First, tell me how to spell your name," he rumbled. I don't meet too many guys from Finland, so I'm not used to the spelling."

"H-A-N-N-U" replied the young man facing him. "But you can just call me Hannu!"

Sean tried not to smile, but couldn't quite help himself – certainly not the full set of enamel that he could flash on a good day, but a mouth-twitcher nonetheless. "Okay, Hannu, let me tell you why I've called you here." His i's sounded more like oi's when he spoke quickly. "You were recommended to me by my bank manager. He said you'd done some work for the bank from time-to-time."

Hannu nodded. "Computer fraud's a boom industry. It's beggarin' tough, sometimes, staying ahead of the bad guys."

"Your English is good."

"So's yours!"

On normal days, the Irish man-mountain appreciated a sense of humour and Sean's tone softened, though it still carried persuasion with its bass growl. "Okay, you cheeky young sod, let me tell you a short story before I tell you what's happened today."

He paused as Hannu settled back in the chair and sipped the coffee that one of the secretaries had placed in front of him a few moments earlier. The chair appeared to be far too large for the young Fin, yet his multi-coloured sweater seemed comfortably at ease against the grey upholstery. A swab of fair hair, parted in the middle, sat untidily on a round face with earnest, slightly slanting eyes and a turned up nose. Sean couldn't help thinking that if his visitor ever had the need to look for work, he could probably make a profession as a Christmas elf. He would have bet that the young man's feet were not, at that moment, touching the floor.

When he had Hannu's full attention, Sean gave him the background to his unhappy state. "Sure and the Isle of Man's a small community," he said. "As makers of industrial handling machinery, Three Leggs Manufacturing is the largest employer here, apart from our wonderful government, of course." His Irish brogue was just enough to be mellow without sounding stereotyped and, despite his annoyance, there was an undemanding lilt in his voice that was easy on the ear. "About a year ago, I considered a sort of semi-retirement. Anyway, to cut a long story short, I sold the controlling interest of Three Leggs to an investment company, then I buggered off for six months of sunshine. When I got back at the end of last year, all hell had broken loose. The guy I'd done the deal with had been fronting for another guy who had put the money up. They'd ripped the Company off, lock, stock and barrel. Stolen the bloody lot they had. Valuable land had been flogged, the buildings had been mortgaged, inventory had been sold off at a fraction of its worth, the pension fund had been completely emptied." He held his hand to his head at the memory. "They'd even mortgaged the damn shares that I'd sold them. In short, they'd cashed in the Company's assets and nicked the money."

He paused for breath and a sip of coffee. The cup looked too dainty in his massive paw. "To this day, no one knows the full truth about what happened, but both these scallywags were found with bullets in their heads. Finest thing that could have happened to the pair of them. The coroner recorded an open verdict - insufficient evidence to track down their killer. Anyway, the company was about as bust as a company can be and then, bingo, almost straight away the money unexpectedly arrived back the bank."

"How?" Hannu asked, raising his blonde eyebrows.

"That's one of the bits we've never puzzled out," Sean said, a cautious smile manoeuvring round the edges of his eyes. "The whole story's well curious and some day I'll fill you in on the details, but up till now the return of the money remains a mystery. Anyway, I'm pretty sure there were others involved in the scam besides the dead guys. I think I know who they were, but I'd probably never be able to confirm my suspicions, and nobody's heard from them since."

"So you got your money back and everything was okay?"

Sean fiddled with a scrap of paper on his desk as the memory lingered. He took the last swallow of coffee and pushed the tiny cup away from him along the polished desk. Gentle though it was, each movement gave the impression of a huge physical force of smooth power, like a great mass of water sliding through a sluice. "Got me money back," he said absently. "Yeah, I got me money back, but didn't the buggerment factor just cost me a fortune. I'm only just getting to a point where I can say that everything's about back to normal. That was, until my bank manager rang me this morning."

"Why what happened?"

Sean looked up at the Fin. "What happened then, young sir, was that this Irishman you see before you got some very bad news. And I do mean very bad. It seems that, overnight, the Company's main trading account has been completely drained. This morning's balance was exactly zero."

"And how much was in there last night?"

Sean checked the scrap of paper that had been waltzing a carousel in his fingers. "Five hundred and twenty nine thousand three hundred and forty six pounds and some odd pence."

Hannu whistled. "Beggar, that's a heap of money," he said, squirming forward and placing his cup and saucer on the desk.

"Sure, but it's not the money so much as the fact that I get the feeling I'm being picked on. Call me neurotic if you will, but I'm beginning to feel like a target in an Aunt Sally stall. Everyone's chucking muck at me and I can't retaliate."

"It's still a load of money."

"That's not my problem, Hannu. I haven't authorised its removal, so the bank will have to replace it. It's the bank's problem."

Hannu scratched at his thatch of fair hair, rearranging the central parting, which appeared to slip neatly towards one ear. "So why have you called me? Why not leave it for the bank to solve? Are they sure that they haven't just made a mistake?"

Sean responded by picking up the phone and ordering two more coffees – laced with good Irish whiskey. He wasn't in the habit of taking alcohol before the sun was past the yardarm, but he could make exceptions to most of life's rules if the situation called for it. "The bank has confirmed that there was no error on their behalf," he rumbled, as he replaced the handset. "They are as puzzled as me because the money has quite literally disappeared without a trace. I called you because, as I say, I feel that I'm the target and can't hit back. Also, I have a nasty sneaking suspicion that the other people who were involved in last year's shenanigans were involved in this thing today, and if I don't stop them now, they may start to think of me as their personal piggy bank."

"What makes you say that?"

"Just a good hunch. A year ago, in addition to the normal trading account, the Company had a pension fund account and a deposit account. The pension fund account is nearly always empty: I only use it for transferring money. The deposit account's the interesting one. About three months ago, I moved my surplus funds to another high-interest account but left the deposit account open. In fact there were a few quid in there – twelve pounds fifty to be precise. That's gone, along with the trading account balance, but the high-interest account is totally untouched. To me, that means that whoever was involved didn't know enough about the current affairs of the Company. It makes me think it was someone who might have known the situation a year ago, but not anymore."

"But they're both dead."

"Sure an' the two main characters of the misappropriation are dead and buried, and long may they stay that way, but that's what makes me wonder if my theory about other people being involved could be true. Like I say, it's only a hunch but my hunches have often proved right in the past and I'm inclined to trust them now. I want them stopped, Hannu, before they try something else, and I need your help finding them."

The conversation was put on hold as a pretty young lady delivered two coffees and a bottle of good Irish whiskey. When she had left, Sean unscrewed the top of the bottle and poured liberal measures into the coffees. He slid one of the cups towards Hannu who wriggled forwards in the chair to reach it.

"The two characters I'm suspicious about are a man and his daughter," Sean continued. "The guy used to work for me as a bookkeeper. His daughter and I had been er… friends."

"What were they like?" Hannu asked, sipping his coffee with respect.

"I always had him down as a likeable rogue," Sean

replied. "If you shook his hand, you'd want to count your fingers afterwards - make sure they're all still there. I employ lots of blokes like that. They usually don't steal from the one that feeds them."

"And her?"

"She is an excruciatingly petite, raven-haired temptress. Intelligent, persuasive, charming and probably completely bloody dishonest. She's too smart to get involved but far too lazy not to. She's shrewd, she's sneaky, she's conniving and, in a peculiar way that only the English seem to have mastered, she's totally bloody scatterbrained just beneath her exquisite exterior. Does that explain her? I'm still not sure exactly what her link was to the dead blokes, but I'm pretty sure she and her father were somehow involved."

"Any names?" Hannu asked.

"I'd rather you discover them and tell me, then I'll know that I haven't blackened their characters unfairly."

"Your description of her didn't sound as though you were holding too much back."

"There's a lot more to that young lady than meets the eye." Sean said with a faraway smile. "But I'm not about to divulge all my secrets."

"Understood, but it sounds as though you don't trust me to be objective."

"It's not like that, Hannu. I don't want you trying to trace people by name then finding you've been following a false trail. You'd only lose time. I'd rather you use your normal methods, whatever they are, and we'll see what transpires at the end. As you might have gathered, I was rather fond of the young lady and I'm hoping that my nasty sneaky mind is just working overtime and that she's got nothing to do with anything."

Hannu nodded. "Fair enough. Do you want me to work alongside the bank's people, or act independently?"

"Stay independent, miboy." Sean usually saved his 'miboys' for longstanding friends, but, despite the younger man having said little, he was beginning to feel he'd known the Finn forever.

"Will the police be involved?" Hannu asked.

"I guess the bank will almost certainly ask them to investigate, but the island's a small place and the police over here have limited resources. I'm not sure how successful they'll be."

"Some pipe-smoking retired traffic cop, you mean?"

Sean chuckled. "I'll tell Angus when I see him."

"You reckon Slooth will get involved then?"

Sean was too slow to stop a look of surprise galloping over his face. "You know Angus?" he asked.

"Sure," Hannu said. "We work on the same side of the fence."

"But he's Isle of Man Constabulary and you're from London."

"When it comes to fraud and money laundering the world is a smaller place than you think. The good Detective Inspector is well known and well respected in Scotland Yard. They've tried to poach him several times but he prefers the anonymity of The Isle of Man to the bright lights of the city."

"Well bugger me backwards with a toothbrush. I never thought the island was important enough to have a top-ranking law enforcer in its midst."

Hannu chuckled. "You live in a sheltered world, Mister Legg. While Angus Slooth spends most of his time solving local crimes just like any regular Detective Inspector, as an offshore low tax area, the island is like a magnet to Mafia money, Colombian cash and Libyan lucre, and that's when Angus really comes into his own."

"Sure an' I'm bloody gobsmacked. He and I have a beer or two together sometimes. He never talks about his work. I just thought he was an eccentric plod."

"Eccentric, most definitely. Plod, certainly not! So now you know a bit more about him, I'll ask you the question again; do you reckon he'll get involved in your problem?"

Sean pondered his fingernails for a moment. "Bearing in mind what you've just told me; for half a million quid, maybe not. For someone crapping on his own doorstep, you can bet your life on it. I don't think Angus will take that one lying down. But I still want you on the case, Hannu. Angus will be using all the official channels and I need someone with the knowledge and ability to get a result. I will personally authorise the expenditure of any reasonable amount of money, but I really am anxious to put an end to this as soon as possible. Will you be needing an office?"

Hannu shook his head and adjusted his hair. "I've a laptop computer and a mobile phone. It's my electronic office. No physical boundaries. The only thing I need from you is your written authority to discuss details of the case with the bank - it's going to have to be my starting point."

Sean slid an envelope across the desk. "I'd already thought of that. The bank are quizzing their own computers even as we speak, but it seems that some clever programming has moved the money and left no trace. What do you think they can tell you? They seem to be baffled themselves."

"They can't tell me anything. But it will let them know you're serious about finding the culprit. That way, when I ask them to let me into their electronic labyrinth, they might agree."

"And if they don't?"

"They probably won't, but I'll sneak in the back door and start looking anyway."

"I'm not sure I want to know any more." Sean said, his usual good humour returning. "You guys seem to walk a dangerous tightrope."

Hannu jumped down from the chair. "There are just a few of us who can access secure networks without leaving any trace. It's a bit like breaking into someone's home; if you don't know what you're doing you'll leave fingerprints or other clues behind."

Sean finished his coffee in one swallow, then stood and offered Hannu his huge hand. "Don't get caught doing anything illegal then."

The young Finn smiled. "Don't worry. There aren't too many beggarin' people who even know how to read my fingerprints - and that includes the legendary Angus Slooth."

* * *

Nick Ferris wiped his hands on the kitchen towel that Sandy offered him. "Safe as a bank." he said, securing the plastic lid of the water storage tank. "Only someone doing a really thorough search would look in there."

Sandy offered her arm to help him as he lowered his gaunt frame off the chair on which he'd been balancing, but her father was like a sure-footed stick insect and didn't need much help. "Hope it's waterproof," she said, nervously.

Her father dropped the towel onto the worktop and closed the cupboard door. "No problem. There's so many layers of polythene and tape round it, it'll be drier than the inside of a submarine."

Sandy followed him into the living room. "What now?" she asked, perching on the edge of the settee and crossing her long, slender legs.

"We do nothing for a week or two then, as you were suggesting the other day, I reckon we should move to fresh pastures."

"Like where?"

Nick reflected for a moment. "How do you fancy the south of France or Northern Italy for the summer months? We can take a break and think about our next move."

"Sounds okay with me. Me and my boobs need a bit of sun after being in this rain-soaked corner of the world. What about renting a villa in Cannes or Nice? I can go and get some brochures tomorrow."

"Sure. Somewhere near a golf course."

"But you don't play golf, Dad. I doubt if you even know the rules."

"I don't, love, but I'm prepared to learn. I think a gentleman of my status should know how to socialise with those to whom wealth comes naturally."

Sandy flung a cushion at him, which he fended off neatly and tucked behind his head. "Socialise with them? You're more likely to rob them than socialise with them."

Her father grinned his not-quite-white grin. "Exactly, Sandy! Find me a villa near a golf club. Someone's bound to ask me to look after their golf clubs while they go take a leak."

Sandy laughed. "Talking of which. Guess who's buying me a drink at the golf club at Nordwijk in…" she checked her watch, "in about an hour?"

"Go on."

"Marcus Foyer. The guy who joined us briefly for a glass last night."

"The big, tall hunky thing? All padded shoulders and bulging crotch?"

"You noticed."

"Could hardly miss it, Sand. Mind you, I always knew that if you were going to date some guy while we were in The Netherlands, it would need to be someone with bulging shoulders and a padded crotch."

"Padded shoulders and a bulging crotch!"

"Same thing."

"Not quite!"

Nick reflected for a moment. "Better not get too friendly, Sand, if we're going to move on again."

"You've never advised me to keep my distance before, Dad. I'm only going for a beer with the guy. And he only asked me because he felt guilty about having to rush off last night."

"I know, love, I'm just being a bit protective. You've only ever been close to one guy and you don't seem too well equipped to get over him."

"You mean Sean."

"I mean Sean."

"Yeah, well Sean's not stupid. He'll probably have guessed that we were somehow connected with last year's Three Leggs rip-off. So that relationship is well and truly finished."

"Is it?"

CHAPTER SIX

Theo swelled with pride as he settled into the bank manager's chair. The manager had taken a day off and, as chief cashier, Theo had requisitioned his office to talk in private to his visitor. It might not have been the promotion he was looking for, but it was the next best thing. After his fiancée's grilling about the bar escapade a week earlier, and the severe written reprimand issued by the bank's internal auditors, he was beginning to wonder if life had not taken a turn for the worse.

But, today, Theo's faith had been restored a little. Today, The Great Mother had given him the gift of Hannu Palernius - in person. Hannu didn't seem to suspect any divine intervention. He was seemingly under the impression that it was he who had tracked Theo down with the help of a little bit of electronic gadgetry that he had built on his kitchen table at home. In fact, he told Theo that he doubted whether Theo's spiritual CEO actually knew the difference between the cumulative binomial distribution probability of a hyperlink and the standard deviation of its exponential inverse hyperbolic sine. On the other hand, whilst staring curiously at Theo's bright yellow hair and dangling monocle, Hannu was sure that Theo's celestial guide had a sense of humour.

No matter who would ultimately claim the credit for putting the Dutchman and the Finn together, Theo vowed to remain eternally grateful for the reinforcements who now sat on the other side of his desk. Though Hannu Palernius had only given the chief cashier an outline of why he was there, Theo just knew that it was going to lead to the arrest of Sandy Ferris and his own exoneration. It was, after all, The Great Mother's will. Wasn't it? "So what do you want me to do?" he asked.

"First, you can help me if I have any language difficulties," Hannu said.

Theo screwed his monocle into his eye socket, wiped his chin, and adopted a bank manager's tone. "I doubt if you will come across that particular problem," he replied, somewhat more haughtily than he had intended. "Almost everyone here speaks English as a second language."

Hannu glowered at him. "In that case, I can move straight on to how I arrived here in your bank."

"But you've already told me. The man you work for was robbed of half a million pounds and you've discovered that the transfer was made using my telephone."

"Not exactly your telephone, just your telephone line."

To Theo, the distinction was negligible - hair-splitting as he would later tell Joska. To him it all boiled down to one thing; Sandy Ferris had been up to something while employed by Alliance Bank and now he had the proof – well, nearly. The fact that Sandy had left the bank three weeks earlier and that the theft had taken place only a week ago was an irrelevant trick of high technology that could easily be disremembered. He didn't see any need to be overly encumbered by the facts. No doubt she planned it all while working for the bank and just triggered it after the bank inspectors had finished their work. "So do you want me to phone the telephone company and see if they can verify the call?" he asked.

"Not necessary," Hannu replied. "I've already done it. That's how I come to be sitting here now."

"You mean you've already spoken with them?"

"I didn't speak to anybody, I just took a quick look in their records!"

"I don't understand," Theo said, feeling that he was on a correspondence course and the next lesson was still in the post.

"Don't let it worry you," Hannu said, maintaining the position of his parting in a way that Theo couldn't work out. "Just accept my word for it that the link was made using your telephone line. The problem is that whoever wrote the programme knows what he's doing. Your line was only used to divert the command connection, it wasn't used to actually divert the funds. That was done using another proxy, so I was totally unable to trace either the recipient bank or the command modem link. The author of the programme obviously knows about firewalls."

Theo was now completely lost. He wasn't sure whether to keep his mouth shut and give the impression that he was stupid, or open it and remove any doubt. Instead he wiped his chin and took a course of action that would trigger a totally unforeseen series of events. "Sandy Ferris!" he said triumphantly. "She's your culprit."

"…?"

"She's the one who took the money. She used to work here but disappeared about three weeks ago. I've been looking for her myself but she's moved. I know she's still around here somewhere but I just can't find her."

Hannu looked as though he was regretting having made the trip to The Hague.

"You don't believe me do you?" Theo asked, reaching for his handkerchief as he planned another chin-wipe.

"Well, we're just a bit short of actual evidence."

"No we're not!" Theo said. "You told me earlier that the man who was paying you thought that there had been other people involved in the previous peculation at his Company, some man who used to work for him, and his daughter. So there we are." He smiled victoriously as he folded his moist handkerchief and replaced it in his pocket.

"Do you mind sharing your thoughts with me?" Hannu asked, after a moment's silence. "I fail to see the connection."

"Well don't you see? It's obvious."

"Please?" - more of a command than a question.

Theo scooped up his ballpoint and jabbed his thumb excitedly on the knob at the end. "Sandy Ferris. She lives here with her father. She knows my telephone number. If they were involved in last year's deception at your employer's firm, they might also have known about your employer's bank accounts. Don't you see, it all fits."

"The fact that both people have a father seems a rather obscure link," Hannu said. "On the other hand," he continued, repairing his parting again, "I can test your theory. Can I use your phone?"

Theo brightened. "Of course. You're going to ring your employer?"

"I'm going to ring the man who's contracted me to find the guilty party or parties. If he can confirm that this Sandy er…"

"Ferris"

"If this Sandy Ferris is the one who he thinks might have been involved in the previous embezzlement, then we might have unravelled a part of the puzzle."

"What do you mean, 'unravelled part of the puzzle'?" Theo said. "We'll have solved the puzzle and we can turn it over to the police… can't we?"

Hannu smiled – a slightly cheerless smile, it seemed. "What shall we tell the police? That we know someone who knows your phone number and who's father used to work for the Company that was robbed? I don't think we have a very convincing case, do you?"

Theo's wet chin dropped again.

"Anyway," Hannu said, "we don't even know yet whether we've made the right connection. I think it's time I called Mister Legg."

* * *

Rolien van der Laan did not even feign curiosity when Hjalmar, for the second time, asked to borrow her spare key to the top flat on Grote Markt. She was well aware that his strange behaviour stemmed from the fact that the Ferris's had withdrawn their ill-gotten gains from their bank before Hjalmar had had a chance to remove them himself. And since it was she who had trashed his computer, she felt sufficiently guilty to pass him the key without questioning. Anyway her agenda did not require his presence so she was grateful that he would be occupied for a while. The first time he'd borrowed the key he'd been gone all day, and Rolien was hopeful that his second visit would take just as long. But she'd be sure to hook the chain on the front door just in case.

Her previous appointment with Marcus Foyer, her clean-cut estate agent, had convinced Rolien that her solicitor was right, and that it would most definitely be appropriate to arrange her second appointment at a time when Hjalmar was unlikely to be there. So, when Hjalmar disappeared down the road clutching a carrier bag and the spare set of keys to the Ferris's apartment, she picked up the telephone and summoned Marcus.

'Straight away.' she said.

'To fill me in.' she told him.

She hugged her knees in anticipation. A little siesta was just what she needed right now.

* * *

Theo listened attentively to the brogue that emerged from the speaker of the telephone. It was the first time he'd heard an Irish accent.

"Sure an' do nothing until I get there," the voice said. "Or at least nothing that might warn that pair of scallywags that we're on to them."

"Understood," Hannu replied, staring quizzically at Theo who couldn't stop himself bobbing up and down in his chair.

"If you can find any way of tracing them without them knowing about it, then fair enough," the Irish voice continued. "But be very careful, I don't want them alerted in any way. I'll get a flight to Amsterdam tomorrow. God I hate flying."

"Let me know what time you plan to arrive and I'll meet you at the airport," Hannu said. "Now we know the name, there's a fairly good chance that I can get an address. I'll do a bit of electronic searching through the utility companies as soon as I get back to the hotel."

"Okay, but take care, miboy, I don't want you getting caught with your nose in someone else's box of binaries."

"They'd have to be beggarin' sharp to spot my thumbprints. I'll be in and out with an address before anyone knows about it."

As Hannu replaced the receiver, Theo looked at his guest with a mixture of awe and disbelief. "What's a binary?" he asked.

Hannu smiled. For the first time since he'd stepped into the bank, he seemed genuinely happy. "All computers represent data as a collection of bits," he said. "These bits can be in one of two states - off or on, nought or one. If one bit has two different states, two bits have four and three bits have eight. If two bits have four combinations, and three bits have eight combinations..."

Theo considered the maths and screwed his monocle a little tighter. "Er…"

"Just multiply eight twos together," Hannu continued enthusiastically. "One two for each bit. Two times two is four, so the number of combinations of two bits is four. Two times two times two is eight, so the number of ..."

"Er…" from Theo.

"Don't you get it?" Hannu asked. "I thought English was your second language. To convert a number from decimal to binary, begin at the leftmost bit position of one hundred and twenty eight. If the number is larger than or equal to the bit's weight..."

"Complicated isn't it."

"Well, there is a simpler way to convert bytes back and forth between binary and decimal; like memorising multiplication tables. The byte can be split into two four-bit halves, each half called a nibble..."

"Would you like a cup of tea?" Theo asked.

"… and the mathematics is so pure; an eight-bit binary byte can be split in half, each nibble converted to decimal and two decimal numbers added together…"

Nothing would now ever convince Theo that The Great Mother hadn't sent him this slightly built young man with a moveable parting that kept the brain of a mastermind warm. The only thing Theo couldn't understand was why, when the genius finally seemed to have run out of binary explanations and he offered to take St. Hannu of Finland for a coffee after work, The Great Mother's messenger preferred to retire to his hotel for a beer.

CHAPTER SEVEN

Big Jack Riley's blue Jaguar drew to a halt in the village square at Wijngaarden. He'd chosen the village from the map as being close enough to Gorinchem to begin his search. Unfortunately, the village turned out to be little more than a skimble-skamble of country houses hovering insect-like around a bicycle rack, and his English-registered car stood out like an Arab at a Bar mitzvah.

An overnight journey from London had left Jack heavy-headed and red-eyed. Dressed in Bentley Platinum sunglasses, camel-hair overcoat and a Roger Dubuis watch, he eased his four hundred pound frame wearily from the car and hauled his eight hundred dollar Louis Vuitton suitcase from the boot. He looked up at the threatening sky and quizzed his thoughts. His quarry was here somewhere, but not close by. He would have known if George were close by. The fact that he had to discipline his own brother gave him no pleasure - quite the opposite. But it was imperative to castigate the offender and ensure that no one else would think it worthwhile to short-change Jack Riley.

It was a Saturday and the village was quiet. Jack lumbered across the empty, tree-lined square towards the steps of the Paleis Hotel, a substantial but neglected building whose better days had passed well before horses had been replaced by bicycles. The wild vine that covered the building was showing early leaf and, like a lazy chameleon, the structure was in the course of metamorphosing from grey concrete into green velvet.

The lobby was dingy and slightly musty. Somewhere in the background was a smell that triggered distant memories; a sort of institutional antiseptic that Jack associated with his catechism days. A brass bell attracted the attention of the proprietor who, despite the suspicion of a moustache, was probably of the female gender.

Jack knew she was watching him. She was staring too hard. Though he didn't make a habit of hitting women, this one probably didn't qualify, and he was tempted to place a well-aimed set of knuckles on the bridge of her nose – teach her some manners. Instead he asked: "Got a room for a few nights? Double would be nice, single if not."

It was about as effective as mustard on chilli pepper. The lady stared at him and shrugged her shoulders. Though Big Jack spoke no Dutch, it was apparent that the lady spoke nothing else.

Jack reached for his phrase book and muttered a string of curses that would have blistered the paint on a nuclear power plant. It did nothing to stifle the spasm of loathing for his brother for having put him in this position. There would be no synthetic grief when he had completed his task. He hoped he would get to George before the man he had hired.

Saving some money and retrieving stolen secrets were incidental to the satisfaction of seeing the fear in George's face when he confronted him with the consequences of his actions.

Jack's eyes turned dark, like the surface of a lake when a cloud blocks out the sun. "Big fat bastard," he muttered, checking his watch. He had an appointment to keep with Wally, his informative driver, who had smuggled a piece of equipment over for him in the back of his lorry. If he didn't show up on time, Wally was dumb enough to assume he wasn't coming and just leave. The last thing Jack needed was to be wasting time asking for a cheap hotel room in broken Dutch from a lousy phrase book.

Mevrouw Modderkolk allowed herself a small smile of satisfaction as the fat English tourist made a pig's-arse out of his effort to speak Dutch. After three attempts, she pretended to understand him, took his deposit, gave him the only key with a room number on it, and pointed him towards the staircase. The man had the arrogance to stand looking at his suitcase, waiting for the arrival of a porter, before realising he wasn't going to get one.

"We don't serve dinner, either," she called after him, in near-perfect English. "We only do breakfast."

She left the lobby and regained the questionable comfort of her living quarters, where the antiseptic faded to a mildewy scriptural odour and a reek of Judas and Jesus. She wasn't usually so rude to tourists – there weren't enough of them who chose the Paleis Hotel to do that. But his arrival had interrupted her while she had been taking one of her regular inventories of the growing stack of money that she didn't dare bank. It was money that had been causing her conscience to serve up sleepless nights for many long months.

"So what's a woman supposed to do?" she muttered to herself whilst pulling at a piece of elasticised stocking that was gouging the makings of a rift valley into her thigh. It was an hour and a half bus journey into the city so she certainly wasn't box-rattling just for the amusement value. The one and only reason for volunteering to make the street collections for The Mission choir was so that she could sneak a few euros out of the box. Something at which she had become extremely adroit.

Convincing disbelievers to part with their money was the easy bit. In fact, she had never been so good at anything in her life. What had turned out to be less easy was to stop helping herself to a large percentage of the proceeds. Fifty percent, in fact. A euro for The Great Mother's earthly mission, a euro for Mevrouw Modderkolk. Now, five years on from her street collecting debut, she was sixty-five thousand euros better off and her conscience was deep in debt. Or was it just the fear of being caught? She wasn't totally sure.

She stared at the wads of notes that she couldn't spend, because she could never explain how she came to have them. Each time she counted the money, she convinced herself that the risk was too great, and that she would stop and hand everything over to the Reverend van Aanroy. But then, if she did that, what would be the point in dressing up and catching a country bus into The Hague each week? And if she didn't get dressed up and catch a country bus into The Hague each week, who would she ever get to talk to except for a few snot-nosed English tourists who couldn't even carry their own suitcases up the stairs?

And so she had continued - a euro for the church mission, a euro for Mevrouw Modderkolk. Worse than that, she'd even invented new ways of intimidating non-believers into parting with their hard-earned cash, which meant that her money mountain had grown even more substantially than before.

Through her dress, she tugged at a strap that was digging into her shoulder, then reached behind and scratched her ample buttocks. She collected up the bundles of notes, wedged them back into the leather hold-all and replaced it under the shelf in the larder. She knew she was going to have to do something soon. She couldn't live the rest of her life as a moral outcast.

Jack Riley watched in silence as the hotel owner sniffed her armpit, then he turned quietly away from the part open door and tiptoed back across the lobby. He'd only come back down to tell the lady to stuff her smelly hotel. Now, having seen the wads of money she was hiding, he decided that it wasn't such a bad establishment after all. Perhaps his overseas mission would turn into a profit-making venture as well as sorting out his wayward brother.

* * *

Hannu turned his back on Theo and fiddled with a connection at the back of his laptop computer, which might or might not have been loose. "The access is on Grote Markt," he repeated for the third time. "But there are six beggarin' apartments sharing the same entrance. Theirs is apartment 'F' which probably means that it's at the top of the building."

"But I still don't see why that's relevant," said Theo.

By nature, Hannu was a peace-loving person, but now he discovered that he suddenly wanted to head-butt Theo, or just sort of smack him round the deerstalker for quite a long time. "It's relevant," he muttered, with as much patience as he could muster, "because we have no idea of the layout of those apartments. If we just ring on their entry intercom and announce what we want, they're hardly likely to open their door and welcome us in. There may be an alternative exit that we don't know about."

"What, you mean just leave without their belongings?"

Hannu sighed and raised his mousy eyebrows to Sean who gave him an indulgent half-smile and picked up the explanation. "I would guess that they rent the apartment furnished, Theo. And in any case, so long as they still have all that money in a bank somewhere, they won't be too worried about a few personal belongings. Hannu's quite right; we have to go a little carefully."

"So what do you suggest?" Theo asked.

"I suggest we wait nearby for one of them to enter or leave the building and have a little chat with them."

"That means we're relying on you," Hannu said, straightening up. "You're the only one who knows what they both look like."

"Yes, but I know what she looks like," Theo said

excitedly, spraying Hannu and his chin with saliva.

Hannu pretended that Theo was invisible and went back to fiddling with his wire, leaving Sean to explain. Maybe grabbing Theo by both ears and smashing his head into the tabletop would be the best approach.

* * *

The previous evening, at an impromptu assembly of the faithful few in The Mission's meeting rooms, Joska had purred contentedly as the Reverend van Aanroy had given a real stem-winder of a sermon. She had listened with delight as her custodian of moral correctness had railed at sinners in the vengeful hands of a merciful Great Mother. Her heart had warmed at the seraphic spirit of the meeting.

But today things had changed and Joska was not in good humour.

Joska and Theo usually spent their Saturdays together, sometimes preparing for special fund-raising events for The Mission, sometimes talking persuasively in the street to people whom they felt might be in need of a new spiritual home. This weekend, as a break, they had planned to clean and tidy the attic while Joska's parents were away visiting her aunt. But this morning Theo had called making some excuse about having to work on an internal audit at the bank – he'd catch up with her later, he'd said - and now she found herself alone in the attic, half-heartedly starting the tidying task on her own.

She opened the door of an ancient wardrobe and peered inside, turning her head in both directions like a squirrel looking for its winter store of nuts. It was empty except for the smell of furniture wax. The door vibrated with a thunk as she slugged it shut. She stared at her own faded image in the tarnished mirror on the door front. Her heart-shaped face stared back at her, expressionless. As if to prove she was still alive, she turned down the corners of her mouth in disapproval. Then she barred her teeth and examined the gap that Theo described as cute.

Joska fingered the silver medallion around her neck and wondered whether she shouldn't just go back to her bedroom and dress up a little. She wanted to feel attractive and she wanted to feel loved. But she knew she was too untidy to be either. Normally she allowed her swathe of red hair to flow free across her shoulders but today, in readiness for attic-cleaning, she had plaited it into matching pigtails that hung down her back like twin stains of rust from a dripping tap. A chequered scarf had been knotted judiciously over her head to avoid hair-cobweb contact, and her normally sensible long skirt had been replaced with a pair of Theo's cast-off trousers that they had planned to give to a needy third world appeal. She didn't like her reflection. She looked too broad-shouldered and too formidable to qualify as anybody's darling, except Theo's.

She clamped her forearms under her bosom and wriggled her shoulders. Beneath the bright orange pullover, she had a young woman's figure, yet, due to the cantilevered effect of sensible undergarments, her breasts always seemed to slide off-centre of their own accord and needed frequent adjustment. She sighed. It could be a hard life being The Great Mother's handmaiden.

She'd done nothing yet, but the stale attic air made her flesh creep. She didn't want to be there. She just wanted to go back down the steep wooden steps, take a long, hot bath and emerge like a wood nymph, smelling aromatic and powdery with salutiferous perfumes extracted from pollens and seaweed, like she'd seen on the adverts. She turned away and headed towards the trapdoor that would return her to the comfort of her parent's home. If woolly-socked feet on dusty wood could sound harassed, hers did.

Exasperated, she kicked aside a long-forgotten doll and stopped to watch as motes of dust swirled through a narrow ray of sun that had no right to be there. Her remorse was immediate and total. There was no justification for treating things that way just because she was moody. The Great Mother wasn't moody: The Great Mother was omnipotent, omnipresent, omniscient …and a lot of other omni's - the Reverend van Aanroy had said so. She picked up the tiny porcelain figure and hugged it better, mouthing a silent prayer of compunction. Placing the doll carefully on an old, battered suitcase, she determined to atone by starting her task without further delay. Maybe Theo wouldn't have to stay at the bank too long, and could join her soon.

As she busied herself developing a plan of action, her peripheral vision registered a slight movement to her left. Startled, she drew a short breath and dared herself to look directly towards the cause of her discomfort. Her eyes traced the beam of light that penetrated the gap in the ragged curtains, and came to rest on the porcelain doll – the one that now possessed a sunshine halo and a rainbow aura. She stared hard at it. She could have sworn that she had lain it on its back on top of the suitcase, but now it was sitting up, looking at her from behind long, dark eyelashes. She blinked to make sure she wasn't imagining anything, and still the doll stared at her.

Joska was not an imaginative woman. In fact, on one or two occasions, Theo had even gently suggested that she was a little impassive. These few criticisms from an otherwise devoted servant had usually come at the end of a heavy petting session when Theo had been in state of total discomposure and Joska had had to remind him that they weren't due to be married for another two years yet. Two years to collect all the linen, cutlery, pot plants and other necessities of married life had seemed like an awfully long time to Theo who would gladly have paid for everything on the spot if Joska had but allowed him bigger embraces. But, much though Joska might have enjoyed bigger embraces, she was The Great Mother's vehicle and not Theo's plaything. Right was right, and there was a time for everything. The Reverend van Aanroy had said so.

Thus it was that she knew that the doll had moved and she knew that she had not imagined it, much though it defied probability. She stared at the sanctified figure, waiting for it to move again, but it stared back at her, inert and lifeless. A minute passed before she breathed regularly again - a minute during which time she could hear her heart beat and the air buzz in her ears like a squadron of mosquitoes. It was only when her muscles relaxed and her breathing returned to near normal that The Great Mother spoke to her. It was then that She told her to look in the suitcase: that the suitcase was where Her message lay. The doll was only the harbinger sent to attract Joska's attention, or at least that's what she told Reverend van Aanroy later.

Joska didn't exactly hear The Great Mother speak; she just felt an incredible urge to look inside the case. It was clear to her that it was The Great Mother's will. Why else would the doll have sat up and developed a sunshine halo? Why else would The Great Mother have sent Theo to the bank this morning and left her alone? Why else would the Reverend van Aanroy have spoken the previous evening about The Great Mother using Her missionaries as the vanguard for Her word?

But the real miracle was that when Theo had suggested having a weekend off from raising money and recruiting converts, she had found the suggestion perfectly acceptable – desirable even. Neither guilt nor remorse had delayed her assent as it had on other occasions when he had suggested a quiet weekend together. Now it was obvious: The Great Mother hadn't wanted her to feel guilty. The Great Mother had chosen her, Joska De Jong, as Her emissary, and The Great Mother had now shown her why She wanted her here, in this place, at this time. Alone.

Joska kneeled reverently in the dust in front of the icon of Her love. Her hands automatically clasped together under her chin like two magnets, and she began to mouth a silent vigil. She'd called them prayers when she was young, but the Reverend van Aanroy had led them to understand that all prayers to The Great Mother were a vigil for the coming of a new world order. 'Dear Mother, to whom all things are known, accept me, a humble sinner, as Thy vessel. Use me as Thou wilt and…' She stopped, mid vigil, and stared in amazement as one of the catches on the suitcase sprung open. 'Yes,

Leader, I hear you.' She reached forward and gently coaxed the second catch. Slowly opening the lid she peered inside…

Morning had dragged into afternoon before Theo decided that he could wait no longer. Though catching Sandy Ferris was at the top of his list of priorities, he knew that it was not particularly high on Joska's list. In fact, it wasn't on Joska's list at all. He hadn't yet plucked up enough courage to tell her that he had received an official reprimand from the bank's inspectors, knowing that, when he did, he would be obliged to explain the repercussions on his career. He didn't want to give up his sentinel; he wanted to wait as long as was needed to be able to lock horns with his antagonist, but he knew that if he didn't respect Joska's needs he might lose her to someone else with a brighter future, and that simply wouldn't do. After summarising his predicament to Sean and Saint Hannu, he excused himself and left the warmth of the café to mingle with the crowds that filled the pedestrian precinct.

Theo peered at the faces of the shoppers who jostled past him, one eye on the shop windows, one eye on the ever-present clouds, and wondered whether The Great Mother really could see into the minds of so many people at the same time; it must keep Her awfully busy. And then fate dealt him an ace. As he turned the corner from Grote Markt into Vlamingstraat, he sidestepped quickly to avoid a running child who was not looking where he was going. In sidestepping, he blocked the path of a young English lady with cherry red fingernails and long black hair. "My goodness, it's you!" he exclaimed, looking down into Sandy's smiling face.

"Hello, Theo," she said, staring up at his hat. "How

are you?"

"Just fine thank you," he replied, unable to comprehend why her speech was perfectly controlled and normal. He had somehow thought that she would be embarrassed - that she would try to run away. "Hoe gaat het U? — Sorry, how are you?" he asked, repeating her own question.

"A little better now. I'm still having to take anti-depressants, but the doctor tells me I can start reducing the dosage soon."

"I'm so pleased," he said, uncertain how to proceed. "You live near here?" he asked, after an awkward silence.

"Not far."

Two policemen were approaching, and Theo considered calling them and having Sandy arrested, but then he recalled that Hannu had said something about having no evidence. He couldn't remember exactly what it was, but it seemed to make some sense at the time.

Theo talked about the weather instead. Then, slowing down his speech whilst desperately beating his brains for some way to permanently detain Sandy, he chatted about the weather in Australia. When he noticed that she was shifting her weight from one leg to another, he talked even slower and changed the conversation to the weather in Belgium. Had she heard that there had been heavy rain in Brussels last night? She hadn't, and he was running out of discussion topics.

"Must be getting along," Sandy said, easing past

him. "Nice to see you again, Theo, byeee."

Whilst Theo had been talking in a manner that made Sandy wonder whether he was slipping in and out of consciousness, she had been aware that her father was leaning on the balcony four floors above – he had waved to her as she had walked down the street. The problem was, she didn't know how to warn him. Though the name of Theo Padmos had been mentioned in conversations, her father had never met the chief cashier and he would, therefore, assume that all was well and that she had simply met somebody she knew. She just had to stay calm and play for time; after all it was only Theo.

She turned the corner and strolled slowly between the wicker tables and chairs that filled the market place, stopping briefly to watch gangs of sparrows strut around the chair legs with their hands in their pockets, chewing gum and demanding titbits or else. After a short detour around the edges of the square, Sandy glanced over her shoulder, satisfied herself that Theo had gone, and headed for the entrance to the apartments. As she felt for the keys in her handbag, she glanced again to make sure that Theo wasn't following. There was no sign of him. Her keys were in her hand when a figure with a long shadow stepped out from the adjacent café entrance.

"Hello young lady. What a pleasant surprise."

Sandy did a double take to verify that it was Sean… it was. "Er, hello Sean. Fancy seeing you here." What else was there to say?

"Coffee?" he asked.

She checked her watch, turned her back to the apartment door, and shook her head. "Mustn't stop. Must be getting home."

"You'll not have far to go then will you?"

For ten minutes, Sandy listened as Sean spoke. He wasn't angry, but he was determined. When she pointed out their lack of evidence, he offered to accompany her to the police station and let the law decide. He made it abundantly clear that, in his view, formal charges with the Dutch police would certainly lead to the police on the Isle of Man taking a closer look at her association with the two dead villains who had nearly bankrupt him.

A small, fair-haired young man hovered in the background, and then Theo appeared from nowhere listening anxiously as Sean issued his ultimatum. Allow them to search her apartment themselves or they would get the authorities to do it. His argument was persuasive, particularly when he took the keys gently out of her hand and led the way up the communal staircase. Sandy held her breath as they mounted the stairs in tight formation and, as Sean opened the apartment door, she felt her heartbeat approaching the rate at which a petrol engine gets valve bounce.

There was a noise from the lounge upstairs, like a door closing. Theo was twittering about something so nobody else seemed to notice.

Sandy pointed to her bedroom. "You can start your search in here," she said, in a voice that could be heard on the other side of the market place.

She watched and listened as they proceeded to

check through her few personal belongings. She even allowed herself a smile of satisfaction when Theo opened the drawer that held her underwear, plunged in his hand, froze, and then closed the drawer again with his eyes tight shut.

But she kept listening.

"This one's my father's bedroom," she said, with the volume still turned up. "And that's the bathroom. You might want to wash your hands, Theo, now you've had them in my knickers."

From the corner of her eye, she caught Sean smiling to himself as Theo fell into the trap and did as she had suggested. When Sean smiled, his wrinkles smiled with him. It was the first thing people noticed about him. Sandy used to tease him that his face looked as though it had been trowelled on and allowed to dry too quickly, but his rugged contours emphasised a certain youthfulness that effused from deep within.

Sandy gave him a melancholy half-smile. She'd missed his warmth, and culpability chaffed in her stomach like a blister in a tight shoe. As Theo dried his hands in his hair, Sean winked at her, sharing the joke. The old Kilkenny creases in the corners of his eyes were still there, though he seemed to have lost just a little weight from round the middle since the last time she had seen him. Sandy had been fleeing the country clutching a suitcase full of Sean's money and he had given her a cheery kiss, oblivious to the maelstrom that awaited him upon his return to the factory. She felt a stab of guilt crawl up her spine - it was a new experience for her. Even now, she couldn't help herself conjuring up moments from their nights of passion, like precious gifts wrapped in tissue paper. If ever she had loved anybody apart from her father, it had been Sean Legg. The trouble was, she was only just beginning to acknowledge it.

She'd heard no more sounds from upstairs so, when they finished their inspection below, she led them up to the living area. She was already feeling more composed, and relaxed visibly when she spotted a few drops of water on the kitchen floor. When she noticed that the glazed door to the balcony was slightly ajar, she began to flash smiles to her visitors, chatting casually about anything and everything.

Her smile broadened as the little foreign guy tried in vain to reach into the water storage tank in the kitchen cupboard. Having found nothing, his shirt cuff left a dripping trail across the kitchen floor, swamping the few drops of evidence that her father had left behind.

She clutched her handbag tight to her side and hoped that they wouldn't insist on searching it. It would have revealed the JoinMyChurch card and the exact details of her alternative banking arrangements. She planned her strategy just in case. Fake a tantrum, reach into her bag, call them dirty names and throw some tampons at them. That should embarrass them enough to back off. It would certainly work for Theo, it would probably work for the foreign guy, but she doubted that Sean would be influenced. She knew that when Sean Legg set his mind to something, it usually got done.

Theo gave her a silly teeth-together beam. "Planning a trip?" he asked, as he picked up one of the holiday brochures of Cannes.

"Might be," she said. "I'll keep you informed so you

can come and poke your nose round the hotel room."

He dropped the brochure as if it had burnt him.

The strange little guy had taken an unhealthy interest in her laptop computer and was waiting as it booted up.

"What do you think you'll find in there?" she asked. "Gold bullion?"

"Who knows," he said, amiably. "Computers have a funny habit of telling their own story."

"Hannu's a computer whiz," Theo whispered, by way of explanation.

Sandy picked up her keys, stepped out onto the balcony and stared over the rooftops. She had the unpleasant feeling that her computer might hold more evidence than her handbag. When she was sure that her three visitors were otherwise occupied, she slipped quietly under the side rail and onto the roof that led to the gay bar and its convenient fire escape. Five minutes later, breathing heavily, she stopped next to her father's car.

"You took you time," Nick said.

"I had to wait till they weren't looking," she said, between breaths. "You've got the package?"

He nodded his head in the direction of the back seat of the car. "Safe as houses. I had an idea you'd run into trouble when I saw you talking to that bloke with the weird hat. When you left him, he was watching you from the doorway of the jeweller's shop and it was more than just your rear end he was interested in. When you didn't come straight up to the apartment I thought it would be best to play safe and make myself scarce."

"Well thunk." Sandy said, as they climbed into the old Ford. "Where to now?"

Her father reached into the pocket of his Bermuda shirt and dangled a key in front of her. "I've just been and seen a friend of mine. She said we can use her cottage for the next few weeks."

Sandy looked at the swaying key, puzzled. "Where is it?"

"Near a golf course!" he said, starting the engine.

* * *

As the sun set, Sean had closed the curtains in Hannu's room in the Corona Hotel. Hannu rubbed his eyes.

"Do you want another coffee?" Sean asked.

"Please. Black and strong."

Sean picked up the handset and dialled room service. "Tough going is it?"

Hannu nodded. His tiny fingers continued their rhythmic dance across the keyboard. He spoke with the air of an absent-minded surgeon in the middle of an operation – never letting his eyes off the patient. "A certain amount of native code was transferred to the root directory when the programme was run, but most of it was wiped off again. That's unusual. When you delete something, it normally only deletes the directory reference, which allows the computer to write over the unwanted segment at a later date, and anyway an exe file can't delete itself. In addition to that, this disk is quite badly fragmented so whatever clues may be left are all over the place. I've managed to resurrect some of the stuff, but it doesn't give us any help so far."

"Never mind, keep trying," Sean said, reassuringly. "If we can find where they transferred the money, we might still have a chance."

"Not much hope of that," Hannu said. "I should think they've long since emptied the account. Even if they didn't, you can bet your life they have now."

Sean shrugged. "I know, miboy, but you're the only chance we've got left."

Hannu, eyes fixed on the screen, raised his thin, blonde eyebrows. "Got something here," he said.

Sean crossed the room and stared over his shoulder.

Lines of code darted across the screen as Hannu flashed his fingers over the keyboard. "He's used bridging which makes it more difficult to track the source."

"Bridging?"

"Yeah, routing or bridging are the two choices, but routing assumes that addresses convey at least partial information about where a host is located, and the addresses are assigned and broken into fields corresponding to ..."

Sean yawned and lowered himself into the armchair.

"On the other hand," Hannu continued, "bridging is a method of path selection where addresses don't imply anything about where hosts are physically attached to the network. It relies heavily on …"

Hannu looked across at Sean whose eyes were fast closing. Must have been a long day for him too, what with Theo chuntering on about nothing of any consequence all the time.

"Tell me about Sandy Ferris," he said, catching Sean unawares.

Sean sat up. "Eh?"

"Tell me about Sandy Ferris," Hannu repeated. "What's she like?"

Sean stretched out his legs and slotted his hands behind his head. "I told you when we first met. She's devious, scheming, deceitful and not at all someone to be trusted."

"But she's got you hooked deep enough for you to leave your business and come trailing round Europe in search of her."

Sean stood up and paced slowly round the bed and back. "You're delving into stuff that I can't even give you an answer to Hannu." He sat down again. "Because I'm not sure I even know the answers myself."

"But you were lovers, right?"

"What's this, men's talk?"

"If you like. I'm just curious what makes a successful guy like you chase after someone as shallow as Sandy Ferris."

Sean perked up again. "Shallow, she is not, Hannu. Don't confuse misdirected with shallow. Sandy had an unfortunate upbringing. Her mother deserted her when she was a toddler and, much to his credit, her father raised her on his own."

"So what's he like then?"

"What, Nick? He's an out and out rogue," Sean said, smiling. "But you can't help liking him."

"Even when he robs you?"

"Even when he robs you! He's the sort of guy that will pick your pocket and offer to buy you a drink out of your own wallet. It's little wonder that Sandy is something of a fly-by-night."

"Unusual pair."

"Certainly. But then none of us is perfect, Hannu. Now, is that the end of question time?"

Hannu adjusted his parting slightly. "For the moment," he said, beaming. "But now I've got your attention, do you want me to tell you about bridge interfaces?"

Sean closed his eyes again. "Think I'll just take a little nap till the coffee arrives."

* * *

Theo took care to fold his hat before sliding it into

his coat pocket. He kissed Joska on the cheek then perched on the settee next to her. The television was on but Joska didn't appear to be taking much notice. Nor did her omnipresent granny who was snoozing in the armchair.

"Have a good day?" Theo asked.

"Yes," Joska replied, "I was in the attic. I had a message from The Great Mother, but it was just to draw my attention to the suitcase. The Great Mother's message will arrive there soon. I think She's just testing my faith first. It will only be a matter of time."

Theo had no idea what she was talking about, but he was beginning to have his own thoughts about The Great Mother. Niggling doubts were starting to creep into his soul, though he still couldn't acknowledge them openly. Particularly not to Joska. He was beginning to wonder whether van Aanroy's Mission wasn't just a do-it-yourself belief. I mean, where was it all written? Christians had their Bible, Muslims their Koran, Buddhists their... well whatever it was that Buddhists had. Where was the book wherein The Great Mother's words had been recorded for posterity? It would make it so much easier if there were a book.

In the armchair, Joska's granny began to snore.

Theo speculated whether he and Joska would ever get a place of their own so they could be alone together. And if they did, what would Joska's attitude be towards a closer union? Would she stick to van Aanroy's vision of a new world order, pushing his devoted initiates to the propagation of The Great Mother's Holy Wisdom?

To Theo, the whole thing was starting to feel like a mumbo-jumbo believe anything you want as long as it made life tough and as long as van Aanroy okayed it first. A mishmash of inspiration, meditation, and salvation. Not to mention guilt, with a capital G. Anything, it seemed, as long as van Aanroy's followers heeded his call and did his bidding.

"Lemonade," Joska said, coming from the kitchen holding two glasses.

Theo took one off her. "Joska," he said, thoughtfully, "have you ever thought about The Mission's monthly levy on my income?"

"Of course, Theo. The Great Mother's Commandment Number Seven: The Great Mother's work is thy work: commit to it one tenth of thy life, as She gave you all of Hers. It's how Reverend van Aanroy helps the needy. How he recruits people into the service of The Great Mother."

"Yes, but I have access to The Mission's bank account and I haven't noticed too many payments to the needy," Theo said. Nor have I had too much help from The Great Mother in tracking down Sandy Ferris, he thought, though he said nothing to Joska about that.

"Oh, Theo, you shouldn't doubt Reverend van Aanroy's motives. Don't forget, we're not party to his conversations with The Great Mother, and this might just be The Great Mother's way of testing your faith. Like She tested mine today."

Theo suddenly felt a little guilty. Maybe Joska was right and his suspicions were just a test. Casting his doubts aside, he said a quick vigil of atonement as he sipped his lemonade.

"Where's mine?" asked granny, opening one eye.

CHAPTER EIGHT

Until he met Detective Inspector Angus Montgomery Slooth of The Isle of Man Constabulary, Joris Duisenberg had always imagined his English to be better than average. He was beginning to reappraise his opinion as he struggled to decipher the unintelligible speech that emerged from the scruffy looking individual in front of him. He might have been less distracted if his visitor wasn't clad in worn jeans, trainers, and a Queen t-shirt with Freddy Mercury's face on the back..

As Chief Inspector for South Holland, Duisenberg had made himself fully cognisant of Slooth's reputation the minute he heard he was coming. What he had expected was an energetic, middle-aged man who exuded experience and guile, who was afraid of nothing and nobody, who wore sober suits and hand-stitched shoes. What he got was a shabby individual with hair that stood to attention like a door mat, it was difficult to take him seriously.

His visitor's police papers indicated a date of birth that put him in his early forties. If he had been asked to guess, Duisenberg would have added at least ten years onto that. Not just because he was talking to a Detective Inspector – a high rank in any police force – but because the skin around the man's eyes was weather-beaten and cracked, and the rugged face seemed to have the words 'well aged' tattooed into every wrinkle and crease.

"It was very clever," Angus Slooth said for the third time, his broad accent catching Joris's attention at last.

Joris wondered what a 'vercliffer' was. Or was it a 'veracleva'? He'd look it up when he got home.

"The money was moved through multiple accounts," Slooth continued, "then reversed out again as transaction errors. Consequently we've no' been able to trace the recipient account. Each trace takes days o' searchin' and we just dinna have the resources."

"And you've no other clues?" Joris asked, as Slooth fingered raw strips of tobacco into the bowl of his briar pipe.

"Just a wee one," Slooth replied.

"A weewun?"

"The program lodged into the bank's computer in order to move the cash on - it's known as worm logic, a bit like a virus. Whilst it can mostly self-destruct after it's done its job, it canna do so completely, and leaves behind lines o' binary code that are used to clear away other traces o' the original program. We managed to decipher a few bits o' the remnants and spotted a thumbprint."

"What's that?"

"What's what?"

"A thomprin. What is it?"

"It's a tadge difficult to explain really. It's a bit like a Modus Operandi that you maybe recognise as belonging t'a particular villain. The style o' programming can gi' a good clue to the programmer. It's no' as good as a handle, but it's better than nothin'."

Chief Inspector Duisenberg fiddled with a shiny button on his dark blue tunic and decided not to ask about handles. The answer would probably be just as incomprehensible. "So whose thomprin was it?" he asked.

"Regrettably unknown," replied the Scotsman, rolling his 'r's off his tongue like boiling water on a stove. "If we knew that, we could put out a trace."

"And where do the Dutch Police fit in?"

Despite the legislation against smoking in public buildings, Slooth fired up the pipe, sending clouds of pungent emissions billowing towards the ceiling. "We've tracked the movement o' funds through a Dutch phone line at a bank here in The Hague. We've notified the bank's Head Office and they're prepared to co-operate. First of all we wanted to let you know that we were operating on your patch, so that you were aware of what was going on, and secondly we could do wi' all the help we can get. I wondered if any of your own people could spare us some time?"

Joris Duisenberg weighed up the possibilities carefully before answering. He had enough problems dealing with an outbreak of shop break-ins without having to worry about a bit of electronic theft – though he was uncomfortably familiar with the concept. "We have very few officers devoted to fraud," he answered hesitantly. "The Netherlands is a small country and, despite a large financial sector, we don't suffer the same problems that seem to affect other countries. I'm not sure that we have the necessary resources or expertise to be able to help you. On the other hand, if you find the culprits we will, of course, co-operate fully in their apprehension and subsequent trial."

"Thanks," Slooth said, though his face said something else that Duisenberg couldn't read behind the smoke. "It's a pity aboot the manpower though. We could ha' done wi' as many people as possible before the trail goes cold."

He paused - a long pause like waiting for a stone to hit the bottom of a well.

Joris fiddled with the shiny button until he realised that he had twisted it off.

"I appreciate your support otherwise," Slooth eventually added, accepting that his counterpart was not about to change his mind.

"Realistically, what chances do you think you have of finding the culprit?" Joris asked popping the button into his pocket.

"I've ne'er lost one yet, and I don't intend to start now."

"The Mountie always gets his man, eh?"

"Something like that," Slooth said, rising from his chair and stretching like a cat.

"So you're going to the bank?"

"It's the only trace we have. Alliance Bank in Wagenstraat. D'yer ken it?"

"Pardon?"

"Do you know it? The Alliance Bank in Wagenstraat?"

"I should do. I bank there!"

"In that case, perhaps you wouldna mind introducing me to the manager?"

"I don't know him particularly well," Joris said, choosing another button to play with, "but I'm acquainted with their chief cashier, a guy called Theo Padmos, totally above reproach, bit of a religious freak."

"And you'll introduce us?"

"Of course. Mind you, I hear a whisper that Alliance has a few problems of its own at the moment. Rumour is they've had an unscheduled inspection. One of their cashiers left in a hurry and there was a suspicion that she might have dipped her hand into the till first."

"Hmm – interesting," from Slooth. "I wonder if there could be a connection?"

"What, between your case and a light-fingered cashier?"

"You never know. It's always as well to be aware of these secondary situations. Thanks for the tip."

"No problem," said the Chief Inspector, donning his coat. He paused to weigh up the Scotsman before he continued. "Can I just ask you one thing?" he said.

"Aye"

He took that as a yes. "Your name," he asked. "Is it for real?"

A hearty chuckle emerged from behind the pipe. "Aye," came the reply. "Slooth by name and sleuth by nature. Now can I ask you a question?"

"Fire away," said Joris, staring at the glowing pipe that was close to melt-down.

"Your manpower shortage. Is it for real?"

Joris nodded uncomfortably. "Every police force could do with more resources," he answered, leading the way quickly out of the office.

* * *

Like an insect with acute antennae, George Riley knew that something was up, that his brother was close by. It was just one of those identical twin things, like choosing the same colour toilet paper or whistling the same tune. Big Jack was in the vicinity and it was time to move on.

George stopped packing his borrowed tent along with his borrowed clothes into the boot of his borrowed car when he spotted a dinghy on the adjacent canal. Something about the boat's occupants drew his eye and he retreated into the early evening shadows of the tall cypresses to watch. There was nothing unusual about seeing a boat out on the canals that ran in straight rows between the polders; the campers played in them all day when the weather permitted. What interested George was the oarsman. The last person in the world he expected to see at Hans Brinker was one of his former workmates.

For a brief moment the thought flashed through his mind that Nick Ferris had been hired by his brother to track him down, but he discounted it almost immediately. Nick was a petty crook, not a killer, and he was sure that the man in the boat was the same Nick Ferris whom Sean Legg had once employed as a bookkeeper. If the razor-thin body, pointed nose and receding hairline didn't give it away, the Day-Glo blue shirt certainly did. Only one person in the world wore shirts like that.

During the five years that followed his escape from Jacks' influence, George had worked at, or at least collected a wage packet from Sean Legg's company, whilst wheeling and dealing with the island's disreputable few to earn a little extra for his daily flutter on the horses. The disreputable few had included Nick Ferris. That was before George's chosen horses had begun to fall, go lame or run in the wrong direction. At that point he had begun looking at other betting opportunities to try to recoup his losses. Then came his brother, Big Jack…

The boat drifted sideways and George held his breath as the other occupant, a young lady, reached down between her feet...

"That's it." Nick said. "Drop it now. I'm exactly in line with those two trees on the left and that big tree and telegraph pole on the right."

Sandy lifted the brown taped package and allowed it to slip over the side. "Do you really think we can find it again, Dad?" she asked apprehensively.

"No problem! I didn't completely waste my three years in the army. You only need a couple of cross-references and it's a doddle. Anyway the water's only six or seven feet deep, I could snorkel to find it if I had to."

"I hope you're right," she said, eyeing the trail of tiny bubbles that floated to the surface from the weed below. "I don't like the idea of chucking nearly a million euros into a drainage ditch."

"Don't fret, love," Nick said, taking half a dozen quick, light strokes on the oars. "Why don't I buy you a beer?"

"I'd rather get something to eat," Sandy replied, eyeing the water that slid under the old boat like oiled silk. "We'll have to do some serious shopping soon, I'm knicker-less and bra-less at the moment."

"Oh well that's a change!"

Sandy grinned. "And you'll be walking around with your wedding tackle on display when I stick those trousers in the wash."

"Jesus H, girl, you'll be getting me arrested."

"We nearly were." Sandy said, as the boat touched dry land. "I still can't get over Sean turning up like that. His bank would have made good his losses, so I don't suppose he was actually out of pocket."

Her father nodded as he stepped out of the boat.

"He knows we were linked to last year's little racket," Sandy continued. "He told me so in the market place before he let himself into the apartment. That's why I didn't have any choice but go along with their search. Theft is one thing, but they take double murder a bit more seriously."

"Do you really think that Sean would see you get done for murder?"

"Don't know. I'd like to think not, but who can tell?"

Nick glanced at her as he unlocked the car door. "You miss him, don't you." he said, omitting the question mark at the end.

Sandy blushed. "That's irrelevant, Dad. We've robbed him twice now inside twelve months, so I doubt he's missing me. Judging by the effort he must have put in to track us down, I think he's more likely looking for revenge than reconciliation."

Her father shrugged and slid into the driver's seat.

George Riley watched the couple drive away in the direction of Kinderdijk, just two miles west. He allowed the low branch that he had been holding to spring back into place, and stepped from the shadows. His fingers fiddled in the lining of his pocket for a sweet while he gave a long, thoughtful stare across the still water of the canal, as if he might be able to see something. Whatever it was that Nick and the girl were doing, he was certain it wasn't legal. Like himself, Nick Ferris was blessed with the uncanny knack of earning a living the easy way. Rumours at the factory after the business nearly went bust were that Nick and his daughter had somehow been involved. That's it! George knew he'd seen the young lady before somewhere - it was Nick's daughter, though try as he might he couldn't remember her name. Mandy kept crawling into his head, but he knew it wasn't right.

George had negotiated several deals with Nick Ferris before his disappearance - Nick was always happy to turn a quick buck. And to see him now, acting suspiciously in the Dutch countryside, could mean only one thing: profit! It had to be either cash or drugs or some stolen valuables, or else some sort of information that could be traded for a gain. At some point, Nick and his daughter would return for the packet and, when they did, George would be sure to be on hand to help them find it. He unpacked the tent again and began re-pitching it. His move to new pastures would have to wait a while.

The rich scent from the new blooms reminded him of his brother's after-shave. A shiver shook his spine. Jack was like a jellyfish washed up on a beach - tread in the wrong place and you were going to get stung. Big fat bastard.

Peering into the windows of the touring caravans as he passed, George rolled and strolled across the site towards the big wooden barn where the site owner spent his days. Money would change hands and he'd rent his patch of grass for another week.

He glanced across to the far side of the park where the tourist with the big motorbike and bright green tent sat in front of a gas stove, frying bacon and eggs. Smelt bloody good too, even from a hundred yards. George had never quite shed the feeling that the man's face was familiar. Apart from the few days when he had left his tent behind and gone off somewhere on his bike, his fellow camper had been on the site almost as long as him.

Just paranoia, George assured himself as he approached the wide double doors of the barn. One of them opened – just enough to let the heavy-built site owner squeeze out.

"What is it you want?"

George told him and handed over a crisp fifty-euro note. He had several more in his back pocket thanks to the generosity of the attendant at the nearby service station, who had left George waiting while he went for a pee. It would teach him that a bit of service and civility cost nothing.

"Nice site," George said, as if to justify wanting to stay for another week. "Very peaceful."

The owner grunted and moved to block his view of the inside of the barn.

"Bit of disinfectant in the lavatories wouldn't go astray," George added.

The owner grunted again and leaned his back against the barn door, closing it with a bang.

"Yeah well I'll be on my way then."

Unsociable git.

Secrets had always intrigued George. Bloody nosy, Jack had called him. But secrets, other peoples' secrets, usually meant profit, and profit meant that he could have a little flutter. His luck had to change some time soon. His horses couldn't fall down every time they got near a racecourse.

Time for a beer and something to eat, he thought. Things were on the up.

* * *

Andy Nottley wiped his hands on his jeans and straightened up. At one stage he thought he'd lost the car he'd been following, but had doubled back and spotted it again as it pulled into a parking space behind the pub on Kinderdijk's main road. It was never easy keeping out of sight on winding country lanes while maintaining contact with a target vehicle.

The contract had been well priced but fraught with risk. As usual, his initial instructions had come by telephone in carefully phrased sentences that would give nothing away to the casual listener. Then, within twenty-four hours, a complete dossier had arrived by courier. The full written description and photograph were excellent, but his client had only been able to give him the briefest of details as to the target's possible whereabouts.

Andy's early hesitation about accepting a contract that was virtually on his doorstep had disappeared now, as the benefits began to outweigh the hazards. Though over 40 miles from The Hague, he knew the area quite well and had known the likely places where a debt-dodger would hide. Bingo! He spotted his mark in double-quick time. Nice neat kill and he could have the money in the bank before the body had time to stiffen. Way to do business.

He climbed back into his rented Citroën. He always rented under a false name when working: anonymity minimised the risks. Reaching a well-manicured hand across to the passenger seat, he flicked a switch on the small electronic tracker that was tuned to the device he had just fixed to the underside of the foreign-registered car. The signal was clear and he adjusted the directional setting before replacing it on the seat beside him. He didn't totally trust gadgets because they seemed not to trust him. They would invariably develop a mind of their own when he approached them. At the moment though, the omens were good as the tracker blipped and flashed an accusing red arrow in the direction of the other car.

Lovingly, he fingered the bone-handled knife in his coat pocket – much more reliable than electronic gizmos. It was one of his collection of deadly sharp Languiole, the French-made speciality knives. Years of experience had taught him that the quarry nearly always clutched the implement after he had made his fatal thrust and, as a service to his victim, Andy always made certain to leave them holding a noble tool. Then, when he was sure that they were dead, he would leave another special 'visiting card'. Perhaps it wasn't sensible to leave clues, but Andy was an artist and it was only right to sign his name to a masterpiece. Pride in a job well done.

A few spots of rain flecked the windscreen as he flipped open the buff folder, which had lain on the seat alongside the tracking device. Andy took a final glance at the enlarged photo of the man he'd been following. Confirmed sighting – absolutely no question. He eased the car out of the car park and into the light evening traffic. It never did any good to wonder about the hit's private life. Was he married? Any children? Was he wealthy? What were his likes? His dislikes? That was all irrelevant. He simply did what he was paid to do, and he did it with merciless efficiency. Now it was time to relax and have a couple of beers. He would pick his own time to fulfil his contract.

It would be soon.

* * *

Joska had skipped her piano lesson to be there. She knelt devoutly in front of the battered suitcase and carefully opened the lid. She was as disappointed as she had been on all the other occasions.

Theo had scoffed when she had told him her story, and made her promise to forget the incident, telling her that it was just a trick of the light. But Joska knew otherwise. She knew that The Great Mother didn't play tricks, and the Reverend van Aanroy had confirmed it to her. And anyway Theo had been acting strangely recently. Consequently, without mentioning it to anybody, she crept quietly into the attic each day to see whether The Great Mother's message had arrived.

Today it had not.

Maybe tomorrow.

She closed the suitcase. Her thoughts were agitated

and she felt lonely and oddly displaced. She couldn't quite pin it down. She was constantly surrounded by people who loved her – Theo and the Reverend van Aanroy and The Great Mother – and yet she felt unhappily hollow. She wondered whether she should be more independent and think more about what happens in life.

But why do that when The Great Mother, in her wisdom, had thought it all out for you?

CHAPTER NINE

Theo had hibernated into that nebulous state where, though he was wide awake, he had neither thoughts nor opinions - like a surveillance camera, just tracking and panning and registering neutral responses. He gazed at his computer monitor, splashing his chin as he whistled to himself. He only knew two tunes; one of them was 'The Old Wooden Cross' and the other one wasn't. He was whistling the other one, because Reverend van Aanroy had messed around with The Old Wooden Cross, adding some Krishna-sounding mantras to the chorus, and Theo didn't like it any longer. He was not even sure that he liked the Reverend van Aanroy any longer. Despite several visits to The Mission leader's home to ask for advice about finding Sandy Ferris, Theo was no longer even getting past the front door. Van Aanroy was treating the Sandy Ferris question as if it were an irrelevance, almost as if he wanted Ms. Ferris to evade punishment. It was beginning to play through Theo's mind that the Reverend van Aanroy and Sandy Ferris were somehow in this together. But that was a silly thought wasn't it? There was no way that an upright citizen like the Reverend van Aanroy would ever get involved in anything illegal like theft.

A weary week of playing difficult questions and evasive answers with the red-faced police detective and his stinky pipe had left Theo little to thank The Great Mother for. He wanted to help the wild-looking Scotsman of course, but if the foreign detective brought Sandy Ferris to justice, he would claim all the glory. On the other hand if he, Theo, tracked her down, he'd be able to show the bank that he merited their esteem. Consequently, he had managed to avoid letting go any information that might place Sandy Ferris's name in the detective's mind. Fortunately, when the man had asked a question about the reason for the recent internal audit, the manager had been nearby and politely advised detective Slooth that it was internal matter and had been resolved internally. That was like telling him to mind his own business, wasn't it?

Theo continued to whistle his not-the-Old-Wooden-Cross tune. Just a few minutes ago, matters had progressed and he felt a little vigil of thanks in his heart, despite the fact that The Great Mother had bowled him some difficult balls recently. Particularly irksome had been his romance with Joska, which seemed to have cooled a little since Sandy Ferris had left the bank. Maybe he and Joska should search for a different type of stimulus in their lives. The word 'sex' sprang to mind, then he batted it back as quickly as it had arrived. You weren't supposed to think things like that, were you?

But why not? What were you supposed to think? He was beginning to feel uneasy about the whole van Aanroy thing. Though he had tried to put it out of his mind, he had never quite forgotten van Aanroy's words to him when his grandmother had been run over by a tram three years earlier. Van Aanroy had reasoned that her untimely death was a mystery, and that if we understood all the things that happened on earth we would be as wise as The Great Mother herself, which of course couldn't happen. And, though Theo knew he was supposed to trust The Great Mother's judgment, somehow, since there was no logical reason why his grandmother should have been run over by a tram, the answer had never seemed quite satisfactory.

He shrugged mentally and switched off his computer terminal. Why worry about it just as things were beginning to look up? Not only was it Friday afternoon, giving him the weekend to look forward to, but also his quest to find Sandy Ferris had taken a dramatic lurch in the right direction for once. Sean had been talking of giving up and returning to his little island while he, Theo, had never lost faith. Well, almost never, anyway.

Sandy Ferris had been careless and Theo had spotted it. She had used her charge card to buy petrol and to draw money from a cash dispenser, both transactions taking place in Kinderdijk, a village about forty miles south. Being a card issued by the bank, the amounts were debited directly to her account, which Theo had been observing with the fixation of a cat concentrated on a mouse. And now it was time to pounce.

A few moments earlier he had called Sean's hotel and broken the news to the Irishman who, psyched-up by the information, had wanted to leave for Kinderdijk without any delay. But Theo had insisted on being with them for the kill.

"Sure an' it might take longer than the weekend to

find her," Sean said.

"So I'll fake some compassionate leave," Theo responded. "Just don't go without me."

Having succeeded in delaying Sean's departure, Theo turned up the volume on his whistle, flicked back a loose hank of yellow hair, swung his legs from under the desk, and marched to the manager's office to demand his compassionate leave. If he was honest, he didn't really care any longer about his career at the bank – that was as good as finished whether he tracked down Sandy Ferris or not – he just wanted to find the cause of his troubles and have her castigated for disrupting his life. She deserved it. He was not sure what he would tell Joska, and it didn't seem to matter any more, she seemed to be otherwise occupied, waiting for messages from The Great Mother that never arrived. It was all a question of priorities, and Sandy Ferris was at the top of Theo's list.

In the Corona Hotel matters were less clear.

"Count me out," Hannu said. "I can't stand the idea of being near that clown any longer. Anyway, I can make myself a lot more useful staying here and carrying on with these binary traces."

"But what more can you hope to achieve?" Sean asked.

"First I can make sure that we have all the evidence to pin the Ferris pair down, and second I can try and find out where the original programme came from." He cast a sideways glance at the laptop on the table. "There are still areas of disk space I've not searched. It's a long process, so I need all the time I can get. The Web Site was set up in a false name but if I can get enough code I might be able to get a handle on the author. Whoever it is, he's no amateur."

Sean had heard plenty about thumbprints and handles over the previous week. He didn't need to ask what Hannu was talking about. "Well okay, if you're sure, miboy, but I would have appreciated your moral support. Theo is certainly a little unusual."

Hannu grinned and rearranged his parting. "You mean he's a ravin' nutter, don't you?"

"Sure an' I'd have to agree that's closer to the mark. And now it would appear that I'm going to have the pleasure of his company for a few days."

Hannu resumed his seat and his keyboard strokes. "Have a nice time," he said, still grinning. "You deserve it!"

* * *

Hans Brinker leaned against the barn doors and watched with growing hopes while the Municipal workers moored a flat-topped boat to the bank. As they steadied the barge with heavy ropes and drove a mechanical excavator aboard, it was clear that they were going to start dredging and clearing the weed from the canal next to the campsite; an on-going task in The Netherlands.

He'd received no paperwork regarding the depositing of excavated spoils so he assumed, and hoped, that the mud and weed would be dumped onto the cultivated polder on the other side of the canal, making the channel deeper and the polder higher and more organic. If nothing else, the Dutch were masters of recycling.

What a break. Now instead of having to make a round trip of almost ten kilometres to dump his earth, he could make a five hundred meter detour to the adjacent polder and get rid of his spoils in double quick time. He spat out another gob of bloody phlegm.

Phthook.

His time was running out. According to his doctor he should have been dead a year ago, but he couldn't afford the luxury of dying until his work was complete. He was getting closer now. Water was beginning to seep through the earth at the face of the tunnel, making digging harder. Another two or three metres and he'd feel safe in laying the charges, knowing that they would do the job. At last, after so many, many years in this dull land of dull people. Twenty dead peasants were nothing compared to the revenge that he would wreak on these godforsaken fools. Only then would his father find justice. Meanwhile, he had to summon the strength to keep digging: strength that came from the vision of billions of tons of water ravaging the land, the towns and the industry in the immense estuary of The River Maas. His moustache gave an anticipatory quiver at the thought of the wholesale carnage at Dordrecht, Ridderkerk and Gorinchem. And, better still, Holland's industrial and port complexes at Rotterdam, less than 10 miles away, would be wiped out as they so nearly had been in the tidal floods of 1953.

Immediately after the blast, the break in the dike

would open into a vast, spewing mouth of liquid death. Within hours, the levels of the River Lek would fall dramatically, grounding the sea-going vessels that served the heavy industry on its banks. The surrounding polders and towns would be hit by a violence of water such as nobody could ever imagine, and this would be followed by a great surge of new water, fed through the Pannerdens Kanaal near Arnhem where the River Waal became the Rhine. The grounded boats would be swept away like balsa flotsam in a monsoon. That would be only the prelude as road and rail bridges were destroyed and warehouses and oil storage facilities ripped out of their foundations. People, vehicles, animals and buildings would all be ground into the black slurry of eternity. And after the blast all the canals and all the dikes and all the pumping stations in the world would not save The Netherlands from its fate.

The Dutch had called '53 a disaster. What would they call this? Armageddon?

Phthook.

* * *

"Hi Marcus," Rolien purred as the estate agent answered after just two rings. "How are things progressing?"

"Better than planned," he replied, in a secretive whisper. "It's looks like we'll get completion on some more of the properties as soon as next week. Do you want me to come and see you to fill you in?"

Rolien hugged her shoulders at the thought. "That would be nice," she said. "What do you have planned for the weekend?"

"Nothing in particular."

"What about Sunday afternoon then? Around two o'clock?"

"Will you be able to get rid of Hjalmar for an hour or so?"

"No problem, he's too engrossed in his damn computers. I'll just rent another room and tell him I'm going out for a while."

"Bit dangerous isn't it?"

"I'll book the room in your name!"

She heard Marcus chuckle at the other end of the line.

"See you two o'clock Sunday," he confirmed. "Put some champagne on ice."

"Done!" she said, and hung up the phone.

Rolien loosened her housecoat and lay back on the bed, splaying her legs and stretching her arms upwards, reaching with the tips of her fingers towards the moulded cornices on the ceiling. The window was tall and wide, allowing rare, precious sunlight to flood onto the bed. She pulled her housecoat open, exposing herself to the sun's rays, basking her naked skin.

The Kaatjes Residence was one of The Netherland's finest private hotels. Though boasting only seven rooms, its associated restaurant, the Kaatje bij de

Sluis on the other side of the canal, earned its two Michelin stars with top quality cuisine. For many, the standard of accommodation and service at Kaatjes Residence came at a price that could cause the casual traveller to hurry away in search of something less majestic. The hotel's bold, square outline dominated the village of Blokzijl, once a small but thriving sea port. When the Zuiderzee had been dammed to form the huge freshwater Lake Ijsselmeer, the huddle of houses found itself ten miles inland, and its few aquatic travellers came by pleasure craft through the intricate cobweb of Holland's canals. There was no police station in Blokzijl, therefore no crime.

Hjalmar hadn't appeared to care where he went, so the hotel had been Rolien's choice. Being tucked away discreetly in the north-eastern corner of the country, it was far enough from The Hague to offer seclusion and privacy, but close enough to Amsterdam to be able to enjoy the city's nightlife if they chose. She had made the reservation in the hope that a few days in a different environment would bring her and Hjalmar closer together, but Hjalmar had brought his plastic box of circuitry with him and they were as far apart as ever. After two days, Rolien had seen and heard enough of her boyfriend's computers and had reserved an adjacent room so she could be left in peace to read or to supervise the sale of her properties.

Hjalmar's insatiable need to perfect his JoinMyChurch programme and her insatiable need for bodily satisfaction ensured that they were both losers. They had argued the evening before when she'd suggested a little cuddle time and he'd wanted to add a few more lines of code to the new, improved, all-singing, all-dancing software.

In an attempt to share their different worlds, she even showed an interest when he took the time to explain how the access codes reset themselves each time the programme was used, and how he'd relocated his web site after the Ferris fiasco. But his excitement at having an audience with whom he could share his secrets had just encouraged him to rush back to the other room so he could test another theory, while Rolien was left to keep herself company between the sheets. They were communicating in Morse code, which neither of them read. The problem was that Hjalmar didn't even recognise there was a problem. He was devoted to her in his own way, but his way wasn't enough to satisfy her needs.

Some positive action was needed to convince him that his computer programme wasn't the best thing since bicycles and orange anoraks had been invented. A little scheme had been fermenting in her mind for some hours but there were still bits missing. Marcus Foyer would probably be the person to talk to.

She stretched in the sun like a lazy lizard and discovered that her right hand had wandered to the soft, downy hair between her legs. Her fingertips explored gently, sending tingles of expectation up her spine and a warm glow to her belly.

Her liaison with Marcus Foyer was just a passing interest. He had a good body and knew how to please a girl, but a couple of hours once a week was enough. She needed more than just a passing interest. Hjalmar was her man and she wanted it to stay that way, but something had to be done to divert him from his electronic wizardry and back into the real world. If only his stupid programme would somehow backfire on him, maybe that would convince him to stop and pay her more attention. Now that she had an idea how it worked, it was something she planned discussing with Marcus on Sunday.

Outside, a young lady with red lipstick, large breasts and soft, dark hair that touched on her shoulders, adjusted the volume on her IPod… and waited.

* * *

Sean sighed with gratitude and quietly thanked Theo's god when Theo finally pulled his yellow Skoda to a halt on the near-empty car park in Kinderdijk. As the two men stepped out of the Lilliputian car, the big Irishman stretched and flexed his body. He wished he had insisted on renting a car and driving himself, but Theo had been adamant that there was no need to waste money on such a luxury.

Sean was seriously considering the possibility of walking the return leg – it would probably be quicker. It would certainly be more pleasant than having to share a car with a driver who insisted on blocking the fast lane of the motorway while cruising at 20 miles an hour. He cast an appreciative eye at the big English-registered Jaguar in the adjacent parking place. At least some lucky devil would be able to ride home in comfort.

"So, where to?" Theo asked.

"I'm not really sure," Sean replied, finishing his stretch. "I don't feel like spending another three hours just going back to The Hague so I guess we need to find a hotel. Though, judging from the size of this place, there might not be too many of those around."

"Don't worry, The Great Mother will provide – she always does."

"Hmmph. I don't suppose we can ask her to provide a proper driver on the way home can we?" Sean muttered under his breath.

But Theo had not heard him. He had spotted a weatherworn bed and breakfast sign and was already trotting across the road towards it, monocle firmly in place and deerstalker sitting on top of his head like an alert tea cosy.

CHAPTER TEN

It was Saturday afternoon when the telephone sounded in the cottage. Something about the ring stirred a bad memory. Sandy closed her eyes and concentrated as she dried her hands, then gave it up, and, in the moment of giving up, found it. A buried recollection of a call from the police when they had found her father in a house that didn't belong to him. "He's being held in custody prior to charges being brought against him in the morning," they had announced. It had been the longest night of Sandy's life. Her father's too. She crossed the kitchen and responded to the phone.

"Sandy, it's me," an urgent voice said. "I need your help."

"Why? What's up Dad?"

"I'm at the police station in Kinderdijk. I've been arrested."

Déjà vu.

Sandy moved from apprehension to alarm like

walking from one room into another. "What for?" she gasped.

"Murder!"

"..."

"Sandy, you still there?"

She whitened as the blood drained from her face. "I think so. I'm not dreaming this, am I?"

"Come and get me out of here."

"What's going on? I left you in town to have a beer. Who did you murder?"

"I didn't murder anybody. Listen, love, it's a long story, but I promise you I didn't lay a hand on anyone, though the cops here are convinced that I did. They don't seem to speak English too well and you know how limited my Dutch is..."

"I'm on the way, Dad. Which police station are you in?"

"Kinderdijk. The one halfway up Main Street, towards the church."

"Be there in ten minutes."

She grabbed the car keys and fled from the house.

Andy Nottley wiped a finger across the condensation on the side of his glass, and then took a large swallow of chilled beer. He had metamorphosed into the city gent on holiday. Sharply pressed slacks had replaced the scruffy jeans he had worn just an hour earlier, a pastel shirt had been substituted for his shabby tee shirt, and his pony-tailed hair was back in place over his natural crew cut. Expensive Raybans and Salamander shoes completed the transformation. It wasn't the first time he'd sat casually watching the police go about their work after he'd completed an assignment. It was his personal confirmation that he was master of his art. Swift, clean, impersonal.

Isolating the mark for the kill was not the only problem to be overcome in his chosen profession. His normal routine was to follow the target, often for days, until he understood the victim's behaviour patterns better than the victim himself – or herself, as the case had once been. It ensured a one hundred percent success rate and allowed for contingencies. On this occasion, understanding this particular target's routine was simple: campsite, café, shops, pub, campsite, café, shops, pub, Ad infinitum, it seemed.

Completing the contract on the campsite was a non-starter, because any stranger on such a tiny campsite would easily be remembered. The shops were out, and the café was too small. So the bar was the logical location. An amateur would avoid a public place like that, but Andy was no amateur, and he recognised a perfect opportunity when he saw one. He was glad it was over. Weekends were busy times and he had people to see and places to go.

His target had been sitting on the terrace of the bar across the road from where he now sat. An earlier recce of the bar's toilets had confirmed Andy's theory that it was the best place to fulfil the contract. Two doors led into the washrooms: one from the front bar facing the street, and one from the rear bar overlooking the polders. A convenient crack in the panel of the cubicle door allowed Andy to keep an eye on the urinals while he rolled on his surgical gloves. The target entered the washroom, and Andy knew he didn't see him. He didn't think about the target's pain when the blade would strike. Those sorts of reactions were for amateurs.

And then something strange had occurred. Andy didn't know what it was or how it had happened, but he had developed a hole in his recollection. The actual moment of the kill – the knife crunching through gristle, the body collapsing under its own weight, the last gasp of the victim - was normally etched permanently in his memory, like carving his initials in the bark of a tree.

This time, after a short wait in the cubicle, all Andy could remember was standing over the body of his man; a big, fat body with a big, round face and a lot of blood. But, as usual, none of it on him. He did remember, though, dropping his stock-in-trade 'calling card' onto the warm corpse, rolling off his gloves and leaving the bar as casually as he had entered it.

It was obvious, as he watched the uniformed men struggling to load the big man's body into the back of a yellow ambulance, that the result was good and that the kill had been executed with his normal efficiency. He'd suffered narcoleptic blackouts for many years, but never during a hit. Perhaps he had no reason to concern himself, after all no witnesses appeared to be rushing forward. He took another sip of beer and stared admiringly at the legs of the pretty young lady with long, dark hair who parked her car next to his and rushed across the street into one of the cobbled alleys that led towards the church.

"What's happened?" Sandy asked, breathlessly.

Her father lifted a hand to his mouth and gnawed at a finger like a hungry dog, his eyes flicking from Sandy to the watching policeman. "I still don't know, Sand. One minute I'm having a quiet beer, next I'm being slammed up in here for supposedly murdering someone."

Sandy looked around the dingy interview room, and smiled politely at the policeman who leaned against the wall and dutifully ignored his wards. "Do you speak English?" she asked. He remained indifferent, hopefully answering the question for her. She turned her back on him and lowered her voice. "So what made the cops pick on you? They must have had some reason."

"You're never going to believe it," Nick said, holding his head in both hands.

Sandy noticed that his hair was not only receding, but that a sizeable tonsure now occupied much of the top of his head. "So tell me," she coaxed, touching his hand gently.

Her father raised his head, slowly. "Did you ever meet George Riley, back on the island?"

"Can't say I remember him."

"Heavy set bloke. Worked at Three Leggs. Used to use a fake Irish brogue when it suited him. We did a few little deals together."

"I think I sort of vaguely remember. Big fat guy

with sideburns?"

"That's him. Anyway, I bumped into George in the street, or maybe I should say he bumped into me. Seems he'd been looking for me."

"Why? What for?"

"Apparently he was on holiday and camping at that site near where we sank the parcel."

Sandy's shoulders slumped. "You're joking."

"Wish I was."

"And he went and got it?"

"No chance," said Nick. "Without knowing the co-ordinates I used to mark the spot, he'd have had a hell of a job finding it. The weed's plenty thick and the water's not that clear."

"So what did he want then?"

"He guessed we weren't just playing games and demanded to know what we were up to. I thought the best way would be to take him for a beer, try a bit of smooth talking, and see what transpired."

"And…?"

Her father paused and ran his emaciated fingers across the top of his head. "And it didn't work. We had a bit of a set to."

"You had a fight?"

"No, Sand. I'm telling you, I didn't lay a hand on

him. We just exchanged a few words, that's all."

"So what happened?"

"What happened was that he eventually went for pee. When he didn't come back I thought he'd left through the front bar – we were in the back bar overlooking the fields. Anyway, I went into the bog to look for him, and he'd been topped – knife straight through the chest."

"And the cops thought it was you."

"Yeah. I'm bending down over him, trying to yank the knife out, and in walks the barman."

Sandy let out a moan. "What the hell were you doing yanking the knife out, Dad?"

"I dunno, love. It was just instinct. There's a bloke I know with a knife sticking out of him and I just thought that the logical thing to do would be to take it out. I thought I was helping him. Anyway, the police didn't see it that way, particularly when the landlord told them that we'd been having a bit of a set-to beforehand."

"I'm hardly surprised."

"Jesus H., Sandy. I'm up to my neck in it here. Whose side are you on?"

"I'm on your side, Dad, but you must see how it looks to the cops. As far as they're concerned, the culprit was caught red-handed, if you'll excuse the pun."

"So get me some help, Sand. Go get the best lawyer

in town. For crying out loud get me out of here."

Sandy touched his hand again as his head sunk into his palms. She glanced at the indifferent policeman and then at the peeling paint on the walls of the tawdry interview room. There was a dank smell in her nose – mouse droppings and fear and something else she couldn't articulate – the smell of hopelessness and despair. She knew that her father wouldn't be able to stand it for long. Like her, he was a free spirit. "You're going to have to remind me how to find the package, Dad. If we're going to get some top legal bod on it, he's not going to give credit to a couple of Brits, he's going to want a wad in advance."

Nick lifted his head from his hands, though he had a resigned look on his face. Sandy couldn't help feeling that he was visibly ageing before her eyes.

He exhaled. "You're right, love. Got a scrap of paper and something to draw with?"

She reached into her handbag.

"Don't go to the canal straight away," he said, as he nodded towards the duty policeman. "One of this lot might follow you. It would be better if you go and find a good lawyer first, then go back to the cottage. Oh, and you'll need to get hold of a boat hook or something to fish the package out."

"Do you really think they'll be following me?"

"I don't know, but it's not worth the risk. In any case, if George Riley was staying at that campsite it'll probably be crawling with feds right now. You'll be safer if you leave it a day or two."

At the campsite, Hans Brinker parked his tractor and trailer to block the entrance of his wooden barn, and then he leaned against the barn doors. One of the police had already commented on its unusual design, the way its walls and roof sloped to meet the angle of the high dike behind. Hans had smiled politely and pointed out that it had been cheaper to extend the roof and side walls than to construct a rear wall.

The policeman seemed to appreciate his good housekeeping policy and went about his business with the other detectives, who were combing through the contents of the English tourist's tent. They appeared to be questioning everybody on the site, paying particular attention to the man with the green tent and the big motorbike.

Naturally, Hans had been co-operative. He told the police how he'd seen the Englishman acting suspiciously behind a French caravan early the other morning, and how he'd checked but hadn't spotted anything out of kilter. Other than that, he said, the fat tourist had been a model of good behaviour: no loud music, no beer or fish and chips, no shouting or swearing. He wished he had more like him, or at least that's what he told the police.

As long as they stayed away from his barn, he'd tell them anything they wanted to hear. He'd moved two trailer loads last night, thanks to the fact that it now only took him ten minutes to deposit the excavated soil, and the attention of the police was about as welcome as a swastika in a synagogue.

Phthook. A glob of bloodstained spit landed on the trail of wet soil that led from his barn door. Hans reached into the top pocket of his overalls and withdrew the old newspaper cutting that he guarded so close to his heart. Carefully, slowly, lovingly, he unfolded it. The date caught his eye, as it always did. May 31st 1943. Just three days left before the anniversary of his father's murder. Three days in which to get the digging finished and lay the charges. The sooner the police buggered off, the sooner he could get on with it. If only he could have used some sort of mechanical excavator, but the noise would have only drawn unwanted attention to him.

He smoothed open the yellowing newspaper page and stared glassy-eyed at the photograph of his father, the adjutant to Reichskommandant Seyss-Inquart. It was so bloody unjust, so bloody unwarranted, so bloody excessive. His father had been shot in the head by the Dutch Resistance whilst doing what all conquering soldiers had done since time began – satisfying his needs on a local girl. And the local girl had been unable to testify to the military command as to the identity of his murderer because it was dark. And anyway she was blind.

The adjutant to Reichskommandant Seyss-Inquart, who had unknowingly fathered Hans Brinker, was found dead on the bank the following morning, his trousers round his ankles and the back of his head blown away. His body had been escorted back to The Fatherland for a military funeral with full honours. Everybody knew who'd done it, but none were willing to testify, so, on the orders of Reichskommandant Seyss-Inquart himself, twenty Dutch males, some of them as young as ten, were shot on the spot where the body of his adjutant was found. Teach them a lesson.

After replacing the old newspaper cutting in his top pocket, Hans wiped his broad moustache with the back of his hand and gazed beyond the gaggle of law-enforcers who were now dismantling the Englishman's tent. Through the trees, in the distance, he could see the outline of his mother's house. It would be one of the first to be wiped out when the river was given its freedom. Not that his brainless, blind mother would know anything about it; she was long dead. His mother's husband too, the so-called hero of the Dutch resistance, who had avoided the Arbeitseinsatz so carefully drafted by his father, his real father, the man whose last act was to sire him from a stupid, blind Dutch girl. A dying gift to an unfertilised egg.

The farmhouse was irrelevant, it was nothing more than bricks and mortar; it was the memories inside the house that would be wiped out. Memories and his two strawberry-blonde half-brothers, both fully paid-up members of the clog wearing brigade. The half-brothers who had ganged up on him even though he was the oldest. The half-brothers who had nicknamed him Adolph, who had made his life a living hell, who had made no secret of their loathing of the bastard child of the adjutant to Reichskommandant Seyss-Inquart. The half-brothers who held him personally responsible for the execution of twenty of their kinsfolk, even for their mother's blindness. The half-brothers who were living together like a pair of bloody poufs in the house that his mother and her devoted bloody husband had built in the shadow of the earth banks of the Lek. Tilling the soil, milking the cows, making the cheese, stroking the tulips. God, how he hated these Dutch. Slow-witted, boring, obstinate straw-heads. Only his half-sister had ever shown him any kindness, and he'd not set eyes on her since her wedding. And that was years ago.

His mother tried hard to disguise her feelings for her unwanted infant but, even as a child, Hans knew the hidden truth. Her damaged eyes could never see her family so she touched their faces and stroked their hair – his half-brothers, anyway. But Hans seldom felt his mother's touch, and her obnoxious husband stared straight through him like he wasn't there. The few times he looked Hans directly in the face, his eyes were black with undiluted hatred.

On Hans's sixteenth birthday, his mother's husband, a man as slimy as the eels he dined on, took him into the barn on some pretext or other and described in graphic detail how he had blown his Nazi father's brains out on the riverbank. How he had used a blunt knife to mutilate the body.

Hans showed no emotion, just smiled knowingly at his mother's husband. The story wasn't new to him; he'd been hearing it at school every day for years. And at school the story had taken on a life of its own. The knife had been longer than a man's arm. His father's brains had been splattered across the whole village and the crows had fed off them for weeks. And Hans remembered the taunting and the hatred and had longed for a chance of revenge.

Phthook.

With his parents both dead, Hans had left his stupid half-brothers to tend the tulips, and gone his own way in the world, turning a buck wherever he could. But the past kept chasing him: never quite catching up but always snapping at his heels. He felt like a stranger in his own country, and his country felt like a stranger to him. Since his father, his real father, was German, wasn't it logical that he, too, was German? Wasn't Germany his homeland?

He surveyed the uniformed police who were combing the site. A grim look of resignation crossed his face as he recalled the uniforms he'd seen on his first visit to his father's home town many years ago but still as fresh in his memory as if it were yesterday. Celle, a little market town near Hanover, dominated at that time by the barracks of a British tank regiment who desecrated the local countryside with firing ranges and tank testing grounds, who drove their heavy armour through the narrow streets and swaggered and staggered from bar to bar like conquering heroes. Was it any wonder that his father had fought for Germanic supremacy? His failure, the failure of the German people, had led to this – The Fatherland invaded by a burger and fries regiment.

Contacts with like-minded Germans had not been accidental. Hans had sought them out. He felt German. He was German. Despite his blind Dutch mother.

He had listened avidly as they talked of the old times, the good times, when they had been so near to victory. One old man, an ageing party member, remembered Hans' father, the adjutant to Reichskommandant Seyss-Inquart, as a fine, handsome man, a man of intellect and charm, a man of high breeding who would have helped lead Germany to her rightful place in the new world order. The old man talked about the Dutch women who he had taken - it was the right of the victor, the spoils of war. Holland had capitulated to the might of the Fuhrer's army and, in doing so, had forfeited its right to determine its own future. The future belonged to the brave, not the defeated.

The old man had given Hans a crusty photograph of his father with his arms around two young ladies. Such a proud man, tall and upright with straight lips and piercing eyes that reflected his unbridled pride in the conquests of the master race. A true follower of the creed. His murder was worth more than twenty Dutch peasants. Much more. He'd be proud of his son's final act of retribution.

Phthook.

CHAPTER ELEVEN

Sandy Ferris was more than just a good-looking girl. Sandy was special; she was sexy, and positively charged energy oozed from every delicately scented pore of her curvaceous body. She was the sort of girl who made middle-aged women weep for their lost youth and middle-aged men stare distractedly at her well maintained curves. She was the sort of girl who made other women steer their husbands across the street because, having set eyes on her, they themselves felt like impostors to womanhood. She was the sort of girl who didn't have to do anything special to look sexy. She just was sexy. And Sandy wasn't exactly unaware of her all-round gorgeousness and the power it bestowed her.

That would adequately describe Sandy Ferris when she wasn't wallowing in a sea of putrid mud. When she was wallowing in a sea of putrid mud, Sandy Ferris was an unholy mess.

She should have given up before she even started, but quitting wasn't Sandy's style; nor was caking her hands, arms and face in stinking river sludge. When she arrived at the polder, she had been wearing a tight Lycra tee shirt over combat trousers, and a pair of trainers that had cost Alliance Bank more than her month's salary. Now, she was wearing swampy weed, and her long hair, which normally flowed like liquid silk, lay knotted and twisted on her shoulders. She shook uncontrollably as defeat stared her in the face.

For almost three hours she had pushed aside the oozing mud with a broken plank, ignoring the stench and the waves of nausea that had twice caused her to swallow back her own vomit. For almost three hours she ignored the warnings that common sense screamed at her, that the task was hopeless. For almost three hours she worried and fretted about what would happen to her father if she couldn't get him a good solicitor. When she had left him at the police station the day before, it looked as though a powerful vacuum cleaner had sucked out his soul; like someone had put a hand into his head and switched something off. He looked as desperate and as beaten as a mongrel dog that nobody wanted. And now she was beaten. Now the futility of the task was obvious.

Staring in disbelief at her hands, she threw down her makeshift shovel, which landed with a smack in the decomposing silt. The cherry red nails that had earlier been perfectly manicured were embedded with ebony slime and were broken and scabrous like the blade of a badly worn saw. Blood seeped through the hardening mud from deep grazes, and jagged splinters from the plank had buried like parasites into the tender flesh between her thumb and forefinger.

It had been obvious to her that something wasn't right as soon as she had arrived. The polder, which had been so combed and orderly just a week earlier, was heaped with piles of black sludge. The canal water, which had been peaty but clear when they had sunk their package, was muddy and disturbed. Someone had been mucking about with nature.

Wrapping her fears in a paper-thin façade of optimism, Sandy had used the same slightly leaky skiff moored in the reeds that she and her father had used when they had sunk their package. Ignoring the obvious, she checked and rechecked that the boat was in exactly the right position and, as time passed, extended her meticulous search over an area of about fifty square yards. But no amount of prodding or poking into the murky sediment would reveal the whereabouts of the parcel that contained their money. She succeeded only in making the disturbed canal muddier than before. In frustration and exasperation she threw the boat hook into the water and watched it drift slowly away from the tiny boat.

As she allowed her head to drop onto her chest, a voice called out. She hadn't noticed the ageing stooped man in denim overalls standing on the far bank next to a tractor and trailer. "Sorry," she shouted back. "I don't speak Dutch."

"What is it you want?"

She called back that her purse had been lost a few days before and that she was trying to find it. It wasn't very convincing, but it was the first thing that came into her head

"They've cleaned out the canal," he shouted, pointing to the adjacent polder. "That's what they dredged out. Now why don't you leave?"

She thanked him for his advice, ignored him, moored the skiff, and began scraping through the slime and mire on the bank. The man eventually left and disappeared with his tractor into a large barn.

From the moment Sandy had arrived, logic dictated that the dredging was likely to be hiding the parcel, but she fudged the issue, preferring instead to believe that she would find the package exactly where they had dropped it. The advice from the old man in overalls had forced her to jettison her optimistic veneer and face reality. That had been three hours ago. Wading calf deep in stinking mire, it felt more like three days.

She tottered and swayed towards a patch of grass a few yards away as she acknowledged the new reality - the reality that the task was hopeless. Almost a million euros lay rotting under a sea of foul-smelling mud and weed. Everything was gone, the money from the Alliance Bank scam and the money from the JoinMyChurch hit on Sean. If only they'd kept the parcel in the cottage. She'd told her father but he'd not listened. They were safe where they were, she'd said. Nobody knew their whereabouts except the owner of the cottage, who her father knew and trusted. But he'd insisted, and now everything was lost. A wave of despair and nausea passed over her and she collapsed with a glutinous squelch into the slime, like a football landing in a fresh cowpat.

With aching limbs, Sandy paused to catch her breath, then pushed herself to her feet again and swayed unsteadily. She wanted to cry in frustration and that just made her even more cross - she was not the crying sort. But she knew when she was beaten and when it was time to give up.

She stomped and staggered in the sticky effluent towards the grass on the canal bank. She should have known better than to try to hurry; she'd already fallen several times as the malodorous goo took possession of her feet. In her haste, she stumbled and fell again. She instinctively reached forward to buffer her fall, and her arm jarred on something solid beneath the semi-liquid sea. Winded, she paused for breath.

Then she paused again, not daring to move. With the last of her strength she freed herself and squatted. She warily pushed her arms back into the mixture of weed and wet mud. Her stomach started to heave ominously as the bacterial stench assaulted her nostrils. Swallowing hard, she fought to hold back another hot torrent that burned the back of her throat. It receded leaving an acid taste that stuck to the roof of her mouth and furred her teeth. She spat and gagged, then allowed her fingers to explore for the concealed object. Her heart pounded as she felt the outline of something regular and rectangular. It was the money parcel. She just knew it was the money parcel. She could feel the packaging tape that her father had wound around it again and again, overlapping and criss-crossing the corners to ensure a watertight seal. She grasped it doggedly like a drowning man grasps at anything that floats then, straining against her aching back, slowly, slowly freed it from the sludge that had imprisoned it.

Elatedly she clutched it tight to her and splashed and staggered to the canal bank. She collapsed onto the grass and hugged the parcel close, wiping off the mud with her sleeve. Injured fingers tore hastily at the tape and plastic wrapping. Another nail broke, but went unnoticed in her excitement and optimism.

Now, at last, it had all been worth it. Her reward was just a few layers of protective polythene away.

But, as she tore at the wrapping, she had a look of concerned concentration on her face, wincing as she struggled to comprehend something. An uneasy feeling clawed at her gut like a razor-toothed ferret. The final layer was in sight but it was not the supermarket carrier bag that they had used to bring the money back from the bank. Something had changed. Something was different. As she ripped and tore at the plain polythene, her exhilaration turned to disbelief.

And then the tears of frustration flowed. It was the second time in her life that she had been robbed of her prize. This time she was determined it would be different. No matter what, she would track down that money.

She didn't know how her father was going to take the news.

Badly, probably.

* * *

For once the sun was shining, and Chief Inspector Joris Duisenberg's wife was making the best of it as she relaxed in a colourful garden chair. She loved the smell of freshly cut grass mingled with the early summer sun, and had long since given up trying to concentrate on her knitting; just happy to enjoy having Joris at home. It seemed that he spent most of his life at the police station and it gave her a warm, comfortable feeling to have him around in his few moments of leisure. She felt secure and at ease, and God knows she needed to feel at ease after all that had happened to the family in recent years. It would be good for him too, what with the pressure of younger blood trying to force themselves into the shoes of the old stags. She waved her arthritic arm to him as he turned the big grass-cutting machine for the last time and headed towards the garage. Easing herself out of her seat, she moved with care, and advanced slowly and painfully towards the kitchen to pour him a cool beer.

As Joris watched her dissolve into the shadows of the house, his countenance changed. The contented family man became a Chief Inspector of Police with a personal problem to solve. A black frown descended on his face as he dismounted the mower and strode into the obscuring shade of the garage.

"What the hell do you want?" he demanded.

"I came to see if there was any chance of making peace," the young man said, extending an open hand.

Joris ignored the gesture. "None whatsoever," he said, in a voice that left little room for negotiation. "You know my position on the matter. There'll be no peace in this family until you change your ways."

"Look, Dad, you can't go on being bitter forever. We've got to patch it up sooner or later, so why not now?"

"I'll tell you why not now, Robert - because you're still up to your old tricks. Nothing has changed. If you'd accepted that what you did was wrong, your mother and I would have welcomed you back with open arms but it seems that you never learn."

"What do you mean by that?"

Joris banged his open palm on the workbench, spreading wood shavings onto the cold concrete floor. "I mean that I know what you've been up to over the last few months. For God's sake, don't you see what a difficult position it puts me in?"

Robert Duisenberg's fists clenched tight. Though he was clearly making an effort to control his emotions, bitterness lay shallow beneath the surface. "Here we go again," he said, "the good cop against the bad guys. For crying out loud, Dad, relax a bit, you're so uptight about everything."

"Of course I'm uptight, you fool. I've devoted my life to catching criminals, and my own son is one of them."

"Oh come off it. You can hardly call me a criminal, I'm just having a bit of fun before I get too old."

"Jesus, Robert, you always were a master of understatement, but that beats it all." Joris folded his arms tight across his chest. "Of course you're a damn criminal. You break the law don't you? And if you get caught, you'll no doubt end up in gaol."

"And I suppose that's where you'd like to see me, isn't it," Robert said, matching his father's raised voice for the first time. "Putting me in prison would keep me out of your hair."

"Grow up," Joris snapped. "You nearly ruined your life once and broke your mother's heart. In her present state, if she found out you'd been locked up, the shock would probably kill her."

"I presume you're going to remind me again how it was you that got me off the hook last time."

Joris grabbed the lapels of his son's jacket and shook him fiercely. "Get out of my sight and stay out of our lives," he snapped. "If I see you again, I'll turn you in myself."

His son pushed himself free, and fell back against the garage wall. "To hell with you." he snarled, straightening his crumpled jacket. "Go back to cutting your grass." He strode out of the shadows and around the side of the building.

Joris waited a moment and listened as his son's angry footsteps disappeared towards the road. He composed himself before facing his wife, and he wondered how she would handle it when Robert was arrested as was certain to happen eventually. What was it about his son that made him so angry? So resentful?

He took a deep breath and peeped through the tiny vent next to the incinerator. On the street, Robert was leaning through the open window of a small car, talking agitatedly to its occupant, whose face Joris couldn't see. But he knew the car and knew that its occupant would be a heavy-breasted young lady with bright red lipstick.

* * *

After two nights in a room the size of a dog kennel, Sean had spent another tiresome day in Kinderdijk with the vocally refreshed Brother Theo looking for any trace of Nick and Sandy Ferris. His frustration and impatience were increasing in direct proportion to Theo's constant blether and blind obsession to resolve the mystery of the missing Ferris's. He seemed unable to do anything in halves. After a fruitless day of dead-ends, as evening set in Sean decided to pay a visit to the local police station in case they had any knowledge of their 'searchees', as Theo was inclined to call them. Theo had been watching too much CNN, he decided.

Much to Sean's surprise, the police had indeed heard of the Ferris pair and had cordially invited him to talk to Nick Ferris, hoping that an English voice would persuade their prisoner to open up and tell them everything he knew. Sean had been as stunned as a sleepwalker who wakes up naked on a busy road. He simply couldn't believe that Nick Ferris and George Riley, both former employees, should have met, argued and killed – particularly in place so far from home.

His mind juggled the possibilities. Had George Riley been involved in the scam six months earlier when two of the scamees - maybe Theo had a point - had ended up with neat bullet holes in their heads? Did Nick Ferris or George Riley have anything to do with their deaths? If so, why would Nick Ferris have disappeared whilst George carried on his life and his job as if nothing had happened? Maybe they'd been arguing over the sting going wrong. It was all too crazy. It just didn't add up.

"George knew nothing about any problems you might have had at Three Leggs last year," Nick said.

Sean believed him.

"Nor Sandy. Nor me."

Sean raised an eyebrow.

After assuring Nick that he would look in on him again soon, Sean watched sombrely as the police sergeant locked the door to the tiny cell. It was sad to see a former employee looking so dispirited, even if he was a former employee with abnormally sticky fingers. Sean wasn't sure why, but something told him that Nick Ferris probably knew a great deal about the deaths of the rogues who had robbed his company the first time round. Though he doubted that Nick would have had his finger on the trigger, he was certain that his former bookkeeper knew whose finger it was. And he was absolutely sure that Nick knew everything about the current computer swindle. His sticky fingerprints were pasted everywhere. Yet somehow, killing George Riley was out of character. Nick could have dealt with any disagreement with George in a manner suiting two minor scallywags. They were birds of a feather. There was no need to kill.

The police sergeant, asking Sean if he would formally identify the body of his ex-employee and translate something for him, disturbed his thoughts.

"It's a tape recording of a telephone call that Mister Ferris received earlier today," he said. "The lady said she was a British lawyer and, although we were suspicious, we let her speak to him. As a precaution, we thought it would be prudent to record the conversation."

"Very wise," Theo said helpfully. "Congratulations on a good job, sergeant."

The uniformed man looked sadly at Theo's hat and shrugged. "Well, anyway," he said, "my English is obviously not as good as I thought it was. They were talking very quickly, so I didn't understand everything. Something about a package mainly. I'll play you the recording, it might help you in your search for your money."

Sean sat down and indicated for Theo to do the same. The policeman pressed the play button on the tape recorder and Sandy Ferris's voice filled the room.

"Bejabers, Dad. Is there anybody in the room wichya?"

Cheeky cow was trying to imitate an Irish accent. Badly.

"Yeah, a copper."

"The same one that was there yesterday?"

"No another one."

"Well don't say nutthin', jus listen. We don't know if this one speaks the English. First of all, Oi don't think it would be safe for me to come to the cop shop. The town's still crawling with the po-leece asking all sorts of questions off of anyone who looks or sounds the sloightest bit foreign, so it's not worth the risk. Anyway, Oi've spent the whole day digging through tons of sloime an' shoite. The loot's gone. The local Council dredged the canal but Oi found the package still intact."

There was a short pause.

"All that was in it was blank paper."

"Blank paper? You mean there was no cash?"

"Keep it shut Dad. Oi was as shocked as you, but don't be givin' the game away at your end."

"But who the hell would make a package with blank paper?"

"Well, Oi've had a bit longer than you to tink about it. The package never left our soight since leaving The Hague, so oither someone found it when the canal was bein' cleared, or it was switched before we left the apartment. If the dredgin' people had found it, whoiy in the name of the good Lord would they be makin' a similar-looking package an' then be buryin' it in the mud? That's not logical. To moi way o' tinkin', the parcel was taken before we left The Hague, and whoever it was left a replacement hopin' it would be a long toime before we found out. Just be sayin' yes if you agree."

Another pause.

"Yes."

"So logically there'd be only one person who could have known that we had the cash, and that would be the fella that was givin' you the card."

"Couldn't be anyone else."

"Then Oi reckon Oi need to try and foind him."

"But how?"

"Oi don't know, Dad. Oi'm going to have to go back to De Hardin's where you got the card and start from there. Is there anyone there you can trust who moight be able to help? If you know anyone, just be sayin' a single name, Oi'll find him."

"Brigitte."

"A woman."

"Sort of."

"Okay, leave it to me. As soon as Oi've got some news, Oi'll call you again, but remember, you be sayin' the minimum possible in case any of them speak the English. Oi'll be back in touch just as soon as Oi can."

A longer pause.

"And take care, eh?"

The dialling tone told the police sergeant that the conversation had ended so he turned off the recorder and looked at Sean.

"Sure an' if she's a lawyer, I'm a bloody astronaut."

Theo giggled.

"The lady whose voice you heard was Nick Ferris's daughter," Sean said. "And I'm hardly surprised that you didn't understand it. She didn't intend you to."

"I understood some," Theo said with an enthusiastic chin full if spittle. "Maybe I'm getting used to an Irish accent."

Sean ignored him. "You were right about the package," he said to the sergeant. "The subject of murder was never mentioned, but it seems that she doesn't have the money either. It looks like someone else got there first."

Theo had a pensive look and an 'I'm-not-listening' smile on his face. "That's that dreadful person in the bar," he said to no one in particular.

"Now what's he going on about?" the policeman asked.

Sean shrugged. "Search me, sergeant. I think his favourite god is at work again."

"Time to go back to The Hague," Theo said. "We'll get ready as soon as you've looked at the body for the sergeant. We need to get back to that bar as soon as we can."

"Well that'll make a refreshing change," Sean said. "If we've got to be quick you'd better let me drive," he added, more in hope than expectation.

"Certainly not. I'm sure I'm a lot more careful than you."

"That's the problem. It's going to take us all night."

Theo looked marginally thoughtful again. "Maybe you're right," he said. "Perhaps it would be best if we left early tomorrow."

* * *

In The Hague, a tall, pony-tailed man with rimless glasses bumped into Sandy as he exited the darkened alley between De Hardin's and the cheap jean shop.

"Sorry," he said, without much conviction.

"Forget it," Sandy muttered, regaining her balance.

She paused to watch him disappear into the gloom only to be replaced by other oddities of the night. One, a long-haired old gentleman, carried two enormous shopping bags with hands clad in oven mitts. He shuffled three paces forward, rested his bags, shouted abuse at some unseen demon, and then graffitied the nearest wall with a worn out pencil. A young dropout, convinced he was a reincarnated witchdoctor, offered to tell Sandy's fortune for two euros. When she didn't respond, he hunched back under his silent ghetto blaster and tapped his feet to the rhythm in his head.

Sandy stepped round a broken bin bag that had spewed its contents across the square. The illuminated hands on the church clock told her it was two o'clock. The chime, somewhat unhelpfully, said it was three. Several night stragglers kept the square company as they made their way to their homes on the wings of blasphemy. The entrance to De Hardin's was just ahead and that was where Sandy was headed.

After tidying the cottage, burning her ruined clothes, and collecting the few personal effects that they had acquired to see them though their short exile, Sandy had embarked on a slow, four-hour drive round the back roads and through comatose villages where humble country dwellings crouched like sleeping sheep, turning and retracing her route time and again to make sure that she wasn't being followed. It had left her drained and depressed and she would have been glad to have gone straight home to bed. But the matter in hand was too important to rest at the moment, and sleep would have to be deferred. She dragged her overnight bag through the door of De Hardin's and entered the smoky bar. The music was deafening despite the late hour and the fact that only a handful of customers had chosen to stay out late on a Sunday night.

She let her bag drop in the corner near the door and pushed her aching legs towards the bar where she recognised the burly owner, a man whose hairy hands Theo Padmos would also have identified.

"Hi Martijn," she hollered above the ear-splitting disharmony of this month's in music.

"Hello, Sandy," he shouted. "What are you doing out so late?"

"Just got back from a few days holiday. Got any coffee on the go?"

Martijn had long since learnt the art of lip-reading. "Sure," he bawled, turning his back to her as he organised her drink at the espresso machine.

"Any chance of lowering the sound levels?" she called. "Your customers don't look as though they'd know the difference!"

Martijn looked over his shoulder, grinned and nodded. "It'd be a pleasure," he yelled back. "Perhaps it'll stop the neighbours from making their usual complaints." He reached down to a switch below the coffee machine and the speakers muted to a quiet background level. One or two of the bar's clients looked up but Martijn Boermans was not a man to pick a fight with, and all quickly returned to the safety of their beer. "So how can I help you?" he asked in a normal voice, as he placed a large coffee on the bar.

Sandy raised her eyebrows. "What makes you think

you can help me?"

"I'm a bar owner. We know everything! It doesn't take much to work out that Sandy Ferris turning up at two o' clock in the morning, accompanied by an overnight bag is not a normal event. When the same Sandy Ferris asks me to turn down the music, I guess that she wants to ask me something – probably not the time, and probably not the state of my health. So, what can I do for you?"

"Dad's in a spot of bother, Martijn. He needs some information and he thinks that someone called Brigitte can help sort things out. Do you know who she is?"

The Dutchman smiled and nodded to the far corner of the room. "You're in luck. He was with a regular client a moment ago, but he's just come back in. Your dad and he got on well so I'm sure he'll help if he can."

Sandy glanced around at the balding fur coat indicated by Martijn. It had the sad look of having been dragged behind a heavy goods vehicle before being ironed with a steamroller. The person occupying it was as pale as a vestal virgin at a sex-offender's stag night, though it was clear that he would have had no qualms about being the evening's star turn if the money had been right. The face was archetypal for the profession – clotted mascara, lipstick as bright as a mail box, deep blue eye shadow, and a give away chin where early morning stubble was breaking the surface like new sown grass. The corners of Sandy's mouth turned up.

"Don't judge a book by its cover," Martijn said, as

she turned back to face him. "There's not a dog breaks wind in The Hague without Brigitte getting to know about it, and he's a good guy to have on your side."

"Oh, I'm not bothered by his sexual preferences. It's just that he could do with a shave or he won't be getting any more clients tonight."

Martijn Boermans did a second take. "You're right," he said. "I'll go and tell him after you're through."

"I'll tell him," Sandy said, jumping off the stool.

"Ask him about the guy who was looking for you earlier this evening. I didn't have time to talk much to him, but he and Brigitte were chatting for quite a long while."

Sandy eyed Martijn curiously then balanced her coffee across the room to where Brigitte and her poodle were sharing a beer. The animal was as threadbare as its owner's coat. "Hi," she said, scratching the dog's ear. "What's his name?"

"Faggot."

She failed to conceal her smile again. "Hello, Faggot, I'm Sandy."

"Yes, I know, my dear," said the man who had been the victim of Theo's outburst. "You're Nick Ferris's daughter. Your dear father pointed you out to me one evening when you came in for a drink."

Sandy looked surprised. "He didn't tell me."

"Probably not," Brigitte said. "He and I are good

friends. But he's in trouble isn't he, bless him."

"How the heck did you know?"

"Instinct. The pair of you leave in a rush and now you turn up at two o'clock in the morning with an overnight bag." He looked at her quizzically, his head slightly tilted to match Faggot's. "You've just come back from Kinderdijk, haven't you?"

"Brigitte! How did you know where I've been?"

He tapped his nose. "Little secret your Dad and I shared."

"Come on," Sandy said. "Spill the beans."

Brigitte looked around to make sure nobody was within earshot - with the music turned down, conversations had become more audible. "The cottage you were staying in," he said in a low voice. "It's mine. I lent your father the keys."

"Yours?"

"Mine. It's security for when I get too old for this game. My earnings aren't generally open to scrutiny by our punitive tax authorities, so I needed something to invest my money in. A property seemed like a good idea."

"I wondered where Dad had found out about it. He just said it belonged to a friend."

"It does, so don't let it worry you. I'm more concerned, though, about your precious father. What trouble is he in?"

Sandy sipped her coffee. "He needs me to track down someone who gave him a business card in here one night. He thought you might be able to help."

Brigitte batted his aquamarine-lidded eyes as he thought. "I didn't see anyone give Nick a card but, if it's the sort of card I'm thinking about, one that gives you a religious outlook on somebody else's bank account so to speak, you should tell your Dad to keep well away. The guy doesn't play honest. He gets his punter to the robbing then takes the cash off them."

"You know who it is then?"

"But of course, my dear. I know most of the dregs of this town, and this one comes in here for a drink from time-to-time. Goes under the name of Hjalmar Linnekar, though that's not his real name. He lives with his girlfriend on Geleenstraat, down near Holland Spoor Station. But don't get involved, Sandy, he's bad news for a whole variety of reasons, and I'm not just talking computer theft."

"I'm afraid we're already involved," she said quietly.

"Oh you poor dears," sighed Brigitte. "And I suppose you've had the money taken out of your bank?"

"No, in cash out of the apartment."

"Oh, good heavens. You have to admire the man's arrogance, just for its size. You must have withdrawn it from your bank before he had time to take it electronically."

"You mean he normally steals it from the punter's bank?"

"He most certainly does, my dear," Brigitte said, adjusting his fur coat as a naked breast peeped out from the folds. "The people who use his system are just tools to create a false trail for the police to follow. Is that what's happened to your dear father? Do the police have him?"

"Yes," Sandy said. "But not for stealing. He's been accused of murder."

Brigitte brought the back of his hand to his forehead, as though he'd been struck by an acute migraine. "Never!" he groaned. "Not your dear father. He would never kill anybody."

"I agree. But now we need the money to get him a good lawyer. This Hjalmar Linnekar guy has not only taken back what we got by using his programme, he's taken all our savings as well."

"Oh, good grief, is there no end to it?" Brigitte said, sighing again, and flicking back a loose hank of blonde wig. He reached into his handbag and took out a business card. "You'd better talk to this real estate gentleman then. He seems to know you and we had a long chat this evening. He was trying to track you or your dear father down because he thinks he can help. He said he had some good news for you but he wasn't very specific. Now I've heard your side of the story I guess maybe he knows something about what's going on. Give him a call in the morning, Sandy. He didn't seem too bad – at least for a male heterosexual."

Sandy smiled. "No, you're right, he's not too bad for

a male heterosexual. Talking of which," she said "if you want to call by the apartment some time, I'll give you some make-up that will disguise the beginnings of a beard."

Brigitte rubbed his chin. "Oh dear, my dear. I usually have a shave about midnight, but I was er… busy earlier. Maybe it would be a good time to call it a night and go home."

"Come to the apartment with me now if you want. You can use one of Dad's razors, then I'll help you with the make-up."

"But you must be tired," he said.

"Not too tired to help a friend. Come on, let's get you respectable again."

He tittered. "Oh my goodness! Presentable, Sandy, but never respectable." He glanced at her hand as she replaced her coffee cup. "In return, perhaps I can help you with those awful nails, my dear. What have you been up to?"

"Gold-digging," she said, staring at her hand.

"Hope you found some."

"I will, Brigitte, I will."

CHAPTER TWELVE

Angus Slooth had known Sean's and Hannu's whereabouts from the moment they had arrived in The Hague. Up till now, he had let them be. But today it was time to push the situation forward a little. He found the young Finn in his hotel room, waltzing his keyboard round the Internet.

"Angus!" Hannu said as he opened the door. "What the hell are you doing here?"

Slooth explained his presence, though he doubted that it would have come as a surprise.

"So how can I help?" Hannu asked, placing a reasonably large glass of malt whisky into the detective's hand.

"Just thought we could share a little information," Angus said. "You tell me what you know, and I'll tell you what I know."

Hannu struggled with his thoughts for a moment before responding. "I'd need to check it with Sean first."

"I think I know Sean well enough to know that he'd be glad to pool our resources. Though I'm still curious as to why he's wasting time chasing around Europe in search of Sandy Ferris"

"You know about Sandy?"

"I know everything."

"So you know that she and Sean were very close once."

"Lovers? Aye. That's common knowledge on the island."

Hannu scratched his thatch then adjusted it so that it sat centrally. "Well I just don't get it, Angus. What would a guy like Sean see in someone like Sandy Ferris?"

"Birds of a feather."

"What do you mean?" Hannu asked.

"They're nay so different," Angus said. "The exception is that Sandy Ferris and her father rob anybody, Sean just rips off the government."

He knew the effect his statement would have, though it was still interesting to see the reaction. He continued, "Sean's calmed down a bit in his later years but, when he was about your age, he was making a fortune in cattle."

"Cattle? I thought he was an engineer."

"Sean's what he wants to be," Slooth said. "He was a cattle man before he got into heavy machinery. It was in the early days of European Community subsidies. Common Agricultural Policy it was called, and there weren't too many people checking on it. As long as you had the right bits of paper with a rubber stamp on them, Europe would donate you huge sums of taxpayer's money."

"You mean Sean was forging documents to get subsidies from Europe?"

Slooth laughed. "He didn't have to forge them, Hannu, his brother worked for the government."

"Christ, Angus, you're telling me that—"

"I'm not telling you anything, Hannu. This conversation is strictly off the record. Anyway, Sean took the sensible option and got out. It's his own hard work that has brought him to where he is today. Plus, maybe, a smattering of Irish labour who don't appear on his payroll but go back to Dublin every weekend to buy their Guinness with tax free cash."

"You seem well versed in Sean's affairs," Hannu said, with a touch of admiration in his voice.

Slooth hung his nose over his whisky. "Not exactly, but Sean and I go back a long way. He's no your perfect citizen, Hannu, but he's way and above a lot of other people I know. He plays the system a bit, but his success is due almost entirely to his sense of fair play. He'll never short-change his friends - particularly friends in trouble. Now, if you want to help Sean, tell me what you know about his friend Ms. Ferris."

Half an hour later, Hannu found himself peering

uncertainly around the curtain as Angus Slooth's jeans and trainers accompanied his pipe and his hair across the cobbled square. Just as it looked as though the associated cloud of smoke had disappeared from view, Slooth reappeared and began re-crossing the square. Hannu wondered what he had forgotten. After Slooth had taken a few steps, a shapely young lady approached him, her dark hair swinging in the wind across her leather-clad shoulders. They spoke briefly, then headed off together in the direction of Slooth's hotel.

What was all that about? Hannu wondered. He had the feeling that it had been no chance meeting. In fact, he had the feeling that the two were well acquainted. Was the young lady providing Slooth with his horizontal pleasures? It somehow seemed unlikely, but who could tell? After juggling the possibilities over in his mind for a few moments, Hannu turned, crossed the room, and logged on to his e-mail programme.

After filling him in on Sean's past, Slooth had spent the last half hour gently grilling Hannu to find out what he knew about the JoinMyChurch scam. Hannu felt obliged to guard the information; after all, he was working for Sean, not for Angus Slooth. Not that he had much information to offer: the site had been closed down and Sandy Ferris's laptop was yielding nothing. But Slooth had let it drop that he had a fix on the author of the programme. Someone rejoicing under the pseudonym of Anthrax, apparently. Hannu's radar leapt into action, though he tried not to let it show on his face.

Now he felt a flush of anger as he started to type. It was time to for The Redeemer to send another e-mail to Anthrax. This time the subject would not be about proving the existence of one-way functions. This time the subject would involve a certain religious site on the Internet. At least he could try and stop Sean from getting ripped off again.

* * *

After a nail session with Brigitte, Sandy had experienced one of those never-ending nights that last a week and leave you wishing you hadn't bothered going to bed in the first place. She hated knowing that she wasn't going to get enough sleep. It had been one of those nights when she had lain thinking, 'If I fall asleep now, I'll get five hours.' Then it was four and a half hours, then four. Until she had fallen into a deep, dreamless slumber that was rudely interrupted before it had begun.

It was just that there was too much to think about: her father, the money, what a mess. Just as a weak sun was trying its best to get some early recognition in the sky, Sandy clicked suddenly awake in the way that meant she'd lie for hours unable to sleep again no matter how tired she was. She had to do something about the situation. Trouble is, she had no idea what.

She stumbled out of bed trying to remember what it was she should be doing, and spotted Marcus Foyer's business card where Brigitte had left it. Before dialling his number, she waited impatiently to give the rest of the world, and Marcus Foyer, an opportunity to wake up in a civilised manner.

It was a while before Marcus Foyer had a gap in his appointments but, by the time the day's first shower had fallen, the estate agent had arrived like an eager racehorse behind a willing mare and, after a long talk, Sandy had the pleasing sensation that, even though she hadn't laid a bet, the odds were good that the bookies were about to pay out. She poured Marcus another coffee and sat close to him, feeling his warmth as their legs touched. For the first time in forty-eight hours, she was experiencing the freedom of optimism; as if she'd taken off a heavy, heavy coat.

"So let me run it past you again," she said. "Make sure I've got it right. This girlfriend of Hjalmar Linnekar's—"

"Rolien."

"This Rolien, who also happens to be my landlady, wants you to rip off her boyfriend so he'll stop farting around trying to improve his JoinMyChurch programme."

"You've got it," Marcus said. "He was a bit phased that you and your father emptied your bank account before he got to it electronically. He got lucky with you being one of Rolien's tenants, because he was able to retrieve the cash physically."

"Enlighten me, Marcus, I've still not puzzled that one out. How did he know to make a similar package to the one we made?"

"Two visits. One to find the money parcel and take it home, and one to replace it with a similar look-alike."

"What? You mean the bolshie little toad broke in twice?"

"He didn't have to break in. He had access to

Rolien's spare keys. If you'd spotted the package was missing straight away, you might have worked out who took it, but I guess he expected you to do a runner clutching the package under your arm and thinking everything was okay."

"We did," Sandy said. "If we hadn't unexpectedly needed some of the money in a rush, we'd probably still be none the wiser."

"Yeah well apparently entering people's houses isn't his normal style, so he's now busy trying to rewrite the programme to make sure that, in future, any money will be diverted straight to his bank. He's not finished that bit yet because he's anxious to completely cover his tracks. He needs the money to go through the user's account, but then to automatically move straight on to his account with no trace. Rolien thinks that if his programme backfires on him, he'll give it up and spend more time with her. Despite him being some sort of computer nerd, she thinks a lot of the guy and wants to get his total attention."

"She'll certainly get his attention, but I'm not sure it'll be the sort of attention she wants."

"That's why she enlisted my help – cover her tracks, so to speak."

Sandy sat quietly for a moment, then put one and one together and came up with two. "So you're her bit on the side and you're going to rob her boyfriend?"

Marcus coughed. "Put like that it sounds sordid," he said. "Got any more coffee?"

At least he hadn't tried to hide behind a denial. Sandy reached for the coffee pot. "It is sordid, Marcus. On the other hand, it's just up my street. I've no sympathy for this Hjalmar guy. He's not exactly an icon of virtuosity, and if his girlfriend is daft enough to think that robbing him will bring them closer together, then she should go out and get herself a few more brain cells."

"She's infatuated."

"I take it she makes up for her state of infatuation in other ways? Ease of access to the body department perhaps?"

Marcus blushed slightly – just slightly. "That's a fair assessment.".

Sandy wasn't a manipulator, but she knew how to manipulate. A fine distinction, but an important one. She handed Marcus Foyer a smile with his coffee and allowed her hand to touch against his thigh. "Okay, so we've established that she's dumb, that her boyfriend is not to be trusted, and that you're just plain horny."

Marcus thanked her for the coffee and smiled back. It was the sort of smile she knew well – a smile that said 'Hey, I might still get lucky here.'

Maybe he would. Maybe it was still worth it.

"So Hjalmar Linnekar dumped the money he nicked from us into his girlfriend's Swiss Bank account," Sandy continued.

"Except for fifty thousand euros that he kept in his own bank here in The Hague; sort of petty cash.

Rolien's given me the details because that's the account she wants me to hit, using the guy's own JoinMyChurch programme. Keep the cash and teach him that computers can't be trusted."

"In the vain hope that he'll knock it on the head and devote the rest of his miserable life to her?"

Marcus nodded.

"She must rate your services highly," Sandy said.

Marcus smiled again, rested his coffee cup on the table, and turned slightly to face her. "She's not after his money," he said. "She's got plenty of her own."

"Apparently so. At least a million euros by your reckoning."

"And that's only the liquid part. There's loads more property that hasn't been sold yet. By the end of the year she'll probably have about 20 million euros in her bank."

"Okay, so she can afford to be generous with her boyfriend's petty cash. Why don't you and she just run the programme yourselves? Why involve me?"

Marcus's hand moved stealthily to the side of his knee, as though he was just thinking and his movements were incidental to his thoughts. When the side of his hand rested against Sandy's leg, she knew that he was testing the ground. She made no attempt to move away.

"Like I told you," Marcus said, "Rolien got as much information as she could out of Hjalmar without him realising what she was up to. She acted interested and Hjalmar told her how his programme works. She knows the name of the new site, she knows which town to pick on the drop-down list, and she knows how the access code rolls forward mathematically every time it's used. What she doesn't know is the original access code that you used to log on to the real programme, the one behind the façade, so she's got no starting point. If she had the starting point, she could calculate what the next code is. So she sent me looking for you to see if I could get you to share the information."

A pause.

"You could get some of your money back," he added.

"What, her bloody boyfriend robs my father and me of nearly a million euros and she's offering us a share of a fifty thousand in return?"

"Almost," Marcus said, with an embarrassed smile.

"What do you mean, almost"

"Well, she told me I could keep the fifty thousand for myself. She didn't actually mention you or your father."

"Cheeky bitch. Did she think we'd just give you our access code and let her thieving boyfriend get away with it?"

Marcus shrugged. "Anyway, she left it to me to come and talk to you. When I didn't find anyone here, I made a few enquiries and ended up talking to that transvestite in the bar."

"Brigitte."

"Yeah. Brigitte."

Sandy leaned back against the cushion on the settee; it allowed her hand to move naturally along Marcus's thigh. "Okay, so you know how the code recalculates and you know the new internet site where we can access the scam again."

"You've got it. The town just rolls forward two on the drop-down list. Amsterdam becomes er... well it becomes whatever's next but one on the list. The programme is now lodged at a new site called find-us-here.com. Apparently Hjalmar has a bit of a sense of humour. He hides his sites where he doesn't think anyone normal will bother looking."

"He's right there! So how does the code recalculate?"

Marcus slowly spread the palm of his hand on her leg, just above her knee. "What was the last code number?" he asked. "The one you used."

Sandy smiled and rested her hand on top of his. "Alright, between us we've got all we need to know to take his money off him. Won't he be able to trace who's taken it?"

"Almost certainly. We're going to have to open a bank account in a false name and move it out straight away when we run the programme."

Sandy was listening but her mind was on other things, and it wasn't just the feel of her guest's hand on her leg. What consumed her thoughts was the considerable wealth that was unsuspectingly accumulating interest in Rolien van der Laan's Swiss bank; an incidental detail that Marcus Foyer appeared not to have given too much thought to. But why had he given no thought to it? Since he'd been paying the proceeds of Rolien's property sales into it for her, he clearly knew the account details. Yet he was ignoring the obvious, which meant that he wasn't a professional. If he'd been a pro, he would have already thought it out for himself. If he'd been a pro, Sandy would have known that she could point out the bigger sting, certain that he would have no spasms of conscience.

What she had to do was to find out more about Marcus's relationship with Rolien. Was the relationship really only skin deep? Was he willing to betray her?

"It was only a bit of fun between Rolien and me," he said, misinterpreting her silence. "Rolien wants Hjalmar's attention and I just made the best of an unexpected opportunity to flex my sexual muscles, so to speak."

It was a situation that Sandy understood well - she'd been there before - but she hadn't yet decided whether he meant it or was just saying it to get her co-operation. Could she trust him to double cross Rolien? She needed to be certain before she would feel comfortable painting the wider picture for him.

From her own experience, Sandy already knew that the world was a smaller place than most people thought, and she had seen nothing ominous in the fact that her landlady was shacked up with the guy who had given her father the JoinMyChurch card. It was no big co-incidence in such a tight-knit community. It also explained how Rolien's boyfriend had managed to switch the packages with no signs of a forced entry. But did Sandy's landlady really think that hitting her boyfriend's bank account would send him into the comfort of her bed? Who knows? To Sandy it sounded somewhat naive.

Sandy had only met Rolien once, a tall girl with hair the colour of set honey, all pelmet skirts, high heels and stocking tops, the ultimate in executive hard-ons but a little too obvious for Sandy's taste. Frilly knickers and Wonderbra cleavages were fine in the bedroom but, worn in public, branded you a dumb blonde. Yet, at their one meeting, when they had agreed terms on the lease of the apartment, Sandy had not thought of Rolien van der Laan as a dumb blonde. Though she had a fruity middle-class accent, unbruised by any trace of Dutch pronunciation, and, though she was irritatingly attractive, she was also streetwise and sussed in an amateur sort of way. If her bank account hadn't contained what Sandy wanted, she could have probably grown to like her, maybe even sympathise with her predicament and tell her to get herself a new boyfriend.

Although distracted by her thoughts, Sandy realised that the tips of Marcus Foyer's fingers had now eased their way under the hem of her skirt. With an outgoing personality and a respectable body like his, it was easy to see why he found the mating process so uncomplicated. But could he be trusted?

There was only one way to find out – further manipulation. Sandy pushed her long, black hair off her shoulders and launched into an act that she had played out many times before.

In a former life, before placing a bullet firmly between the eyes of her father's obnoxious half-brother, and his equally obnoxious business partner, she had spent more time charming the flaccid genitalia of rich old men than she cared to think about.

The only man she'd ever slept with who had meant anything to her other than a source of income had been Sean Legg. He too had been coaxed between the sheets in order to extract information about his business, but the relationship had been a good one. Sean wasn't a wham-bam-thank-you-man, he was a wine-you-dine-you-gentleman and Sandy cherished the memory of his attentions – and the generous, glowing orgasms that they'd shared. If she was honest, it had left her with just the slightest twinge of conscience when they had relieved Three Leggs Manufacturing of its assets. She didn't like to dwell too long on the problems Sean must have suffered after returning from his six-month sabbatical. But profit was profit and she'd gone along with it anyway. Maybe it hadn't been a good idea to go back for a second hit. Maybe, if she got her hands on Rolien van der Laan's wealth, she would give Sean his money back.

Maybe.

Since arriving in The Netherlands there had been no men in Sandy's life except her father, who had looked after her for as long as she could remember; ever since she was tiny; ever since her mother had left them. Her father was special to her. Though he was a thorough rogue (and who was she to criticise roguedom?) there was not an ounce of spite in him. He was as guilty of killing George Riley as the Pope. Of that she was sure.

So now it was time to take whatever steps were

necessary to buy him a good defence and unincarcerate him, and testing Marcus Foyer's loyalty to his wealthy client would be the first step. Sandy knew that if he were unscrupulous enough to flex his sexual muscles with both his employer and his co-conspirator, he would be unscrupulous enough for a bit of financial double-dealing. Sandy was blessed with a deep understanding of human nature. And she knew quite a lot about sexual muscles.

She was glad she'd spent some time on her nails before finally falling into bed exhausted. And she was glad, too, that Marcus was a good-looking guy; it was a bonus she would enjoy. This was going to be his lucky day. Hers too, she hoped.

She was sure she'd not lost the old technique. It was like riding a bike, wasn't it? Something you never forgot.

* * *

Sean struggled to block out the constant background blather that had started earlier than normal. From the little that he bothered to actually listen to, he would have said that Theo Padmos's spiritual umbilical cord was fast unravelling. Worse still, the whole morning and most of the afternoon had been wasted as Theo searched for a sock that was never lost in the first place. And now, at the rate Theo was driving, it looked like they wouldn't get back to The Hague until the following morning.

According to Theo's later version of events, it was Sean's insistence that he change from third gear to fourth that caused the accident. Theo had muttered something about the bend ahead and Sean had pointed out to him that he had time to make a cup of tea before he needed to slow down, and in any case they were already being overtaken by their own shadow. Theo had taken umbrage, moved to the middle of the road and braked instead: ignoring, of course, to check in his rear view mirror if there was anything behind.

The blue Jaguar that had been rapidly approaching from behind, thinking it had a clear opportunity to pass, had swerved and, considering Theo's position in the middle of the road, had done well to avoid nose-diving into the canal. The big poplar tree was less fortunate, proving Einstein's theory of action and reaction by dropping a low branch and crushing the already dented front wing of the Jaguar after it had demolished a fence and mounted a low bank.

Theo braked gently to a halt, and peered curiously at the other car, which had grounded itself on the bank and now rocked gently, all four wheels in the air. "Oh dear," he said. "He must have been going too fast."

Sean jumped from the car and ran towards the other vehicle, his initial shock turning to astonishment when the shaken figure of George Riley staggered from the concave remains of a once proud luxury car. Sean had never stuttered before in his life, but he succeeded without any further training. "Wh-what the b-bloody hell?"

George looked at him with glazed eyes, shaking his head. The shaking reverberated through his whole body, starting at his shoulders and ending at his plump rear, like a wet dog.

"It's b-bloody George," Sean said.

Theo stepped out of his Skoda. "Hello George," he called cheerily, as though he'd known him all his life. The fact that he and Sean had viewed George's lifeless body less than twenty-four hours previously did not seem to trouble him.

"What… how… Jaysus!" Sean was having a less easy time accepting the situation.

George leaned against the Jaguar for support and asked the question that seemed the most relevant in the circumstances. "Which of you bollock-brained cretins was driving?"

Theo discarded his cheery smile and explained that he'd been proceeding cautiously and prudently.

Sean rediscovered the power of speech. "George? You're dead!"

George looked down at his legs, or at least as much of them as he could see past his belly. "Shaken but not dead," he said. "Anyway, what you doing here, Sean?"

"Sure an' that's my question. What the hell's going on? I saw you on the mortuary slab yesterday. You were bloody dead alright then. One hundred percent dead. As a Dodo"

George looked quickly up and down the road. No other vehicles had come into view, but the sound of a motorbike was growing from the direction in which they'd just come. "Let's get out of here," he said, urgently. "I'll tell you all about it as we go."

"What about the car?" Theo asked.

"Not mine," George said, pushing himself away from the Jaguar and sliding down the bank on top of which the car was balanced. "Come on, let's move."

"Now just a minute," Theo said. "You can't just—"

Sean, sensing George's deepening unease, grabbed Theo by the scruff of the neck, pushed him into the passenger seat and helped George into the rear of the car. He loaded himself quickly into the driver's seat, turned the key, pushed the gear lever forward and dropped the clutch. It was the first time that Theo's Skoda had left rubber on the road.

Theo was still protesting loudly when Sean changed from third gear to fourth, keeping his foot to the floor to distance them from the scene. "Shut up, Theo, or we'll have another mishap," he said.

"But it's my car. You're probably not insured."

"Shut up Theo."

"But we might have an accident."

"Shut up Theo."

"But—"

"Shut up Theo," chorused Sean and George together.

Theo fell into a silent sulk.

Sean glanced in the rear view mirror. George's eyes were fixed on Theo's hat. "It's a deerstalker," he said, attracting George's attention.

The fat man shook his head sadly. "Amazing. Is it knitted, or what?"

Sean grinned. "This is Theo. He's helping me trace some missing people. Perhaps you can help as well."

There was a troubled cough from the back seat. "I'm not sure where to start."

"You can begin by telling me why you left the island without handing in your notice to quit."

As George falteringly explained his sudden absence from work and the events that had followed, Theo continued to chant annoyingly from time to time. "I'm still not sure why anybody would mistake your brother for you," he said, from the back of his bright blue hat.

Sean smiled as he heard George's sigh. He answered for him, "The mistaken identity was because George's brother was his identical twin," he reminded Theo. "It was his brother we saw at the mortuary yesterday."

Theo scratched his hat. "So who killed him?"

Sean glanced in the mirror.

"I don't know," came from the passenger. "The only thing I do know is that it wasn't Nick Ferris. Nick and I were having a beer—"

"And an argument," Theo added.

"And a slight difference of opinion. I went for a leak and fell over my own brother on the toilet floor. He was as dead as a crucified Christian."

"So what did you do then?" Sean asked.

"Had a pee. I was absolutely bursting."

"You mean you—"

"Yes, Theo, I had a pee. Nature can be very persistent after a few beers. Anyway, while I stood there splashing my boots and hoping no one would come in, it struck me that the killer had probably got the wrong bloke. Jack and I are well similar."

"But why would anyone want to kill either of you?" Theo asked.

"I owed Jack some money - remember? He probably put a contract out on me. He was nice like that."

"And you think the killer got the wrong guy?" Sean asked.

"That's how it seemed to me while I was pointing at the porcelain. Anyway, I decided to change identity. I figured that it was probably safer being Jack Riley for the time being. I swapped Jack's wallet and passport for mine and took his car key from his pocket, then I left through the front bar."

"Didn't anyone notice you were dressed differently?"

"We weren't. That's not too unusual for identical twins. It's a sort of telepathy thing. Jack and I were used to it. I left through the front bar, and got out of there quick. But the bar was busy and the car I was using was blocked in by another car so I waited a while on the other side of the road. Then the police arrived and eventually took my car away. I didn't dare risk finding a B&B in case the police were checking them, so I slept rough just to be sure of keeping out of sight for a while. Then I went looking for Jack's car this morning."

"You're lucky the killer didn't see you," Sean said. "He might have thought you'd risen from the dead or something."

George glanced at Theo, who seemed to be preparing a theory on the subject. George decided to speak first. "I didn't think of that at the time, I just wanted to get well away. It never crossed my mind that Nick would get the blame."

"And you're sure Nick was with you all the time?" Sean asked

"Positive. We'd been talking for almost an hour. I'd seen several people go to the men's room, so Jack could have only been killed a minute or two before I went in there. He was still warm when I touched him."

"We must go back and tell the police," Theo said. "Mister Ferris might not be a very nice man, but we can't let him take the blame for a murder he didn't commit."

Sean glanced at George in the mirror. "It's a fair point."

The big man leaned forward as far as his belly would allow, and grabbed the headrest of the driver's seat. His voice suddenly had a nervous, panicky edge to it. "No, keep going. Don't you see, if I go back the police will think it's me."

"Why would they think that?" Theo asked.

"Because they'd have no one else to blame. Because I had a motive. To them, it would all be nice and logical, just as it is now with Nick."

"Particularly since you took your brother's wallet and passport and left him there," Sean added, seeing the rationale of the argument. "You'd become prime suspect."

"But we can't just abandon Mister Ferris," Theo said, in a small, anxious voice.

There was an uncomfortable silence as Sean manoeuvred the car onto the slip road of the motorway. "Best we carry on back to The Hague for the moment," he said, as he filtered into the traffic heading north. "Let's go and find Sandy, and take it from there."

* * *

Mevrouw Modderkolk examined the scuffs and scratches on the black leather holdall that she had pulled out from under the bed of the fat Englishman. Not only did it look like hers, it was hers. She unzipped it, then clasped it tight to her mighty bosom in relief when she saw that the money was still intact.

She'd become suspicious about the Englishman when he hadn't shown up for a couple of days, and she had gone to his room to make sure he'd not done a runner without settling his bill – it was one of the hazards of owning a small hotel. What she found was all the usual paraphernalia of a tourist's bedroom – shaving gear, toothpaste, unwashed laundry, clean socks in the drawer. It looked like he'd just gone out for the day, yet the last time she'd seen him had been at breakfast on Saturday morning. Two days ago, and he and his big, shiny car had not been back since.

She zipped the holdall, marched out of the room, and returned to her living quarters on the ground floor to pour herself a large gin. Finding her secret cache under the Englishman's bed had shaken her to the core. Not only had the man taken what didn't belong to him, he now had it in his power to expose her dreadful secret. She suddenly felt more vulnerable than she ever had in her life. The only saving grace was that the fat Englishman was also a thief, so would have no reason to tell anyone about his attempted theft. But she still felt exposed and vulnerable. The fact that the man had somehow discovered the money meant that it was possible for somebody else, someone quite innocent of theft, to stumble over her deception. During the last five years, though her conscience had caused her to lose a great deal of sleep, she had never once considered the real implications of being discovered – the disgrace, prison perhaps – because she had never imagined that she could be discovered. Now the English visitor had proved otherwise.

Mevrouw Modderkolk noticed that her hands were shaking. What on earth had she been thinking about when she began her crusade to relieve van Aanroy's mission of its money? Since she'd lived reasonably comfortably without spending any of it, she was certain that she didn't actually need it.

There was only one thing for it: the cash had to be returned to van Aanroy. The problem was, how? She couldn't just admit she'd been stealing it for five years. If she did that, she might as well keep it and take the risk of being found out.

She splashed another gin into the glass, even larger this time, and set her mind to work to find a way of getting the money back without drawing suspicion to herself.

* * *

Sandy didn't know what made her change her mind. Just a year ago, she would have bedded anybody if it would have advanced her cause, but, having decided to test Marcus Foyer's morals in the customary, time-honoured manner, she suddenly found herself in the unusual role of spectator as, with detached amusement, she watched herself gently but firmly remove his hand from her thigh and get up to make another coffee; which left her in uncharted territory. How, now, to test his scruples?

It turned out to be easier than she could have imagined. Handing him a fresh coffee and looking him straight in the face to judge the sincerity or otherwise of his response, she framed the plan to empty Rolien van der Laan's Swiss bank account in the same way that she would have asked him whether he took milk and sugar. It was difficult to believe that it could be so easy to get a direct answer. Pity she hadn't learned the technique a few years ago.

Marcus thought for less than five seconds before accepting the idea. It only surprised him that he'd not thought of it himself. "Of course," he said, resting his hand on her thigh again as she sat down again. "What the hell am I thinking of, chasing fifty thousand euros when there's your money plus a million just sitting there in Rolien's account? I must be going senile in my old age!" He was obviously far from that, yet, in abandoning her plan to bed him, Sandy had experienced a sea change, as though she should be saving herself for something better. Maybe it was something to do with growing up, she mused. Maybe it was a reaction from having seen Sean again. Or maybe it was because there were a hundred reasons not to climb into bed with Marcus Foyer. The fact that he was as shallow as a children's paddling pool came pretty close to the top of the list.

"Since I know all the computations and Rolien's bank account number, and you know the last used code number, that's 67-33 isn't it?" Marcus asked, stroking her leg. But Sandy had never been a pushover, not even when the glow of desire would have made submission easy, and now she felt she might even have begun to recognise the difference between love and lust. She gently removed Marcus's hand. "No," she said, "we're not getting into that again. You can't do anything without me, and I can't do anything without you. That's 50-50 as far as I'm concerned. Take it or leave it."

Marcus took it.

"Do you want me to go and get my laptop from the car?" he asked as he drained his coffee. "We can do it right away."

Sandy glanced at her watch. "No, I don't want to give Rolien's boyfriend time to spot the transaction and pull any electronic tricks on us. When we do it, we go straight to the bank and withdraw the cash."

"Then we clear out fast!" Marcus said, slipping into

his shoes, which he had earlier kicked off in anticipation.

"Then we clear out fast," Sandy confirmed. "So we need to get packed and ready to go before we run the programme. Let's do it tomorrow." She felt a cautious urge of expectation surge through her veins. For the first time in days, she felt that she wasn't just hanging on by her fingernails.

As a slightly disappointed estate agent left the apartment, agreeing to return the following morning, Sandy couldn't help herself, not for the first time, admiring the contours of his bottom. She shrugged at her own change of attitude, climbed the stairs up to the lounge, and poured herself a large glass of wine.

Reaching into her handbag she took out the JoinMyChurch card and carefully copied the access code on a note pad. As she slid the card back into her bag her eyes fell on a small, folded computer printout that she couldn't remember being there. She unfolded it and read the name, address and balance of an account that had attracted her attention when she worked for the bank. She remembered having put it there now. It was an account that had received regular credits and almost never any withdrawals. Even during the six months she had worked for Alliance, the balance had risen from about three hundred thousand euros to almost five hundred thousand. And then she remembered why she had printed it. It was to give to her father to see if a bit of nocturnal snooping would reveal anything about the account-holder that would leave him vulnerable to a little blackmail. Something her father was quite good at.

Sandy screwed it up and winged it into the wicker wastebasket that she kept by the bureau. Pity she hadn't thought of it when they were running the JoinMyChurch scam, it might have avoided much of the mess they were now in.

As she was about to close her handbag, the corner of an old, dog-eared photograph peeped from the inner pocket. She eased it out and gazed at it glassy-eyed, feeling that a crumb had lodged in her windpipe. It was a photo of an innocent nine-year old girl holding a large ice cream with one hand and her father's hand with the other. Though the faded picture was black and white, she could still visualise the shocking pink of her father's shirt. She knew without looking that his shoelace was undone. She wondered how he was coping in his dismal prison cell. Give me time, she asked. Just give me a little time.

Nearby, the pretty young lady with the bright red lips turned off the IPod and pulled her anorak tight around her shoulders. Despite it being almost June, her high perch made the wind as keen as a fresh razor blade. The old buildings leaned against each other like a badly organised rugby scrum, and she picked her way warily across the leaded valleys between the roofs before grasping the iron ladder that served as a fire exit from the gay bar. She was tired and needed a shower. Time enough to deal with this in the morning.

* * *

Theo's yellow Skoda pulled to a halt in front of the Corona Hotel. Sean left the engine running as he hauled his overnight bag and a slumbering George Riley from the back seat. Theo cocked his leg over the gear lever and slid into the driving seat, grateful to be in charge of a steering wheel again. As Sean and George bade him farewell and disappeared towards the hotel entrance, Theo eased the gear stick forwards and manoeuvred circumspectly around the corner towards Grote Kirk.

What a terrible day it had been. First of all there had been the loss of his sock. Then there had been that terrible accident that wasn't his fault, then learning that Sandy Ferris's father had been unjustly imprisoned, then the awful drive home.

As he braked and moved down to second gear to allow a lone cyclist a wide berth, he wondered how Sandy was coping with her father being imprisoned. He told himself that she deserved it, that she was a thief who had to be punished. Then he felt a belt of common sense squeezing his thoughts and realised what a stupid idea it had been. She might not be the most honest person he'd met in his life, but she certainly didn't deserve a punishment like that. But there was still a niggle deep in his mind that things weren't quite what they seemed. It was obvious that Sandy Ferris was guilty of something, though he just wasn't quite sure what it was. All this Irish talk about parcels wasn't getting him any nearer finding out what she had been up to when she worked for the bank and he felt that everyone was losing sight of the real mission.

Damn it, why couldn't he just let it go? Why couldn't he put the clock in reverse and not tell his bank manager his suspicions about their recently departed cashier? But then The Great Mother would know, wouldn't she. The Great Mother would look into his head and know he'd not been honest with his employers.

Or would she?

Who was this big woman in the sky who was supposed to be watching his every move? The Great Mother never slept, it said in van Aanroy's hymn. "No careless slumber shall her eyelids close". Instead she roamed the streets spying on people, seeing if they'd been good enough, or sending plagues to finish them off, or pushing them under trams, or indulging in some other whim. Theo felt a needle prick of guilt about thinking of The Great Mother in that way. He had been taught… no, he had been told that The Great Mother was an ever-present, ever-watchful force, and now he felt accountable in case The Great Mother was listening to his thoughts. But where was the evidence, the proof, of her existence? How was the acceptance of an unseeable deity supposed to explain the mysteries of the universe? Why replace one mystery with another? And why should The Great Mother be any different to all the world's other gods?

Theo put his questions to the back of his mind and concentrated on navigating the traffic lights. He wasn't sure whether his shifting views were a good thing or not. Even Sandy Ferris was beginning to seem less mephistophelean nowadays: she was just a very original person; bigger than life you could say. It was obvious, now, that she had been gently pulling his leg for months, bending over to give him a better view of her delightful bottom, leaning forwards so that he couldn't resist peeking down her well-formed cleavage, blatantly disregarding the truth and saying anything that came into her head just for its amusement value. She had none of the fragile self-pride that would prevent her from telling a joke against herself. She didn't seem to care what sort of impression she left behind, just so long as she did leave an impression. In her own carefree way, Sandy Ferris took life as it came and twisted it to suit her own standards and sense of fun. Why couldn't he be the same? Why couldn't he 'pull a Ferris' and charm life instead of chastising it? But that would have meant breaking the The Great Mother's rules, wouldn't it?

'Oh Great Mother, born of your own creation,' Theo began; then realised that, despite years of repetition, the prayer had failed to enter his heart. 'Oh Great Mother, born of your own creation,' he began again, 'what on earth are you playing at? I know you are supposed to be invisibly manifest at all times; but if you are invisible, how the hell do I know you're there?'

As Theo rewrote his prayer, Sean Legg was not a happy Sean Legg. Three days of Theo's blatterooning had set his nerves on edge, and the fact that the door lock was being truculent was not improving his mood. "Damn things never work first time," he muttered, swiping the card through the reader for the fourth time. This time the lock light flashed green. He heaved against the door, flicked the light switch, and looked around the hotel room. Something was wrong, different somehow. It was too tidy. When he'd left, cables had been draped across the floor and a modem sat mid-carpet waiting to jump out and trip an unwary maid. Papers had been strewn across the bed. Now the room was bare. Only Sandy's laptop computer sat on the table: no wires, no papers, no Hannu.

George followed him into the room and opened the door of the wardrobe. It was empty.

Sean glanced over George's shoulder. "He's gone,"

he said. "All his gear has gone."

Though he didn't know it, Sean Legg would never see Hannu Palernius again.

CHAPTER THIRTEEN

A second restless night left Sandy's unmade bed looking like a war zone. After several short bursts of shallow sleep, between which she punched, turned and wrestled with her pillow, and flicked agitatedly through the channels of her thoughts, she arose and took a bleary-eyed look out of the window over the roof- tops. The softened edges of daybreak were thinking about lightening the sky and, as she sipped her morning coffee, a yawning sun made up its mind, sending a faint glow of light from beyond the horizon and tinting the soaring tower of Grote Kirk in shadowy hues of pink and grey.

Sandy and Marcus met early as agreed but, despite Marcus' initial enthusiasm, events had not proceeded as planned and his reactions had moved from curious head scratching through keyboard-stabbing frustration, to incomprehensible forehead smacking.

"Reboot?" Sandy asked, for the third time.

"Hardly seems worth it," Marcus replied, pushing back his chair and staring out across the rooftops.

"You're sure you got the code changes right?"

"Sure. I wrote it down as Rolien was telling me. The location rolls forward two on the drop-down list, the code numbers and letters all roll forward one, except Z's which become D's and 9's which become 4's."

Sandy rechecked their calculations from their own code that she'd written on the scrap of paper. "Damn it. Hjalmar must have reset the convention when he relocated the web site," she said, shaking her head. "Why the hell does he use access codes anyway?"

"So he can control the whole scenario, probably."

"But you said he'd just moved the site and not reset the codes."

Marcus sighed and turned back to face her. "That's what Rolien told me. Perhaps Hjalmar changed his mind. Perhaps Rolien got it wrong. Who knows?"

"You're going to have to go back and see her," Sandy said. "Maybe she can get the information out of Hjalmar. She can hardly just ask him straight out, so she's going to have to use her womanly wiles, and from what you tell me about the current state of their relationship, that might not be too easy."

Unwillingness and doubt reflected in the depths of Marcus' eyes.

"On the other hand," Sandy said, "you could always go and ask Hjalmar for the information yourself."

"What do you mean?"

"I mean, just ask him outright. Tell him you heard about his programme through a friend. Tell him you know a good account that's worth hitting and ask him if he'll give you the code. You wouldn't even be lying."

Marcus eased his chair back to the table and swivelled his empty cup in the saucer. Sandy noticed that it went clockwise, a quarter turn each time. Twelve o'clock – three o'clock - six o'clock - nine o'clock … "What about if he asks me to run the hit there and then?" he asked when he reached twelve o'clock on the third lap.

"Tell him the account is due to have a large sum of money paid into it in the next couple of days and that you don't want to run the programme until you know that the funds have been transferred. Tell him it's the proceeds of some property sale you've negotiated."

Six o'clock – nine o'clock - twelve o'clock – three o'clock. "Who shall I say told me about the programme in the first place?"

"Say it was Brigitte. That's the bloke - the woman - you talked to in De Hardin's on Sunday evening. She seems to know most things that go on in this town. Apparently Hjalmar and she vaguely know each other, so he probably wouldn't be suspicious."

Marcus reached for the phone with his free hand. "I'll give him a call."

Sandy placed her hand over his, stopping the clock. "Go and see him," she said. "He'll be suspicious if he gets a call out of the blue. If you go and meet him face-to-face, he'll be much more likely to trust you."

Marcus nodded, and then his frown disappeared. "Do you trust me, Sandy? If Hjalmar gives me the code, I'll have all the information I need to do this on my own."

"I don't have much choice, do I?" she said, quietly. "On the other hand, Marcus, if I find out I've been done over, you don't think I'd let my share just disappear, do you? I wouldn't hesitate to let the authorities know who was responsible. You and I need to stick together, my friend. It's safer for both of us that way."

He offered her a half-hearted smile and closed down his laptop computer. "Birds of a feather, eh?"

Sandy laughed. "On your bike, birdbrain. Give me a call if there are any problems. Otherwise, I'll see you back here this afternoon."

She ushered him down the stairs and out of the door, anxious to move her plan forward and get back to her father in Kinderdijk. As she closed the apartment door behind the estate agent and he began his descent of the communal stairs, the entry intercom buzzed. Sandy trotted quickly back up to the living room to answer. The voice that replied caused her to look anxiously towards the balcony.

"Hello, my dear, it's Sean. Now don't you go panicking and climbing over the rooftops again, I just called round to return your laptop computer."

There was a faint crackle of static through the earphone as Sandy tried to weigh up whether or not to let him in. And then her decision was taken from her as, through the speaker, she heard the street level door open and Marcus Foyer's voice pass a casual greeting as he left.

"The door's open now," Sean said into the speaker grille. "I'll come on up if that's okay. Don't worry, Sandy, I'm on my own and I'm not here to cause you any problems – I promise."

Sean had always been scrupulous in his promise-keeping but Sandy still opened the door to her sanctuary with caution. She could hear his heavy footsteps on the wooden staircase that served the six apartments. He was, it seemed, unaccompanied.

"Hello, my dear," he said cheerily, bending to kiss her on the cheek as he closed the door behind him with his foot. "What's the state of the coffee pot?"

Sandy smiled, as much in relief as in welcome. "Always available to a friend," she replied. "Come on up."

As she busied herself with the coffee percolator, she glanced back over her shoulder towards the towering Irishman whose bulk was blocking the kitchen door. Sean was looking at her yet not looking at her as their eyes met. It was as though his eyes and his brain were working on two different levels. She'd only ever seen such a look once before, and it had come from Sean then. Interest, concern and affection were built into the expression but his eyes related something that was greater than the sum of all three.

There was something else that Sandy couldn't read, yet she had the wacky feeling that she was mirroring the look, and that she too was communicating more than she understood. It was as though they were both reaching out with tender fingers into concealed but cherished areas of their past. Sandy gave herself a mental prod. "Did you find what you were looking for on my computer?" she asked, unassumingly.

Sean smiled and his eyes engaged gear. "Enough to be certain that you're the guiltiest little thief I know," he said, unloading her computer from under his arm onto the kitchen table. "And the prettiest," he added quietly.

Sandy's face broke into a smile that was blocked only by her ears. If ever she needed a friend, it was now. She turned and hugged him. "Sorry," she said simply, snuggling into the warmth and comfort of his chest.

Sean returned the hug. "An' so you bleedin' should be, you cheeky little cow." He squeezed her shoulders gently then held her with imperceptible firmness at arm's length. His face lost the smile. "I want you to promise, Sandy, that you'll never use me as a target again. The police might not be able to prove anything against you, but you and I will always know the truth."

She nodded and wiped a moist eye with the back of her hand. "I know it was wrong, Sean, but I always thought it would just be a case of you claiming on the insurance or something."

"No, you're brighter than that, Sandy. You might have fooled yourself that that's what you thought, but you knew deep down you were dropping me in deep shit. None of us are perfect, Sandy, and to some extent you're right; this time round, I've lost nothing. The bank has already replaced the money.

But have you any bloody idea of the grief and worry you and your friends caused me the first time you screwed Three Leggs? You put at risk the jobs of hundreds of men and women, just to satisfy your own greed. Not to mention long, sleepless nights for me while I tried to sort out the mess you left behind. It's true I got the money back, but—"

"You got the money back?"

"Sure. The money your little group of conspirators stole. You mean you didn't know?"

"No. We knew that we didn't have it, but we had no idea where it had gone."

"Well then, it remains a mystery," Sean said. "But it still doesn't let you or your father off the hook. I don't know what your level of involvement was in last year's scam and, frankly, I don't care anymore. I just want you to promise you'll leave my finances alone in future."

She nodded again. "I promise. Right at this moment, I wish I'd never got involved. It's caused more trouble than you can imagine."

"Like your father being accused of murder?"

Sandy jumped as if his fingers had emitted an electrical charge. "How the hell do you know about that, Sean?"

His smile returned, and this time it was the full keyboard. His green eyes twinkled and the twinkle smiled too. "Let's just say that I had a bit of help from an old friend of yours and someone called The Great Mother."

"Theo?"

"The very same. Our Mister Padmos spotted some charge card transactions in Kinderdijk. We went down there in search of the elusive Miss Ferris. Stumbled over your dad and a dead body, we did."

"He didn't do it," she said, leading him by the hand into the living room.

"I'm well aware of that. That's why I'm here."

Sandy searched his face for a clue, a myriad of questions entering her mind.

Though Sean was clearly enjoying the silence, he saved her from having to ask. "Right at this moment," he said, "your father's alibi is snoring soundly in a room at The Corona Hotel." He continued in detail to explain George Riley's identity switch and the reasons for it. "George thought his brother had been mistaken for him; that he was probably the target and that, if he went back, he would probably be accused of the murder."

"But we can't just leave my dad to take the blame."

"I'm well aware of that," Sean replied, touching her arm gently. "But if we transport George back to Kinderdijk against his wishes, he'll just deny everything and we'll be back where we started. I want you to come to the hotel at lunchtime and we'll see what we can do about things. There must be some way we can get your father out."

Sandy nodded. The magic of Sean was that he was encouraging and open and generous. He embraced life, whatever its problems. "You're using 'we', like you're involved as well," she said.

"So I am. It was my idea to track you two down and it was me that caused you to bolt." He paused for a moment. Normally, Sean was unafraid of conversational pauses or holding a gaze - his self-confidence was powerful and lethally attractive. Now, however, he seemed to be examining the air behind Sandy's head, and his eyes had the same look that she'd seen when they stood in the kitchen. "Anyway," he continued, "do you really think that Sean Legg would leave a damsel in distress? Particularly a damsel who's shared his bed and his…" The colour rose high in his cheeks and his normally strident voice softened, like it was wearing carpet slippers. "…and his affection."

"Sit down and I'll pour the coffee," Sandy whispered, standing on tiptoe to kiss his cheek. She took his words with her to the kitchen and came back carrying two steaming cups, but was just in time to hear the apartment door click shut, down below in the entrance hall. She smiled to herself and stepped onto the balcony. A moment later Sean strode around the corner from the market place into the shopping street. "Lunchtime," she called down.

He looked up and returned the smile, though the blush was still on his face like a Caribbean sunset. "Lunchtime," he shouted back.

She continued watching for a few moments as Sean mingled with the shoppers before turning up a small side street towards his hotel. Then Sandy crossed the living room to the kitchen and scooped up her laptop computer. Sean didn't know it, but he'd just saved her from having to go on an urgent shopping expedition.

She plugged in, booted up, and logged on to the Internet.

* * *

Joris Duisenberg looked up from his papers as his daughter strode into the office. "What's the news?" he asked.

"He's about to be taught a sharp lesson by his girlfriend and her estate agent," said the heavy-breasted young lady with the bright red lips. She placed the iPod look-alike on the desk in front of the Chief Inspector, removed her shoulder-length wig and shook free a bundle of alabaster-blonde hair. "Do you want to hear the recordings?"

"No need," Joris said. "You can give me the general gist.

Detective Sergeant Jolanda Duisenberg explained quickly and efficiently how Rolien planned to regain her man's attention.

"Serves him right," Joris said. "It would be better if he lost the lot."

"He will, Dad. I managed to bug the Ferris place and it seems that the estate agent and Sandy Ferris have changed the rules. They're planning to take everything, including Rolien's money. In fact, they're probably doing so right at this moment."

Joris kicked back his chair. "We can't let that happen, Jolanda. Standing by and watching your brother being taught a lesson is one thing, but we can't let them rob Rolien as well."

"That's why I came to see you."

He smiled, but it was a smile of resignation. "You're a bloody good copper, Jolanda, you know when to use your initiative and when to pass the problems up the ladder. Unfortunately, the buck stops here with me and, to tell you the truth, I've no idea what to do next. I want Robert to see that crime doesn't pay but I can't have innocent bystanders getting hurt."

"You could hardly call Rolien innocent, Dad. She's two-timing Robert and she's planning to rip-off the taxes."

"I know, but a phone call to the tax office would soon put that straight. As far as two-timing Robert is concerned, it's hardly illegal, no matter what you and I might feel about it."

"So we go and rescue him again? We can't keep mollycoddling him for ever, even if he is family."

"It's not for him, Jolanda, it's for your mum. For all I care, they can throw the book at Robert, or Hjalmar, or Anthrax, or whatever he likes to call himself nowadays. He's had his chances. But your mum…" His words trailed off.

"Well we need to do something," Jolanda said. "At the moment, they're all double-crossing each other."

Joris picked up his peaked cap. "You're right. Get yourself down to Grote Markt and pull Miss Ferris and the estate agent in for questioning. I'll take a squad car up to Blokzijl and bring in the other two. It's time we threw the book at the whole lot of them."

"What about Mum?" she asked.

"It's too late for that now. Like you said, we can't keep mollycoddling Robert for ever. Come on, let's get moving."

* * *

Mevrouw Modderkolk didn't know and didn't care what had happened to the English tourist; she was just grateful that he still hadn't returned. When he did, he would find the hotel locked and bolted and his belongings in the dustbin in the back yard – that is, if he got back before the dustbin lorry arrived. She scuttled across the square to the bus stop, struggling to tuck the black hold-all under her arm as she dragged her suitcase behind her. She knew now what she would tell the Reverend van Aanroy; that the money had been given to her as a donation from a well wisher who preferred to remain anonymous. And then, to avoid any embarrassing questions, she would disappear to her brothers' farmhouse out in the countryside near Ridderkerk. As far as she was aware, no one even knew that she had any brothers, so she would be safe there. She'd leave it a few weeks, then make a decision about the hotel. Maybe it was time to sell up and find herself a little cottage somewhere even more remote.

She just had time to take one last look at The Paleis before the bus turned into the square.

* * *

It had been copiously clear since the inspectors finished their audit, that the bank had pulled the plug on any evolution in Theo's career. There was no need to discuss the matter or commit the facts in writing, his progression up the ice-smooth managerial ladder had lost all traction and he was free-falling at a terrifying rate. Responsible tasks that were normally assigned to him were now being delegated to others more junior than he. He had lost the bank's trust, and they his. His annual appraisal was due in a few days and his manager, a man given to dreaming up lurid catch phrases that were so lame they needed wheelchairs, was probably practising his speech already. 'Hero to Zero, Theo. Hall of Fame to the Wall of Shame.' Theo was quite sure he didn't want to have to listen to the reprimand that was undoubtedly in store for him.

What had also become apparent to Theo was that, if The Great Mother really did exist and was not just some vapour wave of his imagination, she, too, was chastising Theo by trashing his life. Unfortunately, The Great Mother needed to brush up on her communication skills, since she seemed to have overlooked telling her loyal servant what he was being disciplined for. Apart from a few little untruths in his search for Sandy Ferris, Theo had tried his hardest to obey The Great Mother's ordinances and, whatever his crime, the punishment didn't seem to fit. Life was seeming damnably unfair.

Theo picked up his pencil – the bank's pencil – examined the point, and very deliberately broke it against the edge of his desk. He exhaled noisily and brushed back a lock of yellow hair that had wedged between his face and his monocle. His desktop computer was, as so often in the past weeks, logged on to Sandy Ferris's account. One hundred and thirty three euros and twenty-seven cents. Hardly the proceeds of grand larceny. Deep inside, he knew that she was guilty, that she'd been up to something;

or at least he thought he knew. Yet where was the evidence? The bank didn't seem to be missing any money and Sandy Ferris didn't seem to have any. So what had all the fuss been about? How the hell had he got himself into this mess?

True, Sean seemed to think that she was involved in taking his money, and it was certain that she and her father were up to something, otherwise why had they run away, and why all the telephone talk about parcels and packages and things? It was hardly going to be a parcel containing her underwear, was it? Theo felt his ears burn at the memory of his hand in her private clothing drawer.

Another glance at the screen. One hundred and thirty three euros and twenty-seven cents.

He pushed aside the loan application that lay unprocessed on his desk and aimed himself towards the staff rest rooms to get rid of the three cups of tea that the lady with the sensible dress had brought him. Sensible? Boring, more like. No fleshy bits on view like there used to be when Sandy Ferris was around.

Damn her, why did he have to keep thinking back to Sandy Ferris? What was it about her that kept him awake at nights? Was it just that she had an indefinable quality that Joska lacked? A sort of casualness? Was that why he was being punished - for wanting Joska to be a bit more natural?

The toilet smelt wholesome and clean, like the bathroom at Joska's parents' house; a high nose of lavender and bleach with undertones of soap and clean towels. He stood before the urinal and exhaled noisily as the pressure released from his bladder. He knew what his flaccid appendage was capable of, apart from draining off cups of tea, yet Theo's sex life was as empty as a new bank account waiting for money to be paid in before it could be activated.

Joska had given him a severe reprimand once when he had made a suggestion that they could activate their account before they were married. Well, in fact it wasn't just a severe reprimand, it was a damn good bollocking. The Great Mother this; The Great Mother that. Why the hell didn't she just say what she thought? If there really was a Great Mother… But then maybe that was the nub of the problem. Theo's physical discomfort was real and The Great Mother wasn't. And maybe, just maybe, Theo had known it all along.

He zipped himself up and sidestepped to the hand basin. If somebody had asked him to explain what a weak-willed wimp looked like, he would have described the man he saw in the mirror.

He'd read Reverend van Aanroy's book 'The Great Mother into the Future' once. Joska had told him how, by reading it, it would convince him that The Great Mother's way was the true way.

Read it, Theo had. And the book had turned out to be the electrician that reconnected part of his brain and enlightened the darkened parts of his head. Until now, Theo the puppet had short-circuited the obvious and had gone along with van Aanroy's ideas. 'There's always a price to pay.' He could hear van Aanroy intone. 'Why?' he'd often wanted to ask. 'Why is there always a price tag on just being yourself? Why this reward and punishment system?' Up till now, he'd believed the 'price to pay' system. Up till now, he'd thought it was real.

"Heaven is not at stake here," Theo mouthed, looking in the mirror into the eyes of an imaginary congregation. "All that's at stake is the influence of the power-seekers like Reverend van Aanroy." He gripped the sides of the hand basin as they became imaginary pulpit rails. "Reverend van Aanroy, who talks of the punishment that awaits the sinner. The enemy of pleasure who uses the powerful language of sin and hell." He paused before summing up, and lowered his voice for effect. "The reward of a hereafter is uncertain," he said. "And the cost is high. So much guilt, so much cruelty, so much pain."

His congregation, led by Joska, murmured their approval before melting out of sight. Only van Aanroy remained, shaking his fist.

Theo blanked out the image and searched his own face in the mirror. He realized that, in one short discourse he'd converted himself back into a human being. Joska, too, he hoped. He finished washing his hands and wiped them in his hair. He allowed his monocle to fall onto his chest at the end of its silk cord. And there's something else that's going to change. Ordinary spectacles from now on, or contact lenses even. Don't care what The Great Mother thinks about it.

With a final shove, Theo closed the door on his past. His decision was made.

Though the imaginary Joska had nodded her approval along with everybody else, Theo wasn't sure how she would receive the news in real life. He didn't want to lose her, but it was a risk he was willing to take. Perhaps she could learn to be just a little bit more like Sandy Ferris.

Suddenly, without his constant moral guardian of many years, Theo was the loneliest man alive, though he left the rest room feeling better – physically and mentally. He felt more like Theo the bold, like he could start making his own decisions from now on. Pass the kryptonite, Superman; I'm immune. He planned a chin wipe, discovered that his chin was dry, and put his handkerchief back in his pocket.

The manager was standing by Theo's desk, peering at the loan application that had been awaiting Theo's attention. "It's taking a long time, Mijnheer Padmos," he snapped, his voice like a cinder under a door. "A little urgency if you please."

'Go to hell.' mouthed Theo to the thinning patch on the top of the retreating head as his boss marched back towards his office.

"Oh and I want you to go to the Bezuidenhoutseweg sub-office today," added the manager, turning back to face him. "Nobody else to do it. No security clerk either, he's off sick. I'll try and get someone up there during the day."

Theo nodded noncommittally. More demotion. The sub-office was usually staffed by one of the cashiers, not the chief cashier. Definitely time to consider another vocation in life.

He dumped himself into his chair and exchanged his monocle for his spectacles. Goodbye monocle. A final glance at the screen and Sandy Ferris's account. Two million six hundred and thirty three thousand, one hundred and nineteen euros and sixty-six cents?

Whaaaat?

Two million six hundred and thirty three thousand, one hundred and nineteen euros and sixty-six cents.

Something wrong with the damn computer now. He checked the account name and number. Sandy Ferris all right. Pushing back his chair, he crossed the banking hall to a colleague's desk and leaned across the young clerk's arm. He typed the account number on the keyboard – no exchange of pleasantries – and read the result on screen. Two million six hundred and thirty three thousand, one hundred and nineteen euros and sixty-six cents – confirmed.

Back to his own desk and reboot the computer. Still no change. Two million six hundred and thirty three thousand, one hundred and nineteen euros and sixty-six cents. It had even been converted back into guilders for the old and the politically incorrect.

Ye Gods, now what was she up to? Sandy Ferris had struck again.

Theo read the numbers slowly. 2 – 6 – 3 – 3 – 1 – 1 – 9 – 6 – 6. Then backwards as if to verify. He closed his bad eye, slid his specs down his nose and read them again squinting through his good eye.

There was no doubt about it: Sandy Ferris was up to her old tricks.

He checked the incoming credits. Three of them; one from Commercial Bank in Geneva, one from a bank in Amsterdam, and one from – WAIT A MINUTE – one from Alliance Bank in The Hague?

Theo looked up the account number and folded into his chair when he read the customer's name. He felt physically empty, as though all the wind had been knocked out of him. The entire balance of the Reverend van Aanroy's personal account had been transferred to Sandy Ferris. Surely they weren't in this together? How could that be? Theo pulled his thoughts together and tapped quickly on the keyboard. If nothing else, the bank had taught him how to use their computer systems.

He scanned van Aanroy's account history but, after reading from the screen for several minutes, could not recognise any sort of pattern. He knew that each member of The Mission paid a tithe, a scutage as van Aanroy called it, and that these were paid into the Mission's bank account: after all, Theo had been paying it himself until now. And he knew that the gospel singing and other collections were paid into the Mission's account. But, as he scrolled back through the records, he could make no sense of van Aanroy's private account. It had received large sums of money, certainly more than the Mission members were soliciting. Theo drilled down to the details. All of them were electronic transfers from various other European countries. He guessed that van Aanroy would have a problem explaining them to his followers, but he felt suddenly very determined to have them accounted for.

He pushed his specs onto the bridge of his nose when he realised they were about to fall off. His thoughts were as clear and fresh as spring water now. It was just a pity he had not realised earlier that Sandy and van Aanroy were accomplices. It was no wonder that van Aanroy had been impatient and less than helpful whenever Theo had asked his advice about his search for Sandy. It was no wonder that Sandy had eluded him all this time. They were in it together and van Aanroy had been tipping her off; letting her give him the slip each time he was closing in.

But what of the other two credits, one from Geneva and one from Amsterdam? Sean's missing money surely; although it seemed to have grown somewhat, because he felt sure that Sean had mentioned a sum of money that converted to about seven hundred and fifty thousand euros. For the moment though, the amount was unimportant, he could check it all out with Sean later. What mattered now was to remove it from the clutches of Sandy Ferris – even if he had started to like her a little bit.

Theo stared at the screen, cudgelling his brain for a solution. Transferring the money to his own account was too obvious; it would look like straight theft, and he was not a thief. In fact he was preventing a theft. Telephone Sean? Not very bright if he were caught breaking bank secrecy. Anyway, what could Sean do if the money was locked into Sandy's account?

The answer formed in Theo's head slowly, like condensation on a window. As long as he could reduce the balance of Sandy's account to its former level and get the money off the premises in cash, he could sort it out later. At least it would enable him to put the situation on hold for a while and, though it was only semi-legitimate, it was better than any of the other options. Mainly because he couldn't think of any other options.

It was left to Theo, as chief cashier, to decide how much money to take to the Bezuidenhoutseweg sub-office. Normally about thirty thousand euros was enough to last the day, the office was never that busy. Today, though, if he took the 'Ferris' money with him as well, he could hide it on his way to the sub-office, demand an explanation from van Aanroy, and return Sean's portion to him later.

Meanwhile, a forged cash withdrawal slip slid into the pile of daily entries that were currently being processed by the sensible dress lady would ensure that the bank's books balanced and that Sandy's account remained unchanged from its level ten minutes ago. It was brilliant. Sandy Ferris would no doubt call at the main branch in his absence, discover that the balance of her account was unchanged and go away again scratching her head. She was hardly in a position to complain about a phoney withdrawal slip or the loss of stolen money.

Theo took the cash from the vault in five hundred euro notes – the largest denominations in circulation. Even so, over five thousand of them proved a tight fit in the Livingstone bag, along with the cash that was normally taken as a float. The bag was bulging and heavy in his hand as he stepped back into the brightness of the banking hall.

He pulled his deerstalker tight on his head, then had second thoughts and tossed it into a drawer in his desk. The monocle stayed there too. Then he had third thoughts, pulled out the hat again, dropped it on his head and tilted it slightly to one side. Jaunty.

Some days were like that – make a decision, think again, change the first decision. He picked up the leather cashier's bag, strode out of the bank and marched with some purpose towards the car park, whistling a little tune that wasn't The Old Wooden Cross and that didn't wet his chin.

Had he troubled to look over his shoulder, he

would have seen Sandy Ferris dodge into a shop doorway to avoid being spotted. But Theo wasn't one to take backward glances when his mind was made up.

Sandy waited and watched as the blue head disappeared around the corner, then she caught her reflection in the shop window. She was smirking. She wasn't sure if it was the rear view of a pin-stripe suit, blue deerstalker hat and bright yellow hair, or whether it was her overactive imagination painting silly pictures of a wet chin and a gleaming monocle. Either way, all she could visualise was Theo Padmos looking like a Magritte painting. But her smile was good-natured and not at all vindictive: after all, Theo had never done her any harm, and she wished none on him.

She entered the fluorescent banking hall, wishing that she'd not closed her account at Avrobank. Though she knew she'd not be bumping into Theo, she also knew that eyebrows would be raised when she asked to withdraw over two and a half million euros in cash. The bank usually required a short period of notice for withdrawals of that size. If Sandy had had the time, she would have re-opened her other account and had the money transferred there, but time was of the essence now that Marcus Foyer was out of the way. She'd already placed her few personal belongings in the car, and all that was left to do was to withdraw the money before going to see Sean at the Corona Hotel. After that, it would be back to Kinderdijk to extract her father from his prison cell – one way or the other.

After a short drive, Theo let himself into Joska's house, removing his hat and tucking it into his jacket pocket as he stepped over the threshold. He called Joska's name. No response. Joska's parents both worked, but Joska had devoted her life to The Great Mother's labours, and working for a living didn't fit too well with her grand plan. That would have to change if they were to stay together.

He wasn't sure where grandma was, but he was secretly pleased that the house was empty. He didn't have time now to explain to Joska the full details of how he happened to be carrying two and a half million euros of somebody else's money. It could wait until this evening. Meanwhile, he just wanted to find somewhere safe to leave it, somewhere where nobody would be likely to look.

Five minutes later he left the house, donning his hat before climbing into his Skoda and easing gently away from the kerb. If he had glanced into his driving mirror, he would have seen Joska bustling round the corner some fifty yards away. But Theo wasn't one to take backward glances when his mind was made up.

Joska waved to him. It was easy to recognize Theo's yellow Skoda with the bumper sticker that said 'I'm going to meet The Great Mother. Are you coming with me?' She'd given it to him just two weeks before, though he had seemed less impressed by its message than she had hoped. She waved again as Theo slowed for the traffic lights. If she had run, she could have easily caught up with him, but she, too, had other things on her mind. She was sure that today would be the day when The Great Mother's message would arrive.

* * *

It was Hannu who saw the police squad cars pull to

a halt in front of the Kaatjes Residence. There was no scream of sirens, no squealing tyres, no blue flashing lights swathing across the net curtains, just two quiet little cars pulling quietly to a halt in a quiet little village in front of a quiet little hotel - at least it had been a quiet little hotel until Rolien's estate agent had arrived. Hannu adjusted his parting in appreciation of the speed of the police response; after all, the hotel had only dialled the emergency number two minutes earlier.

As Hannu listened to the banging of car doors outside, he sped through the events of the previous twenty-four hours, wondering if it was something he'd said or done that had brought the situation to such a violent head.

After Angus Slooth's visit to the Corona Hotel, he had contacted Anthrax by e-mail and agreed to meet in the civilised surroundings of the Kaatjes Residence. At last, Anthrax and The Redeemer came face-to-face, and Hannu discovered that Anthrax was called Hjalmar, and Hjalmar discovered that The Redeemer was called Hannu. And Rolien, it seemed, discovered that her boyfriend wasn't the only person in the world who knew how to use immutable arbitrary-precision integers to provide analogues to primitive operators for modular arithmetic. Though for some reason, she didn't appear to be over-impressed by her discovery.

The previous evening had been spent in digital pleasantries as Hannu, Hjalmar and Rolien had enjoyed some of Holland's finest cuisine in the Katje bij de Sluis on the other side of the canal. During the entrée an interesting discussion evolved as to whether a common encapsulation mechanism would eventually be selected for Ethernet. Hannu had wondered whether Proxy ARP or Reverse ARP would become the norm. Hjalmar had thought that Reverse ARP was a simpler bootstrapping protocol, which he preferred to the risks of bridged and routed network segments not being clearly delineated. Rolien didn't seem to hold an opinion either way.

Then Hannu and Hjalmar spent the rest of the meal comparing notes about the upgraded 16-byte Ipv6 addresses and whether full replacement from Ipv4 would develop or whether it would be possible to assign a host both Ipv6 and Ipv4 addresses, allowing multi-version interoperability. Rolien hadn't been following the conversation, preferring to push her food round the plate instead

It was only when Hannu prompted Hjalmar into talking about his background that she perked up, letting her coffee go cold as she joined the discussion. It seemed that she wanted to know more about what made Hjalmar tick. What made him the person he was… or wasn't. But it was obvious to Hannu that Hjalmar was still concealing more than he revealed. He claimed that he had not had a happy home life. Then, under interrogation from Rolien, admitted that he had never been abused, never been short of anything, never felt that his parents didn't love him.

"So what made you so unhappy?" Rolien asked.

"Oh you know."

"No I don't."

"You know. Sort of pressure."

"What sort of pressure?"

"Just pressure."

"Pressure to what?"

"To achieve. To be like my father."

"He's successful, I take it?"

"Yeah, sort of. In his own way."

"But it's not the way you wanted?"

"No, I just want to do my own thing. I guess I just resent the demands to follow in his footsteps."

"What, like inherit the company or something?"

"No. No company. Just to be like him, that's all."

"But what's he like?"

"Proud. Successful. He irritates me."

After that the conversation ground to a halt. Hannu thought he understood what Hjalmar meant, but Rolien, it seemed, didn't.

This morning, however, Rolien had again taken a lead role in the discussion when Hannu had raised the issue of Hjalmar's Internet scam. During the exchange of views, Hannu came close to convincing Hjalmar that Anthrax and The Redeemer should join forces to resolve the enigma of the one-way function. Hjalmar would have gladly agreed had Hannu not insisted, as a precondition, that he scrap his Internet site and stop messing with viruses.

"But it's the only way I know to earn a living." Hjalmar said.

"Rubbish!" from Rolien.

"There are ways to use you computer skills legitimately," Hannu said. "Look at me. I get paid very nicely thank you for solving other people's problems."

"Then you should thank me for creating those problems for you," Hjalmar responded.

"How would you like it if you were on the receiving end?" Rolien demanded.

"Wouldn't give a damn," Hjalmar snapped back. "Money isn't important to me, like it is you. I do what I do because I'm the best. But I still have to live."

"You're on the wrong side of the fence," Hannu said, quietly. "First of all, there are plenty of idiots who can write viruses, but there aren't enough of us who know how to identify and quarantine them. Secondly, I get paid for what I do. You don't."

"Yeah, well, okay," Hjalmar said, begrudgingly accepting the logic, "I suppose the virus bit is a bit naughty."

"So why not join with me and we'll work as a team? We can pool our knowledge."

Hjalmar pondered for a moment. "And what about my JoinMyChurch programme? It still needs perfecting."

"Dump it." Rolien said.

"Yeah, that's all you ever say. Just because you're financially sound, you rail against me doing what I want to do."

And then Hannu realised the conversation had gone full circle. Hjalmar resented anyone who succeeded in their own field. Particularly if it was something he knew nothing about. He needed to work with an equal. But before Hannu had time to air his views, Rolien had chipped in again.

"This damn obsession of yours about computers is totally destroying our relationship. You know that, don't you?"

And that was when Hjalmar exploded.

"The only thing that's screwing up our relationship is your bloody infidelity," he shouted. "My sister told me all about you and your goddamn real estate agent."

To Hannu's surprise, Rolien didn't try to deny it.

"I wouldn't have needed to find comfort elsewhere if you hadn't been so involved in your stupid computer programme," she replied angrily. "Someone had to satisfy my needs and he just happened to be available."

As the slanging match continued, Hannu sidled into the corner clutching his laptop computer.

All in all, it was probably the wrong moment for Marcus Foyer to arrive on the scene, and it was definitely not the moment for him to tell Hjalmar that his attitude was childish.

As the wrestling pair crashed to the floor, Hjalmar's elbow smashed against Hannu's arm causing him to let go his laptop which landed on Marcus' head, leaving a new-born bruise throbbing painfully on his right temple. Hjalmar found the situation amusing until Marcus returned the punch – and the laptop. Hannu looked with dismay at the remnants of his keyboard.

When, due to the uproar, the hotel manager opened the door and surveyed the state of the room, and the kicking and wrestling combatants, he clasped his hands to his head and the telephone receiver to his ear.

"The police are on the way," he whispered to Hannu as he returned to block the doorway.

He, Hannu and Rolien were then unable to do anything but watch as Hjalmar and Marcus spat and scratched like alley cats. For a brief, impulsive moment, Hannu considered trying to separate them but, discretion being the better part of valour, noted that two of him would hardly make one of them, and settled for keeping an eye on the window for the arrival of the police.

It was one of those peculiar spontaneous moments that happen from time to time in life. As the doors of the police cars clicked open and banged closed, the combatants, without any verbal communication, called a truce. For two or three seconds they stood facing each other looking sheepish, then burst out laughing. Hannu juggled with his hair. "The police have just arrived," he said, quietly.

Like naughty school children caught having an illicit cigarette, a look of guilt crossed both their faces. "Best be going then," Marcus said, and bolted past the manager, sending him sprawling into the corridor.

Hjalmar pushed the net curtain aside and glanced out of the window to where the police were fanning across the lawned gardens like dandelion seeds in the wind. "Bloody hell!" he said, letting go of the curtain. "I don't think I want to be here." He grabbed Hannu's arm. "Come on then, let's go prove the existence of one-way functions."

"No more JoinMyChurch ?"

"No."

"No more viruses?"

"No."

"No more—"

"Oh for crying out loud, Hannu. No, no, no. No more nothing naughty, okay? Now let's get the hell out of here."

The hotel manager, a big man whose moustache had achieved a wingspan in proportion to its owner, had chased Marcus Foyer into the reception area and was too intent on pinning him to the wall to notice Hannu and Hjalmar slip quietly through the service door behind the main staircase.

"Where are we going?" Hannu asked breathlessly as they ducked behind a yew hedge that separated the patio from the garden.

"Let's try and get to my car," Hjalmar whispered. "It's just over there." He pointed to a blue Audi in the roadside pull-in that served as parking for the hotel.

They ran, crouched, towards the car.

"Have you got your key?"

Hjalmar helped Hannu over a low wall. "Hope so," he said, feeling in his pocket and producing a small bundle of keys. "Come on, amigo. You and me are out of here."

As Hjalmar started the engine, Hannu, climbed up into the passenger seat. "Where to?" he asked.

"I think it's time—" Hjalmar didn't get to the end of the sentence as his door was wrenched open.

Joris Duisenberg pushed the top half of his body into the car. "Going without saying goodbye, Robert?"

Hannu held onto his hair with both hands. "I thought you said your name was Hjalmar."

"Only since he changed it after the last time he was caught," Joris said. He turned his attention back to his son. "Listen quickly and listen carefully, Robert. I'm about to go into the hotel and act surprised when I discover that you've got away. Do not be here when I come back out."

Hjalmar nodded.

"If you can get your act together and keep your nose clean for a couple of years, your mother and I would be delighted to see you again. Meanwhile, I suggest you leave The Netherlands; in fact, I insist you leave The Netherlands, otherwise I'll be obliged to arrest you." Joris offered his hand. "I can't stay, the others will be wondering where I am."

Hjalmar hesitated a moment before shaking his father's hand. "Sorry, Dad," he said. "Maybe, Hannu was right. Maybe life can be just as interesting on the right side of the law."

Joris glanced across the car. "If you're Hannu, thank you for your good advice." He paused then added quietly; "Take care of him for me." The car door closed and Joris Duisenberg hurried towards the hotel entrance.

"Come on," Hannu said, smiling. "Let's move, Bobby Baby."

Hjalmar started the engine and reversed out of the parking bay. "Let's just stick to Robert shall we? - Baldy."

Hannu clutched his hair to his head again. "Robert, you're a beggarin' plonker."

"I know," he said. "But I'm a plonker who is closer than you to proving the existence of one-way functions, only it will have to wait 'till we get to beggarin' England."

"Why? What's in England?"

"Your apartment. I thought you might be pleased to accommodate me while we get our new business established."

At the same time that Joris Duisenberg took charge of the situation inside the hotel, the Reverend van Aanroy caught an incurable dose of religion. It wasn't exactly a blinding spear of light on the road to Damascus, but at least the question of whether a god really did exist momentarily passed through his mind. It was something he'd never given much thought to in the past. Van Aanroy believed in a lot of things, but a god had never been one of them; so he decided, whilst fingering slowly through the money that Joska had given him, that today was just his lucky day. And if it was something to do with religion, well God bless Jesus.

He fanned his face ecstatically with a wad of notes then stopped and dropped them back in the suitcase when he caught Joska staring strangely at him. The five hundred euro denominations smelt slightly stale and musty, a smell that money acquires by constant passing from hand to hand. He was glad for that. He would have been suspicious of virgin banknotes. He'd never seen so much money in his life, and it was all his. A gift, Joska had said, from The Great Mother. Yeah? But who cared where it had come from, it was his now and no one was going to take it away from him. No one. He wanted to hug it, to caress it, to count it – to spend it.

But not until he had rid himself of The Great Mother's indomitable handmaiden.

Van Aanroy strove to appear calm and humble as his mind raced through the possibilities. "Your faith has been rewarded," he said, fiddling absently with the tassels on his twisted cord belt. "You were right to bring it to me, Joska. It was clearly intended to further The Great Mother's Mission here in The Hague." He'd already told her the same thing twice, but he'd not been able to think of anything else to say. "Who else have you told?" he asked reassuringly.

"Joska seemed surprised, though her voice retained its excited tremor, "Why, no one, Reverend. You were the only person who believed that The Great Mother was sending a message. You were the only person I could trust. But it's different now, isn't it. Now we have the proof that The Great Mother speaks to us."

It was the answer he'd wanted to hear – she'd told no one else – bye, bye Joska.

He knew what he had to do now. From past experience, he was aware that he couldn't just quietly disappear and change identities; that took considerable planning and preparation and he didn't have the time. He would have to dispose of her, and quickly. And he had to leave no trace; that was the important thing, nothing that could lead back to him. No clues. No evidence.

"I can't wait to tell Theo," Joska said, disturbing his thoughts.

"Of course, my dear. Of course." The good ideas bulb illuminated in his head. "But perhaps we should thank The Great Mother for her bountiful goodness first."

"You mean a vigil?"

"We must thank Our Leader for this miracle."

Joska's face lit up like a beacon in the night sky. "Of course, Reverend. I was so pleased to have been proven right that I completely forgot about thanking The Great Mother. How very selfish of me." Predictably, she dropped onto her knees in front of van Aanroy's stained settee, clamped her forearms under her bosom and wriggled her shoulders to centre her breasts. Her hands clasped themselves together like a pair of magnets and her eyes closed tight on autopilot. "Oh Great Mother, have mercy on me, a humble sinner—"

Standing behind her, van Aanroy dropped his corded belt around her neck and pulled it tight. Mercy wasn't in his vocabulary when two-and-a-half million euros were involved..

He didn't like this. It should have been clean and clinical like in the movies; the ones he liked to watch in the privacy of his study. There was nothing clinical about this wretched girl who was struggling and squirming and tearing at his hands and gasping for breath. Why couldn't she just submit to the inevitable?

He pulled harder on the cord, perspiration breaking out on his forehead like raindrops on a windowpane. He forced and strained every muscle. His hands shook, but still Joska did not yield. Her fingernails cut deep gouges into his flesh. Van Aanroy dug his knee between her shoulder blades to force more leverage. He closed his eyes as the effort made his arms shake. Death should be cold and quick and instant. This was too muddled and chaotic. Too personal. He could feel the rasp of air in her throat through the tightened cord. He could smell the fear and panic in her pores. He could hear the whimpering, unasked question in her head. 'Why?'

She had let go of his hands now, though her arms were flailing wildly around at her sides, like a windmill in a hurricane. Her shoulders had begun to sag and her head rolled forwards. At last she was submitting to his power, to his superior strength.

Then a gut-wrenching bellow of nauseous pain roared and blethered in van Aanroy's crotch as Joska's flailing elbow caught him full in his most vulnerable region. He let go of the cord and grabbed instinctively at his burning testicles.

Eyes watering, he staggered backwards. His heel caught on the turned up edge of the hearthrug, and he felt himself fall. But the sensation lasted only a heartbeat until his head struck the marble fire hearth and he came to earth with a sickening thud at the base of his skull. Blue-white light splattered the backs of his eyes. He gasped upwards for air as he faded into darkness. He struggled against it, but it was like being dragged under water in a fast-flowing river. He was disorientated and couldn't tell where the surface was. He was being swept uncontrollably downstream, tumbling over and over in the current, his head banging on hidden rocks and submerged debris. It was dark and it was cold and he couldn't breath. He knew he had to, everybody had to breathe, but a boulder blocked his throat as the band of pain at the back of his head tightened mercilessly. He forced his lungs, like bellows that had to be pulled in and out.

Finally he broke the surface, but briefly; just long enough for one gasp of air before being dragged back under. His limbs were wooden and useless as he tried to break free. He could see daylight above him but it seemed to be fading. His mind was hauled back into the black abyss below, and a deep weariness overtook him.

Slowly - very, very slowly - like a weighted corpse released from a riverbed, his mind rolled back the claustrophobic waters that imprisoned it. He gasped for breath as though the waters had been real. His arms and legs felt as though they'd been amputated. And somewhere in the blackness of the room he could hear Joska gasping for breath and sobbing uncontrollably. He gasped with her. Goddamn her, why couldn't she just have died without all this suffering? Disposing of her body would have caused no problem in Holland's watery wasteland.

He opened his tear-filled eyes and found that everything was out of focus. The room was grey and blurry. Somewhere through the film, he could make out the girl's outline, supporting herself on the settee. She, too, was coughing and fighting for breath.

Van Aanroy forced himself into a sitting position, leaning his back against the wall for support. His nerve ends reconnected and he hugged his legs to ease the torture. But there was no time for self-comfort. He had to stop her. He had to finish the job.

He blinked away the tears to clear his vision. Joska was standing now, her back to him, still bent double, clutching her throat and coughing. Van Aanroy tried to stand but collapsed as his legs gave way. Crawling was all that was left. Crawling to get to her, to stop her, to kill her. Crawling for the money. His face screwed tight as he suppressed the urge to sit quietly and comfort himself.

But it was not to be that easy. All he wanted to do

was to stay there, curled in a comforting spiral. But he couldn't stop now: he had to finish what he had started.

He forced himself forward…

He was only a few feet away…

Just one more effort…

If he could just grab her…

Joska turned her head as the hand took hold of her ankle. It was the demon again. She screamed. She'd wanted to scream from the moment the tension round her neck had been released, but she couldn't. No noise would come. She could only gasp to fill her bursting lungs in a rapid, rasping panting. The hand round her ankle gripped tighter, trying to pull her off balance. She stifled the next scream, desperately trying to think, trying to work things out. How could The Great Mother have deserted her like this?

Van Aanroy reached for her other ankle. Joska raised her foot and stamped on the grasping fingers. Somewhere in the background she heard him shout. She turned around, staring down at the top of van Aanroy's head with a blank expression. There was no time to think, to weigh things up. Why was this monster whom she once treasured as her closest counsellor trying to kill her? What was she doing in this room? She kicked at his head, and watched dispassionately as the toe of her shoe connected with the side of his mouth. It was like watching a slow-motion replay. It couldn't have been Joska De Jong who just kicked another human being in the face.

She knew now that if she didn't get away she was going to die. It was the money, that's what it was, the wretched money. How could she have been so stupid? Now, instead of thanking The Great Mother for it with a full and happy heart, she was mortified by her own naivety.

In desperation, she shuffled sideways the length of the settee, stumbling over the arm and onto the floor. Her ankle cracked against the wooden leg and she let out a gasp as pain seared through her foot. She rolled over and looked behind her. Van Aanroy was standing, though leaning forwards, shaky and unsteady. Behind him was the door through which they'd entered. It led into the long hallway that spanned the depth of the building. No way out. Her ankle hurt like hell. Just behind her was the door that she knew led into van Aanroy's study at the back of the house. Struggling to her feet, she reached for the handle, yanked the door open and hobbled through the opening. Her mind wouldn't focus. Everything was happening too quickly. Nothing was rational anymore. Stupid, stupid, stupid.

As she slammed the door shut, she caught a glimpse of van Aanroy staggering towards her, his eyes gleaming with anger and hatred, snot slugs crawling out from his nostrils. It was a vision that would remain with her till the moment of her death.

Thank goodness there was a lock. The old, brass handle was wrenched from her grasp at the same moment that she turned the key. The lock block slid smoothly into place. The handle might have been old, but the lock was well maintained and strong. A shout from the other side. More filth – more oaths. Three large, black, metal bolts at the top, middle and bottom of the door, which Joska whipped firmly into place. Bang. Bang Bang. More swearing from the other side. "Bitch. Stinking ugly bitch."

With her face against the door, Joska sobbed uncontrollably, clasping her own shoulders with both hands. Van Aanroy kicked and thumped on the door, screaming obscenities, but the bolts held firm, showing no signs of strain. Then the swearing and banging stopped abruptly. With a supreme effort of will, Joska stifled her sobs and strained to listen. All she could hear was an ominous silence. She waited, expecting a fresh onslaught at any moment.

The onslaught came two minutes later, just as Joska was taking her first look round the room. The banging on the door had not recommenced, but something else had replaced it - not a sound, but an expectation that something was about to happen. Instinctively she turned her head towards the window at the exact moment that a loud crack heralded the arrival of a thrown brick. Shards of razor-sharp glass spun across the room. She screamed in shock. Then screamed again in terror as the enraged face of the Reverend van Aanroy appeared at the shattered window.

He reached through the broken glass and fumbled for the window catch. "No escape now, you bitch."

Joska searched the room frantically, seeing what she needed in an instant. It was a letter-opener with a rabbit's foot for a handle and a nasty-looking metal blade for slitting open the letters. Despite her fear of approaching the enraged cleric, she stepped to the window where van Aanroy was too concentrated on his task to monitor her actions.

She gripped the rabbit's foot and swung with all her strength at the hand that was groping with the window catch. Co-ordination was not one of Joska's natural assets. Today, though, coordination could have been her middle name. She knew from the moment she began to swing her arm that the blade was going to find its target. Her eyes fixed on the exact spot at the back of van Aanroy's hand where it was going to make its entry.

Thunk.

The cutting edge seared through the peachy flesh like a steak knife through butter. There wasn't even enough resistance from the veins and ligaments to slow it down as it emerged through van Aanroy's palm, bedding itself deep into the timber of the window frame.

A screaming, "Oh shit. Fuck!" from van Aanroy before instinctively yanking back his hand. Then an abrupt gasp as the knife held tight and the steel tore his flesh. He reached through the broken glass and wrenched at the handle with his free hand. But his tug brought him no relief; the letter knife was too deeply embedded in the wood. With a grunt of unsurpassed hatred, he began to wriggle the knife handle. Joska stared at him for a second, then reached down and took off her remaining shoe. She beat at his hands with the heel, drawing a string of oaths from van Aanroy who, with clenched teeth and veiled eyes, flexed his elbow and heaved again.

This time the blade and his arm came free. Joska thought she could hear the flesh tearing and the sinews ripping. Van Aanroy staggered backwards, clutching his hand to his gown. A stain of crimson blood spurted onto his face and across the remaining shards of glass in the window.

Joska knew that she had bought some time, though it wouldn't be long before he came back to the attack. She knew now that she had to die; that the money meant more to van Aanroy than any of The Great Mother's commandments. But she wasn't going to make it easy for him. She watched as the preacher closed his eyes, gritted his teeth, and slowly, slowly drew the metal spike from his lacerated hand. The pain must have been unbearable but his lips were clamped tight, his face expressing nothing. When he opened his tear-moistened eyes, they reflected only a cavernous loathing.

Then Joska spotted the window shutters. Big, old, heavy, wooden shutters.

She sprang quickly, grabbed the nearest handle and heaved. There was no need, the shutter opened with simple ease and banged firmly against the remnants of broken glass on the inner window ledge. As she reached across to the other side of the window, van Aanroy, realising what she was doing, took the final step forwards that placed him next to the opening again. He reached out to push the shutters back, then let out another oath and pulled his arm away when a shard of glass pierced his palm, drawing more blood from his tattered flesh.

Joska banged the second shutter firmly into place, plunging the study into almost total darkness. She leaned hard against them, hoping that van Aanroy's broken hands would leave him with insufficient strength to prise them open. Her shoulder rested on something cold and metallic that dangled like a pendulum. Catching the loose end in one hand, she immediately understood its function and swung it over to lock into the metal cups. A bang on the wood and a cry of pain from outside as van Aanroy attempted to knock the shutters open.

"You stinking cow. I'll fix you."

Joska breathed deeply. It felt as though she'd been holding her breath since the brick had smashed through the window. She stumbled forward, reaching blindly in front of her, trying desperately to remember the layout of the room. Shards of glass fragmented further under her weight. She was conscious that her bare feet were cut, but not particularly aware of the pain.

The room echoed to another loud crack as something struck the shutters from the outside. There were more muffled curses. Another crash and the shutters vibrated. A faint tinkle of broken glass falling onto the paved yard outside.

Her hand touched the back of an armchair which she gladly collapsed into, sobbing uncontrollably. In the space of five minutes, her tranquil life had been turned completely upside-down: her soul had become a prison and had sprung out to club her without mercy. She'd been so happy when she'd knocked on van Aanroy's door. Such a large amount of money in the place where The Great Mother had told her to look. How stupid she had been. How irrational to believe that The Great Mother had somehow placed it there, that it had been intended to help van Aanroy's mission. How foolish to believe that there was such a being as The Great Mother. It was obvious now that it had all been an invention of van Aanroy.

She wiped her eyes with the back of her hand and

tugged at the collar of her blouse, as if to give herself more air. She discovered that, as if in search of reassurance, she was fingering the silver medallion that hung around her neck. With a violence that she would not have believed herself capable of, she tore it loose and hurled it across the room. Her life was falling apart – what little of it there was left. And where was Theo when she needed him?

Theo was in the bank's sub-office, which normally closed at one o'clock, re-opening from two until four. Today was going to be different, Theo decided. Today he would close early and go and have a meaningful discussion with van Aanroy about his financial affairs. Then, once he had cornered van Aanroy into confessing his connections to Sandy Ferris, he would collect the cash from Joska's home and return Sean's portion to him. Today, Theo was in charge. A different, changed Theo, but an in-charge Theo nonetheless. If Joska was at home after he'd spoken to van Aanroy he'd be able to share his news with her.

He locked the cash drawer, tossed the key in the air and failed to catch it, watching with disinterest as it bounced under the polished mahogany counter. Making no attempt to retrieve it or look back, he donned his hat and marched through the door, slamming it behind him, then strode from the building for the very last time.

Van Aanroy threw the hammer at the study door and wiped the tracks of sweat from his face, leaving a dark smear of blood on his cheek. One hand was still bleeding profusely, the other was bruised and aching where Joska had stamped on it and beaten it with her shoe. If he'd had the proper use of them, he could have hammered a hole in the study door in minutes.

It was tempting just to take the cash and leave. Though he didn't particularly want to be trailed by the police, he knew that, in normal circumstances, he could buy a fresh identity elsewhere – he'd done it before and could do it again - Switzerland or Malta maybe. Dealing with Miss de Jong was the least of his worries.

What concerned him more, and what kept him from running, was the mass of evidence in his wall safe that would lead the police into a manhunt for his close friend, which would, by nature, implicate him too. There was no way he could risk that, and time was against him now. What a mess. He closed his eyes and tried to let his mind relax. Good ideas often came to him while his mind was empty.

He came to with a jump. He had no idea how long he'd been there and glanced at his watch – it was almost one o'clock, so he'd only blacked out for a few minutes. Something had disturbed him and he didn't know what it was. Then the doorbell rang again to remind him. He jumped up and slid behind the settee with his back to the wall: he knew that the inner darkness of the house would hide him from view. Inching slowly towards the window he could see a man's arm, then a swathe of bright yellow hair. He didn't have to look any further; the answer to his dilemma was standing at his entrance. Somehow, he had to get Theo to believe he wasn't there and enter the house without being invited.

Joska did it for him. As Theo rang the bell a third time, she began to bang on the study door and scream for help. Van Aanroy ducked down between the settee and the wall as the front door burst open. He listened as Theo blundered from the hall into the living room. Joska shouted again.

"Is that you?" called Theo.

"Is that you?" she called back.

On his hands and knees, van Aanroy shuffled slightly to ease the pressure on the injured hand on which he had been leaning. Something soft and hairy rubbed against his wrist. What the hell? He pulled away instinctively. Then, as he remembered what it was, his eyes turned black and calculating and he pulled the pony-tailed wig tight on his head.

It didn't feel right somehow. The space in his head was totally absorbed. His characters had never mixed before. Andy Nottley was a different person to The Reverend van Aanroy. They shouldn't come together. They couldn't come together. It didn't work like that. That's why the wig had been thrown out of sight. Andy's glasses would probably be somewhere nearby.

He swept his flattened hand through the dust under the settee. Got them. Spectacles in place. Voila, Andy Nottley disguised as a preacher… or was it Reverend van Aanroy disguised as a killer? Same thing – no?

Too complicated…

A cacophony of noise in his head...

He had to move into the darkness of his mind for a few moments...

Eyes closed…

Nothing…

When he opened his eyes, Andy Nottley knew that he'd been in a blackout situation again. But he knew instinctively that van Aanroy had been protecting his interests, that there was a shitload of cash in the room, and that the wall safe had to be emptied at all costs. There was too much evidence in there that would tie him to too many dead bodies.

The door to the study was open. The sobbing voice of the handmaiden from hell wafted through the opening like the sebaceous fumes of a deep fat fryer. Good, he'd not been in limbo for too long then. He reached for the back of the settee and pulled himself to his feet, swaying unsteadily as a wave of nausea swept through his body. The stupid cow had caused him more grief and pain than any he had experienced, including the knife in the gut when his spleen has been punctured. His crotch throbbed, his head ached, his face hurt and his bloodied hands burnt like charcoal on a barbeque. She'd pay dearly for that.

Clean termination wasn't possible now. Van Aanroy had screwed it up. It was too late to try to tidy up and pretend that nothing had happened; he'd just have to leave the bodies here, clear the safe and emerge somewhere different as somebody else. The police could quickly forget two corpses when their enquiries led nowhere, but the mass of evidence in his wall safe would be enough to start a major international enquiry that would never go away. He had to retrieve everything from the safe.

In the study, a man's voice spoke urgently,

explaining how he had come to talk to van Aanroy about his bank account, and how he thought that van Aanroy was in cohorts with Sandy Ferris. The female voice said, "Never mind being in cohorts with Sandy Ferris, he's in league with the devil." Andy knew the owners of the voices but he couldn't puzzle out who Sandy Ferris was. Though Andy had never met Theo Padmos or his fiancée, his alter ego knew them well and, if he was honest with himself, he was not totally sure now whether he was Andy Nottley or Reverend van Aanroy. The hair and glasses belonged to Andy: the bloodstained gown and injured hands belonged to the good Reverend. Today, his mind belonged to neither. He didn't know who his mind belonged to. He didn't like it. It wasn't clean and clinical. Come on brain, work for crying out loud.

Kill them. No other option. There were some good, sharp knives in the kitchen. He just hoped that van Aanroy's damaged hands wouldn't let him down. Stupid man, why couldn't he stick to preaching and leave the killing to a professional? Goddamn amateur.

* * *

Sandy tapped urgently on the door of room 213. After a brief wait, while she shuffled agitatedly from one foot to the other, the rugged Irishman stood before her. He kissed her cheek then dropped his hand to the small of her back and steered her into the room.

"Come on in, Sandy. Come and meet George."

She allowed herself to be led into the room. It reflected the wood-panelled warmth of the rest of the Corona Hotel. Normally Sandy would have felt comfortable and at ease, in contact with the only man who had ever meant anything to her - the man who had forgiven her so readily for robbing him - but she was still stewing over her near-empty bank account.

The scheme had worked exactly as planned, or so she had thought. As soon as Sean had left the apartment, she logged onto the internet, searched for the 'JoinMyChurch ' site, remembered that it had been changed to 'Find-Us-Here ', then re-run the programme, recalculating the correct code from the card that her father had been given. The code on the note she'd written, the one she'd shared with Marcus Foyer, was a few digits out, as well she knew when she had written it. Marcus might have been the harbinger of good news, but he wasn't worth fifty percent of these pickings. Anyway, he scored low on the reliability ratings.

And then, just as she was packing away her laptop computer, she remembered the computer printout that she had thrown from her handbag in the wastebasket; the account that had caught her attention when she worked for the bank. Why not? Why not take the opportunity for a little extra bonus? Now she knew how to recalculate the city and the access code, there was nothing stopping her from making use of Find-Us-Here until she ran out of accounts to hit. She straightened out the crumpled ball of paper and, within five minutes, added another five hundred thousand euros to her account. And then a further fifty thousand as she drained Hjalmar Linnekar's local 'petty cash' account, as Marcus had called it. A total haul, with Rolien's and her own money, of over two and a half million euros. Good day's work!

When, in the bank, she asked to withdraw two million, six hundred and thirty-three thousand euros in cash, the cashier, whom Sandy knew well, checked the balance of her account, smiled sadly at her, and asked if she was feeling any better these days. Sandy blushed, realised that all was not well, and beat a strategic retreat to the automatic cash point in the street. There, having checked the balance and account details for herself, it became clear that her plan to divert Rolien's money had failed. It seemed as though Hjalmar Linnekar had already succeeded in filtering the funds elsewhere. The three incoming credits had landed and then been withdrawn in one transaction.

Now, it would mean some drastic rethinking of strategy if she was to find the necessary resources for a good lawyer. Maybe even going to see Hjalmar Linnekar and begging for the return of their own money. She would do whatever it took. She owed it to her father.

She was aware of Sean's hand moving from her back as he placed a caring arm around her shoulder, as though he could sense her mood. Pushing his considerable bulk from the depths of a well-upholstered chair was a man Sandy had seen a few times before. He looked vaguely embarrassed to meet her, as though he were guilty for her father being incarcerated in a Dutch prison cell. As he stood, he brushed crumbs of food off his belly and raked at his long sideburns, like he was combing them with his fingers.

"Hello, Sandy."

"Hi, George. I remember you now. You and Dad used to do a few little deals from time to time didn't you?"

George smiled. "We did that. Good, reliable man, your dad."

"So do you think you can help clear his name?" she asked, skipping the formalities. George was her last hope and she wasn't in the mood for pleasantries.

The telephone rang as George opened his mouth to speak. Sean picked up the receiver in his ham-like fist. He listened then smiled. "Come on up," he said. "There's someone here who'll be mighty glad to see you." He rested the phone back on its hook.

Sandy and George looked at him quizzically.

"Fancy a drink?" he asked, opening the door of the mini bar.

Sandy watched him in curious silence as he proceeded to loosen the wire around the neck of a bottle of Moët et Chandon.

"You'll have to put up with ordinary glasses," he said, as the cork came out with that delicious pop that only champagne corks can make. "I forgot to ask room service for crystal flutes."

Sandy scratched her nose, a reflex she was not aware of when people acted in an unexpected manner. "Do you want to give us a clue, Sean? Who was it on the phone?"

There was a tap on the door.

"Answer it," Sean said, still smiling.

A white fur coat wearing a poodle greeted her. "Hello, my dear," Brigitte said, planting a kiss on her cheek. "Brought someone to see you."

Sandy stared open-mouthed as the razor-thin face of her father appeared around the doorframe.

"Hi, Sand," he said, giving her an off-white grin. "Bet you didn't expect to see me here."

"Jesus H."

"Cut it out girl. That's my line."

Sandy grabbed him and hugged him, dragging him into the room like a playful bear cub.

"But how…?"

"Anyone for champers?" Sean asked.

"But…?"

"It's beautifully chilled."

Sandy discovered her voice nestling deep in her chest. "It's you, Sean, isn't it. You've pulled this off."

Sean handed her a smile along with her glass.

"But how?"

"Money!" he said. "Bail money. Lots of it. And an element of gentle persuasion by Brigitte."

Sandy looked at Brigitte questioningly.

"I'm personally acquainted with the judge," he said with a titter. "But the judge would prefer that no one else knew about it."

"But how did you and Sean get to know each other?"

Sean winked. "The Great Mother works in mysterious ways."

Sandy didn't know who to hug: her father, Brigitte or Sean. She settled on all three, and then hugged as much of George as she could get her arms around, so that he didn't feel left out.

After sipping her champagne and making a fuss of Faggot, she allowed Sean to guide her gently to a chair. He dropped into serious mode as he addressed both her and her father.

"Now listen, you two. I won't give you the lecture again about targeting my bank accounts and me, but I do want you to know that the bail money has to be repaid. It's a loan, not a gift."

Sandy nodded and noticed that her father was nodding in unison. He had lost weight, if that was possible, and his pale skin stretched across the dark hollows of his temples like a tambourine.

"Also," Sean continued, "we've got to remember that this is only a temporary reprieve. There'll be a trial and we've got to make sure that Nick is well represented. Now, I want you to tell me honestly, do you have any money for a good brief?"

Her father looked at Sandy. She shook her head and suffered the same attack of anxiety she had experienced in the bank earlier. "We had some savings but it's all gone now," she said quietly. It was as close to the truth as she wanted to go for the moment.

"Right, so with George's help we've got to start piecing some form of defence together," Sean said. "First of all you, Nick; tell me everything you know, and I want the whole truth this time."

Sandy's father put a skeletal hand flat on his chest. "On my baby's eyesight, Sean, I've told you everything I know about the murder. I went looking for George and found him lying dead – at least I thought it was him at the time. I never laid a finger on the guy."

"And there's nothing - absolutely nothing – you've not told me?"

Nick thought for a moment. "One tiny thing," he said, reaching into his pocket. "I found this lying on the dead bloke's chest, like it had been placed there. Looks like it's silver so I sort of put it in my pocket."

He held out his clenched hand and slowly opened his fist. Peeping at the world from inside was a silver medallion shaped like a Celtic cross.

Sandy poked at it curiously. "Looks a bit like the one Theo Padmos wears. I've noticed him fiddle with it sometimes."

Brigitte took a closer look. "Your friend Mijnheer Padmos is not the only person who wears one of these," he said. "I know of others who wear them, particularly one of my regular clients"

"Any idea where this regular client lives?" Sean

asked.

"I know exactly where he lives. But be careful, I know most of my clients and I know most of what goes on in The Hague, yet I know virtually nothing about this guy that I could swear is accurate. The simple fact that he uses disguises would suggest he has something to hide. I hear rumours and, if there's even an element of truth in some of them, this is not someone you should mess with."

Best be paying your client a visit then," Sean said, matter-of-factly.

* * *

Joris Duisenberg steered slowly through the leafy lane that circumnavigated Wassenar. The main road, the A44, was heavy with traffic after an accident between two trucks; and Jolanda, his daughter, had radioed him from the office to warn him of the blockage. She had also told him that she had arrived at the apartment on Grote Markt too late to apprehend Sandy Ferris. The loose ends were still not coming together; there was still a load of cash to be tracked down. Then Jolanda had called back; she'd just had news that Nick Ferris had been bailed from prison. Most unusual for a suspected murderer. She'd muttered something quite rude about balmy liberal judges before signing off again. Now the loose ends were becoming even looser.

Joris tutted and shook his head. At least Robert was safely away from the action. Rolien and the estate agent would have some explaining to do to the tax authorities regarding certain offshore bank accounts, but Robert was, hopefully, on his way to a more sensible future with the help of his funny little friend. If Rolien decided to confess what she knew of Robert's Internet site, it would muddy the waters somewhat, but the burden of proof would rest with the police which, of course, they would be unable to devote sufficient resources to: he'd make sure of that. Anyway, so far as he knew, Rolien had only ever known Robert as Hjalmar Linnekar. There would be no connection to the Duisenberg family.

The remaining issues centred firmly round the Ferris pair who were both on the loose again and probably clutching a bundle of money that didn't belong to them. How the hell to track those two down?

His answer came more quickly than he could have hoped for. Jolanda buzzed him again on the radio. A telephone call from the Corona Hotel had advised the police that a group of people were on their way to an address close to Holland Spoor Station and that the police might be needed. The call, apparently, had come from the Irishman whose empty bank account had caused the arrival of the Scots detective with the smelly pipe.

Oh dear, it looked like being a long day. Why the hell couldn't all these bloody foreigners bugger off and cause problems in their own countries? Why did Joris Duisenberg have to sort it all out?

He dropped the engine down a gear and sent a lone cyclist wobbling dangerously towards the roadside canal.

* * *

Theo kept a protective arm around Joska's shoulder. The Reverend van Aanroy was waving an wicked-looking kitchen knife towards the cubist painting that he had told them was The Great Mother.

"Take it down," he shouted. "Now!"

Theo responded sullenly, prising himself away from Joska as she clung to his arm and trembled. He moved crab-like towards the wall, never letting his eyes off van Aanroy. He cursed himself for being so slow when he'd first found Joska locked in van Aanroy's study, shocked and sobbing. If he'd just grabbed her and left the house they would have easily made it to the police station. Instead, he had listened as Joska had explained what had happened to her. Before she had finished, they had turned round to find the evil Reverend standing behind them wearing a strange wig and glasses and threatening their lives.

Theo reached up to the painting, lifted it off its hook and laid it on the floor.

"Now back away."

He did as he was told, retreating in reverse gear to the far side of the room and offering Joska the comfort of his arm again. He watched as van Aanroy, eyes never leaving them, reached for the combination dial on the safe. He spun it slowly, first one way and then the next. Judging from his dextrous touch, he'd done it many times before. The door swung open with ease and Theo pulled Joska closer as van Aanroy reached inside and pulled out a small cardboard box. He waved the knife towards a green carrier bag lying in the corner. "Bring it here"

Theo followed instructions, easing his arm off Joska's shoulder again. As he neared the bloodstained cleric, van Aanroy said, "Stand there."

Theo obeyed.

"Now lean against the wall."

He took a step forwards.

"No!" screamed van Aanroy. "I said lean, dumfuck. Lean, not walk. Under-bloody-stand?"

"But the wall's a long way away."

"Exactly. You'll not be able to make any sudden moves if all your weight is on your arms."

Theo took a step back so that he stood a little more than three feet into the room, then leaned forward like a buttress to rest on his hands against the wall, just a couple of feet to one side of the wall safe. He couldn't help feeling that the painted cubic of The Great Mother, who seemed to be staring up at him with her one octagonal eye, was having a laugh at his expense. Should have got out while you had the chance, moron.

"Lean your head forward," van Aanroy snapped.

"Leave him alone," said Joska from the far side of the room.

"Shut up, bitch. Do as I tell you Theo or I'll bury this knife so far in your belly you'll be able to see what you had for breakfast."

Theo lowered his head until it, too, rested against the wall.

"Now hold the bag towards me."

He held out the plastic bag, his weight transferred to his head and his other hand. He turned his face and watched van Aanroy tip the contents of the cardboard box into the bag. Tiny silver medallions spilled out, like the one around his neck that denoted his membership of The Mission. Mixed with them was an assortment of expensive looking knives. Van Aanroy continued to empty the contents of the safe into the bag - a wad of buff folders, two passports and a diary. Theo couldn't see why these things should be so important.

Van Aanroy snatched the bag off him. "Now get back with the slut."

Theo bit his tongue, impotent against the man with the knife. He didn't like hearing Joska referred to that way, but there was nothing to be gained from antagonising this lunatic. He pushed himself away from the wall and offered Joska his arm again, which she wrapped round her shoulders like a woollen shawl. Theo noticed that she had stopped shaking.

Van Aanroy transferred the carrier bag to his knife hand and reached into the wall safe one last time. When he withdrew his hand he held a small revolver. "Now where's your Great Mother?" he asked, spitting out the words.

"You tell me," said Theo, in a show of defiance.

Van Aanroy swung the muzzle of the gun in line with Theo's head. "Time to go meet her," he sneered.

Theo battened down his eyelids when he saw van Aanroy's finger start to close around the trigger. It was as though a cold hand was squeezing his stomach, and his mouth felt like it was stuffed with dry leaves. To say that his life flashed before him would be untrue - just a feeling of great sadness that so much time had been wasted and so much living had been missed.

Did he believe that he was about to meet The Great Mother? Absolutely not. He expected just to hear a loud bang followed by nothing. Oblivion, courtesy of a damn fool cleric in a ridiculous wig. What an exit.

Was he afraid? Funnily enough, no. Fear was being chased down a dark alley in the early hours of the morning. Fear was waiting for the unknown to catch up with you, when your imagination runs wild and paints bigger and bigger pictures of the demons that are gaining ground. Fear requires time to infect the system, and time was something that Theo didn't have.

Instead, he was struck with an insufferable wave of regret for the things he would never do, the experiences he would never be able to share, the parents to whom he would never be able to bid farewell, the wife he would never marry, the children who would never call him Dad. What a waste. And what was worse was that now his ship had arrived in port, he found that he couldn't even look back on a pleasant voyage; it had been neither eventful nor satisfying.

Even so, he sent up a small prayer of penitence, like an insurance policy, just in case anyone was listening.

Andy Nottley swung the gun towards The Bitch. A knife was his tool and there were plenty of them in the supermarket bag. But there were two targets and, with his hands in the state that they were in, there was no telling what might happen if he tried for a clean kill. Guns were messy - they made a lot of noise and attracted unwanted attention. This was one that van Aanroy had insisted on acquiring in case of emergencies. Damn his alter ego for being in such a hurry to snuff The Bitch. If he hadn't, Andy could have made a clean job of it, and the body would be sinking neatly into the mud at the bottom of a canal somewhere with nobody any the wiser.

Which one first then, The Bitch or The Idiot? The Idiot still had his eyes closed. No fun there, he wanted his target to see what was happening. Eyes open, cold fear, nothing like it for pumping the adrenalin.

The Bitch stared at him eyeball to eyeball.

Joska didn't want to die, but she felt calm and at peace with Theo's arm around her shoulders. When van Aanroy had tried to strangle her and to smash his way into the room, she'd been terrified and she'd struggled and fought in sheer desperation. But now, staring down the barrel of his gun and watching his silly little piggy eyes behind his silly little piggy glasses, there was something farcical about the whole situation. Why on earth was he wearing that stupid ponytail wig? It wasn't even on straight.

She wasn't going to give him the pleasure of an anonymous shot. She wanted him to be looking straight into her eyes when he pulled the trigger - not that she was fooling herself that it would scare him off, a new wave of realism had forced itself into her consciousness in the last hour and she wasn't trying to kid herself that they weren't about to die.

She waited for the bone-splintering thud that would end it all.

Van Aanroy blinked as Andy Nottley screamed at him to pull the trigger. He'd never killed anybody before, that was Andy's job, and it was so confusing having his alter ego shouting at him inside his head. Why didn't he just shut up and give him time to think? He knew what had to be done; he just needed to prepare himself.

The Bitch had stopped sobbing and shaking now, and was just staring at him coldly with eyes like black stones, as though she could see right through him. Why couldn't she do the same as The Idiot and close her eyes? It would be easier if she'd just stop staring. He pointed the gun at Theo.

That's better, just a lump of meat to shoot at.

"Missing the party are we?" Sean asked as he stepped into the room.

The preacher pivoted on his heel, swinging the gun towards him. "Who the bloody hell are you?"

"Friend of Theo's"

Theo opened his eyes. "Sean, what on earth are you doing here?"

Sean felt a slight shove from behind.

"Thought you'd like a bit of company," Sandy announced, stepping past him.

Van Aanroy swung the gun again and stepped backwards until he rested against the wall.

"The front door was open so we thought we'd come and join you for a chat," Nick said, squeezing through the paper-thin gap between Sean and his daughter. He stared at van Aanroy, who was waving the gun in an arc, trying to cover everybody at once. "Jesus H, you want to get them hands looked at, Reverend. Seen his bloody hands, Sandy?"

"Horrible isn't it," she said. "You could do with a sticky plaster on that, Reverend."

"What the hell's going on here?" van Aanroy screamed.

Sean moved slightly to one side to allow the minister a free exit if he chose to flee. Brigitte had told them all he knew about his client, including the various rumours, so Sean knew they were entering a potentially explosive situation and had warned the others before they left the hotel, though the warning had done nothing to dampen their enthusiasm to face down the man who had been responsible for the death of George's brother and for Nick being imprisoned. Sean weighed up the enraged ecclesiastic. He seemed to be changing characters or acting out a different role. Now, it was a combination of two; a religious uniform and a killer's clinical eye

"Come on," screamed van Aanroy. "What the hell is going on here?"

"Reinforcements," Sean said quietly.

"Very funny, big man, now get over there with your

friends."

"I think you're outnumbered, Reverend. You can't get us all."

"Maybe, maybe not. Do you want to be the first to find out?"

"Is that your own hair or are you playing charades?" Sandy asked, smiling politely.

Van Aanroy aimed the gun directly at Sandy's face. Sean sensed the imminent danger signal as he saw the trigger finger tighten, and herded Sandy and Nick to join Theo and Joska on the far side of the room. He positioned himself closest to the gun-waving cleric so as to be in a position to act if needed.

Sandy put her arm round Joska. "Okay?"

"Never better," she replied with a pale smile.

"So now what?" Sean asked.

"You've complicated things," the preacher said.

Sean noticed that his manner had changed abruptly. He seemed to be suddenly calmer. His eyes had lost their apparent panic and had turned hard and black, seemingly calculating the odds. He'd switched characters again "You reckon you're going to shoot all five of us?" Sean asked, moderating his voice to a soothing rumble.

"I might just have to do that. My ecclesiastical friend has made a mess of this and it looks as though I'm going to have to tidy things up for him.

It's my job, you know, tidying up loose ends for other people."

"What sort of loose ends?" Sean asked.

The man with the gun didn't have time to answer as a white fur coat bobbed into the room, followed by a scruffy off-white poodle. "Oh my word, you're all mixed up. Who are you today? Look at your hands. What have you been up to?"

The preacher's mouth fell open. "What the hell are you doing here?"

"Just looked in to say hello," Brigitte said. "If it's inconvenient I'll call back later."

"Sure an' we'll all call back later if you want to be on your own," Sean added.

Van Aanroy-Nottley didn't have time to answer. When he turned to see George waddle into the room behind Faggot, his eyes glazed over and the colour drained from his face – like he'd just seen a ghost.

Sean peered curiously at the dazed look and the blank eyes. The cleric's facial muscles appeared deactivated, as if someone had switched off the power supply to his head, though he remained standing, swaying even, with the gun seeming to aim at everybody at once. Sean took a tentative step forward. No reaction. Another step. Still no reaction. The cult leader didn't move: just stared empty-eyed into space.

"I think he's a bit confused," Sandy offered.

"Perhaps he doesn't like crowds," added Nick.

Sean gently eased the gun from van Aanroy's frozen fingers, looked around and handed it to Theo. "Keep him covered," he said. "If he so much as blinks, shoot him."

Theo gave him a little upside-down smile.

Van Aanroy blinked.

Theo shot him.

It was another 20 minutes before Joris Duisenberg arrived at the house near Holland Spoor Station. He wasn't certain what situation he would face when he strode through the front door. All that Jolanda had told him on the radio was that she'd had a call from the Irishman whose money was missing, and that he had told her that they were on the trail of the man whom they thought might have committed the murder in Kinderdijk.

Joris had advised his daughter that he would deal with it himself and that he wouldn't need any backup. Normally he would have humoured the amateur detectives by assigning a couple of uniformed guys on bikes to go and take a look, but, with the famous Ferris pair involved, and consequently a possible link to Robert's stupidity, this was one where he would be inconvenienced into doing his duty. Against his better judgement he'd given Robert one last chance, and now he had to make sure that nothing pointed back to him. The front door was wide open, so he invited himself in and found that the living room was deserted. Muted voices drifted from the room beyond.

He stepped into the open doorway.

At first he thought it was just a bad dream but, after a minikin shake of his head, he could see that it was for real. He was well used to the unusual in a city like The Hague. Drugs, sex, rock 'n roll; gays, prostitutes, all-night bars; euthanasia, voluntary or otherwise; it was all available here in the land of laxity, but usually he came across these things in small doses that could be easily absorbed and integrated. The scene before him was confusing even by Dutch standards.

Joris surveyed the occupants of the room with a sad, depressed countenance. Whatever was going on, it was going to take some sorting out, and it would be Joris Duisenberg who would have to do the sorting. Though normally a hard-working cop, it was times like this that he wished he'd chosen a simple career, like accountancy or bus driving or inspecting people's tax returns to make sure that the full stops were in the right place.

He registered his surroundings, taking in the scene with a well-practiced eye. Seven people, a dog and a body, packed like dates in the tiny study. To his right, a round-faced body of obesity was perched on a tall stool like an elephant on a mushroom. His attention was fully focussed on forcing cookies into his mouth as fast as his podgy fingers could flip them out of the packet. Next to him was his antithesis, a skeletal figure who looked like he needed the biscuits more than the fat man, but who had the resigned air of someone who knew that he wasn't going to be offered any. He was chatting furtively to a well-known local transsexual whose tiny breasts were peeping from the folds of a battered fur coat, which, if had been offered back to the animal that it came off, would probably have been refused.

On Joris's right, at the far end of the room, the window shutters lay flat against the walls - thrown back but not folded away. A cool breeze was blowing through a broken pane of glass, the jagged edges of which were splashed in a substance that was either tomato ketchup or blood. Considering the circumstances, tomato ketchup seemed the less likely choice.

Next to the window, the chief cashier of Joris's bank, who appeared to have a gun sticking out of his trouser pocket, gave the distinct impression that his hidden hand was surreptitiously exploring the bottom of a young lady, whose face was consumed by a far-away smile. Neither of them looked too concerned that, from the floor, the painted eye of an octagonal old woman was watching them with apparent disapproval, nor that the young lady was shoeless and that a small quantity of dried blood (or was it tomato ketchup?) was stuck to her toes.

From behind the only armchair in the room, the extravagantly large fingers of a rugged battle-tank of a man were gently massaging the shoulders of a pretty young lady who was sitting in the chair in front of him. Her long, dark hair, café-au-lait complexion and cherry red fingernails would have made a hunchback look attractive, and she seemed to be in charge of a heavy wad of five hundred euro notes, which she was guarding with parental determination.

Then Joris looked down to the floor. A meandering trail of seemingly unconnected objects - knives, videos, medallions, document folders - led towards a scruffy, off-white poodle that was sniffing the shredded hand of a comatose preacher with a funny wig and a bullet hole in his forehead.

It was hard to remain detached and professional. "Shitty death," he muttered, to nobody in particular. "Indulge me, someone. What in the name of crusty cow dung is going on here?"

Some people fit into a chaotic scene and some people don't. The huge man with the massaging fingers was one that did. "Sure an' you must be the law," he said.

"I'm Chief Inspector Duisenberg," Joris replied by way of introduction. He didn't have to ask whom he was addressing: he'd heard an Irish accent before. "Maybe you'd like to introduce me to the rest of the group," he suggested.

The Irishman waved a large hand in a vaguely clockwise semi-circle. "That's Nick Ferris who's wanted for murder. That one is George Riley who's dead – Nick killed him. Over here is Brigitte. The dog is Faggot. They live together. They're friends of ours."

Joris nodded to Brigitte. The police knew him well and, unfortunately, he knew the police even better. He had close contact with a lot of people in The Hague. Too close, many would say.

"This here's Joska de Jong," the Irishman continued, though Joska seemed not to notice as she burrowed her face into her fiancé's neck. "And she's engaged to—"

"Theo Padmos," interrupted Joris.

"Your already acquainted?"

"I bank at Alliance Bank. Theo's the chief cashier there."

"Used to be," corrected Theo. "I just quit."

The Irishman finished rotating his arm and concluded by waving loosely towards the young lady in the chair. "The pretty one here is Sandy Ferris, Nick's daughter. She had an accident with an internet site after getting acquainted with your son."

Joris frowned and felt a hood of cold sweat break over his brow. "Who?" It was the only thing he could think of to say. He found himself suddenly able to identify closely with the criminals he had interviewed who, when confronted with the irrefutable facts, still refused to admit to the crime.

"Your son Robert," Sean said. "Calls himself Hjalmar Linnekar. But then you know all about that, don't you."

Joris looked at the army of expectant faces. Even Theo's girlfriend had detached herself from her fiancé's anatomy and seemed to be watching him accusingly. He didn't know what to say.

"Sorry Chief Inspector," Brigitte said, pulling the folds of his coat together. "I usually keep my nose out of other people's business, particularly police business, but this was a situation where innocent people were getting hurt. That doesn't mean it was all Robert's fault, he was just one of the links in a long chain, that's all."

Joris Duisenberg found himself breathless: a

sensation of coming into unexpected collision with something much bigger and more powerful than himself. He allowed the Irishman to help him to the chair, which the dark-haired girl vacated, money clutched tight to her admirable bosom. He knew it had been wrong to let Robert go free, but it was his own son, damn it. Now it seemed that he was facing an early and dishonourable end to an illustrious career. He still didn't speak. He had nothing to say.

"Sure an' we're not quite through yet," Sean said. "There's this other party on the floor over there, but I don't think he's up to sayin' too much at the moment 'cos he's a bit dead."

Joris glared at the body, as though the lifeless preacher was responsible for his own death. Eventually, he found his voice and discovered that it had lost its usual authority. "And I suppose you're going to tell me that this guy was already lying there when you got here."

"Not at all," Theo said. "He was threatening our lives so I shot him."

"You?"

"Yes me. Why are you so surprised?"

"Because I thought you were of a deeply religious persuasion," Joris said. "Who is he anyway?"

"Our spiritual guide."

"Oh God!"

A beat.

"Anybody feel like explaining?"

The Chief Inspector listened as Sean Legg summarised the 'facts'. Somehow The Reverend van Aanroy, alias a contract killer named Andy Nottley, had got hold of a load of money belonging variously to Robert's girlfriend and the Ferris pair: some internet scam that was never going to be resolved according to the Irishman. Seemingly Theo and Joska had stumbled across the Reverend's dishonesty and the Reverend had tried to kill them. In self-defence, Theo had shot van Aanroy with his own gun. Turned out that the good Reverend's alter ego had disposed of more people than the bubonic plague – complete dossiers available – and that it was he who had killed Jack Riley, mistaking him for his twin brother George, who had finished the biscuits and excused himself to go and look in the kitchen to see if there were any more.

"And what of your own missing money?" Joris asked, having assimilated Sean's version of events.

"No trace," Sean replied. "Must have been a different scam."

"Of course! I can understand why you wouldn't like Mister and Miss Ferris to be implicated."

Sean nodded. "Nor your son."

Joris permitted himself a half-smile - the Irishman seemed to have it all worked out. "And how did Theo and Joska just happen to stumble across van Aanroy counting other people's money?" he asked.

"I hadn't thought of that," Sean said, beaming happily. "But I'm sure you'll come up with something."

"I'm sure I shall," Joris replied, breathing a sigh of relief as his mind's eye conjured up a few more years of illustrious policing before an honourable, fully pensioned retirement.

* * *

Hans Brinker tightened the screw until the head split and fell away. It was designed that way, leaving sufficient bevel to hold the cover tight but no means of unscrewing it.

Everything was set for midnight.

A single digital display blinked at him like a one-eyed cat in the dim light of the barn, 09:59:46 then 09:59:45 then 09:59:44. Ten hours to midnight, the exact hour of his father's murder.

He held his chest and spat onto the floor of the barn, Phthook, leaving a bloody oyster dripping down the side of a wet stone. Sweat dripped from the end of his nose and his eyes burned in their sockets like hot coals. He knew that he couldn't hold out much longer, but it didn't matter any more: the digging was finished and the charges were laid. Nothing could now stop the inevitable. Water was seeping through the tunnel face in a steady stream, and the ground in the barn was sticking to his feet in heavy clods that made walking difficult. Further into the tunnel it was pure mud, deeper than his boots in places. The massive river Lek was anxious to escape its restraining banks, and was tugging at the leash like a dog with a lamppost to sniff.

May 31st, the anniversary of his father's murder,

perfect! Even though the digging had been harder than he could have anticipated, probably due to his age and his health, he had achieved his goal. His father would have been thrilled with his efficiency. Soon, very soon, the world would know who had devastated this flat, boring little land. Just ten hours left before the antlophobic Dutch would learn about Hans Brinker's revenge. No need for any preposterous bloody folklore then – they could savour the real thing in reverse.

Phthook.

He slammed the barn doors behind him and stared across the fields at his mother's house. His brothers were out, it seemed. The building was unlit and there were no cars parked outside. Never mind, at least the house and their precious flowers would be history ten hours from now.

He'd already taken steps to set the record straight. Safely in his solicitor's vault in Amsterdam was the full history of the injustices that had led to the carnage that would descend upon these unholy people. He'd left hand-written instructions on where to send it and when. The newspapers would get to know the facts only after Hans's death - or assumed death, he'd added, knowing that he intended being close at hand when the charges blew, and that his body would be evaporated into the atmosphere. Any pieces recognisable as human remains would be washed away as the surge of billions of tons of water scoured the face of the land.

Phthook.

At last his father would be revenged. His friends in The Fatherland, too, the ones who had supplied him with explosives and detonators and advice and encouragement, would have their own victory to celebrate. There would be glasses raised to Hans Brinker tonight. The cruel murder of the adjutant to Reichskommandant Seyss-Inquart would have been avenged at last.

Teach them a lesson.

Phthook.

* * *

Sandy stepped out of van Aanroy's house into the watery sunshine. She closed the front door behind her and took a deep breath. She quite enjoyed a bit of excitement in her life, but normally only when she was controlling it. The last few hours had been as hectic as she wanted, particularly since she hadn't been orchestrating the plot. She looked round at the quiet street that backed onto Holland Spoor Station and wondered if the residents would ever guess what sort of neighbour they had had in their midst.

Everybody else had gone, except Sean and the Dutch police inspector who she'd left haggling over the division of the spoils. Sean had been adamant that Rolien should only get back what belonged to her, not what Duisenberg's son, aka Hjalmar Linnekar, had taken from Sandy and her father. Sandy had omitted to mention that the cash included van Aanroy's own bank balance, and Theo had apparently been too engrossed in Joska's anatomy to even give it a thought - he'd simply departed the house saying 'I'll leave you to sort it all out then'. The Chief Inspector appeared to think that the Dutch police should take care of the Ferris money until such time that its source had been established, but Sean was having none of it.

Sandy smiled to herself and walked to the gate. If Chief Inspector Duisenberg had known of Sean's legendary powers of persuasion, he would have given up before he even started. When Sean made his mind up, trying to change it was as effective as peeing into the sea to make the tide come in. And anyway, if things got tricky, it wouldn't take Sean long to remind the Dutchman of his son's involvement.

A menacing shadow crossed Sandy's path. Its owner blocked her way and spoke to her in Dutch.

"Sorry," Sandy said, "my Dutch is not that good."

"I wondered if the Reverend van Aanroy was at home," said the black-dressed pyramid.

"Don't I know you?" Sandy asked. "You're the lady that collects money for the gospel singers, aren't you?"

"And who might you be?" Mevrouw Modderkolk asked, her eyes reflecting a mixture of suspicion and foreboding.

"I'm a friend of Reverend van Aanroy, his personal banker you could say, but he's a bit preoccupied at the moment, he has the police with him."

The big lady's face turned ashen. "The police? Why, what for?"

"Ah, er, it seems that some money has gone missing. The police are looking into it now."

Mevrouw Modderkolk thrust a black holdall into Sandy's hands. "Give him this. Tell him that I didn't intend to take it, I was just saving it up for a worthwhile project," and then she disappeared as quickly as she had arrived, dragging a large suitcase behind her.

Sandy's smile widened. Seemed like the lady was having some sort of conscience attack, poor soul. She looked curiously at the holdall. It felt supple and comforting, the way a well-worn woolly jumper feels after it's been in the wash a few times. She couldn't help feeling that she was in for a pleasant surprise.

After she'd opened the zip and peered inside, she scuttled off up the street as fast as she could. After all, there was no point heaping further confusion on an already confused Chief of Police.

It was early evening by the time that Joris Duisenberg had dealt with the scene of crime, returned to the police station, and finished updating his daughter.

"I don't believe a word of it," Jolanda said, "except maybe that Theo Padmos killed van Aanroy in self defence."

"Nor me," replied Duisenberg, "but since Sean Legg's bank is now the only known loser, I'm inclined to let matters lie. If we were to suddenly turn up with their money, they'd want to know how we came by it and how we knew it was theirs. Since I can't think of any plausible excuse that wouldn't implicate Robert, I think we've got to leave things as they are."

"And do you really think that van Aanroy, or whatever his real name was, was responsible for that murder in Kinderdijk?"

"Positive," Duisenberg said, sliding a black and white photograph of the dead preacher across his desk. "The forensic team have gone over the place with a fine toothcomb and it's obvious that van Aanroy was guilty of just about every unsolved murder in Europe. He kept a file on all his contracts. And anyway the M.O. was always similar - expensive Languiole knives and the same silver medallion left on the body. I've already sent copies of the non-Dutch files to Interpol and our own lads have re-opened the local cases. As far as the police in Kinderdijk are concerned, the issue is closed and all charges against Nick Ferris have been dropped."

Jolanda took a long, hard look at the picture of van Aanroy's body. "So that's it then," she said, "the whole world goes free?"

"That's it," he confirmed, "and if you're in contact with Robert any time, you can tell him that if he ever returns to The Netherlands and gets even so much as a parking ticket, I'll break his dumb neck."

"No you won't, Dad. I'll break it first. Hopefully we can consign this whole charade to the dustbin of our memories. What's happening with Rolien and the estate agent?"

Joris smiled economically. "They're going to be busy for the next few weeks explaining certain property transactions to the tax authorities."

"Serves them right. I'll be glad when they've all gone and left us in peace."

"I think we might just be left with one of them," Joris said. "Father Ferris seems to have made his mind up to stay in The Netherlands. We'll have to keep an eye on him."

"And the others?"

"Theo Padmos and his girlfriend have apparently discovered the meaning of life. I'll lay odds that, at this moment, they're secreted away in an anonymous bedroom somewhere, making up for lost time."

Jolanda smiled. "What about Sandy Ferris and Sean Legg? And George Riley and Angus Slooth?"

"What, Fat Fart and Pongo Pipe?"

The red lips parted slightly. Jolanda glanced over her father's shoulder. "I'm not sure Angus would appreciate that particular description," she said, with a chuckle.

"Noo, Jolanda, I'd have to agree with your father there - George Riley is a fat fart!"

Joris spun round in his chair and blushed like a virgin bride on her wedding night. "Oh God, Jolanda, why didn't you say something? I'm sorry, Detective Inspector, I didn't really mean it. I was just—"

"Yes you did, you cheeky wee policeman. But don't worry; I've heard a lot worse than that in my time."

Jolanda stood up and reached out her hand to Slooth. "I hoped you'd call in before you left," she said. "I wouldn't have liked you to have gone without saying goodbye."

Slooth squeezed her hand gently, then offered his own to Joris, who shook it complaisantly, knowing that it was expected.

"No offence meant," Joris said, twiddling his button furiously.

"None taken," laughed Slooth. "When you act eccentric, as I admit I do, adverse comments go with the territory. People have a habit of underestimating me, which suits me well in my line of work. So eccentricity can have its advantages. When folk look at me and think 'thick'," he tapped his forehead. "they forget that a stinky pipe, an unruly mop of hair and a scruffy pair of trainers can hide a passable brain."

"And a decent man," added Jolanda, noticing her father's puzzled look. "We have a lot to thank Angus for, Dad. Possibly my brother's freedom for a start."

"What do you mean?" Joris asked, as his daughter perched on the corner of his desk and offered the Scotsman her seat.

Slooth remained standing and eased his smouldering pipe from between his teeth. "Your daughter's trying to tell you that I spotted Robert's involvement fairly early on in the enquiry, and she came clean wi' me about the family connection." Joris noticed that he had dropped the strong Glaswegian accent in favour of a gentler one that seemed more natural.

"So Angus did his best to make sure that Robert's

activities remained undetected," Jolanda said. "But we had to try and find a way of getting Robert to stop. Angus paid a visit on the little Finnish guy and let him know that someone called Anthrax was involved. He had a shrewd idea that the Finn would know who Anthrax was. Since he's always worked on the right side of the law, we banked on him persuading Robert to give up his black hat stuff and use his computer skills legitimately."

"And it would probably have worked," added Slooth, "if it wasn't for events moving forward at the pace they did."

"So you stayed here just to help us out?" Joris asked.

"No, I'm not that charitable. Your son was a wee bit of litter you could have easily picked up by yourselves. I was over here to bag a real load of rubbish: a guy by the name of Jack Riley." Slooth checked the time and turned to leave. "So having already stood by and watched most of the garbage get binned by you, I think it's time I went and did a wee bit of tidying up of my own now."

He left as quickly as he had entered, leaving a room full of blue-grey smoke. Jolanda chased after him, "I just remembered something," she called to her father over her shoulder.

As Angus opened the door to his rental car, Jolanda came behind him, put her arms round his waist and hugged him. "It would be nice if you could stay a little longer," she said. "I'm going to miss you."

Angus turned to face her. "Me too, Jolanda. You've certainly made my stay in the Netherlands something I shall always remember - and cherish."

She kissed him, long and deep. "Why don't you stop for a few more days. I've got some leave due to me. You could take a short vacation. We could do what people do."

"What, spend all day in bed?"

"That works for me," she said, laughing, "although there are lots of other things we can do and see as well."

Angus was quiet for a long moment, six or seven seconds, right to the moment when the pause become uncomfortable. Then he smiled and said, "You know what, I think that's the sort of invitation that would be very discourteous to turn down. But there's something I have to do right now. It might take an hour or two, but I'll explain when I get back to yours. Do you want to go arrange for a few days off while I'm gone?"

Jolanda kissed him again. "It will be my pleasure!"

CHAPTER FOURTEEN
Just before midnight

Mevrouw Modderkolk tutted to herself. She should have telephoned first - it never crossed her mind that her brothers might have gone away. What in heaven's name was she going to do? It was too late now to walk back to Kinderdijk and catch another bus. She was going to have to find somewhere to spend the night. She strained her eyes across the polder to where her half-brother's campsite lay. It looked peaceful and calm, but it was too dark to be certain. As if to oblige, the protuberant face of a gibbous moon launched itself from behind a loitering cloud, casting clean-cut shadows across the grass.

Half a mile away, George Riley would have preferred no moon at all as he sniffed the air, which smelt slightly woody and comfortable, like wet peat or rotting leaves after a gentle shower. A few lights still broke the semi-darkness from some of the caravan windows as satisfied campers finished the chapters of their books before succumbing to sleep. Somewhere across the flat polders an owl screeched to his mate, who returned the call. Even the working boats on the river high above his head were moored and silent until the factories and warehouses on the far bank awoke in the morning.

George dusted the soil off his notebook and tucked it into his pocket. He balled up the supermarket bag in which he'd buried it, threw it back into the hole and carelessly kicked some loose earth over it. He'd been concerned that he wouldn't be able to find the spot again in the dark, or that the police had found the notebook and removed it. He needn't have worried; it was exactly as it had been when he'd hidden it. He brushed the remnants of soil off his hands.

Now he was in business; now he could catch a flight to London and return as Jack Riley, ruler of everything he surveyed. It shouldn't be too difficult; he still had his brother's identity and he now had everything he needed to understand and control his brother's empire. Not that he wanted anything to do with racketeering or thuggery, but there was a high value attached to controlling a wealthy patch in London, and George knew that he could soon turn the information into cash with one or more of the other gang-land bosses. They could have a little auction to divide the spoils. Big Jack's retirement auction. Nice thought. Bye-bye Jack the villain; hello Jack the retired gentleman. A cosy little villa sounded good, somewhere warm like The Bahamas.

First, he'd have Jack's body shipped to the Isle of Man and quietly cremated. Name on the registrar's list? - George Riley. Bye-bye George. Even if some of the gang bosses got wise to the switch, what could be more natural that a brother taking over his deceased brother's business interests? He was, after all, Jack's only known relative.

George eased from the cover of the tall cypresses, which stood against the night sky like black exclamation marks. He scanned the site for any movement. The last caravan light was extinguished and everything fell quiet. He illuminated the face on his digital watch. Eleven forty-eight. He could be back in the hotel before one o'clock, maybe have a crate of beer sent up to the room to celebrate his new identity. Burger and fries first at the all-night Big Mac opposite the hotel.

An urgent rustling sound echoed in the undergrowth as some tiny creature went about its nocturnal business under the cloak of seeming silence. George looked up to see a faint needle of light stretching across the grass from the cracks around the cumbersome doors that guarded the secrets of the barn. The owner was busy again. He stole another quick glance around the site to make sure that he was unobserved, then, like a human globe, hovered casually across the sward towards the building. Like many heavy men, George walked with a certain grace and delicacy as though he'd been practising in front of a mirror. He was not, he was convinced, fat. Poor people were fat and he was no longer poor. He had metamorphosed into a man of imposing stature. Like a prodigious pumpkin, the wider the girth the greater the flavour… well the greater the wealth, anyway.

He was glad Jack was dead. There was no point feigning sorrow over the demise of his brother. George's only regret was that it had fallen to him to do the deed. Though bumping off his brother had eventually turned out to be as simple as hijacking an ice cream van, it would have been more comforting and more convenient if Jack had died accidentally - a car crash or drowning or something. Strange, though, that the guy with the knife should turn out to be the schizophrenic leader of some weird religious sect.

George approached the barn. He'd been dying to

know what the old boy did in there all the time, and this would be his last opportunity to find out. A lifetime of natural curiosity had brought certain benefits, as the notebook in his pocket testified. He glanced around the site to make sure he was not being observed. By the light of the smiling moon, he could see that the man with the green tent and the big motorbike had moved on, his space having been taken by a long touring van.

As he neared the barn doors, George raised his heels and balanced on the balls of his feet. He was a miserable old sod, the site owner, and George didn't want to give him any excuse to splatter him in phlegm while he cursed him for being there. Anyway, being nosey was an art form: if you wanted to find things out, you had to go about it in the right way. He found a spot where the crack was widest and placed his bulbous cheek against the wood, screwing up his eye against the light inside. It was only a single bulb, but his eyes had grown accustomed to the darkness and the light pierced his retina like a can opener.

When his vision had adjusted, he found that he could see only about half of the inside of the cavernous barn. Against the one side wall that was exposed to his gaze, the Dutchman's tractor and trailer were parked. Tools of various shapes and sizes littered the floor near the trailer wheels – mostly digging tools; spades, shovels, plastic buckets, a small pneumatic drill like the ones people rent for a day to break up hard ground in their gardens. At the far end of the barn, directly in line with the doors, a hole had been dug into the face of the riverbank. About five feet high by three feet wide, it clearly went some way into the bank before darkness obscured its true depth: more like a tunnel,

George thought. He peered to the right until the timber of the doorframe obscured his vision. He could see a man's shoulder and arm and part of his back, all squatting on a wooden chair. The denim overalls of the site owner were easily recognisable.

George pulled back and stepped away from the door, afraid that he might be discovered.

He was.

"Och, Jack Riley. At's a funny place to be meetin' you."

George gawped at the figure facing him. The man's face was craggy like granite rocks - somewhere between Lee Marvin and Clint Eastwood without the romance. And his hair… well, his hair… words failed him - it was like coconut matting, shredded by the dog while his owners were out. And he was wearing a 'Kiss me Quick' T-shirt. George hoped he was wearing it for a bet; otherwise it was a catastrophic fashion statement.

"Who the hell are you," he whispered.

"Detective Inspector Angus Slooth of the Isle of Man Constabulary," in a strong haggis accent.

"Sure, and I'm the Archangel Gabriel. Now who are you and what do you want?"

"I've told you, I'm Detective Inspector Angus Slooth of the Isle of Man Constabulary, and you're nicked, as they say."

"Bugger off."

"That's noo way to be talkin' to the law, Jack Riley. My friends at Scotland Yard have been lookin' for an excuse to nick you for years and now they've got it."

"Like what?" George asked. "Sneaking a look into somebody's barn?"

"No, Jack. Like murrrder." The 'r' rolled like marbles scattering down a wooden staircase.

At the word 'murder', a blade of cold fear, like a shard of ice, ran down George's back, starting at his collar and stopping only when it reached his knees. He turned and moved a few paces away from the barn. If he was going to be forced into a conversation with this guy, the last thing he wanted was the site owner taking part or listening in. But what did he know, and why was he calling him Jack? Was he really a copper? Despite his appearance, it seemed feasible. Surely he couldn't possibly know who had killed his brother? There had only been three people in the lavatory at the time, and the other two were now dead. It just wasn't possible. The guy had to be bluffing. Years of scallywag training scampered instinctively to George's aid. Lies could tumble from his mouth with the reassuring beat of raindrops on the window and, when in doubt, bluff back. "So who am I meant to have murrrdered?" he asked, imitating the Scotsman's accent.

"Your brother."

George held his breath, though his pulse was off the blocks and rapidly gaining speed. He did his best to keep his voice controlled. "My brother's murderer was killed earlier today, and not by me. You can check it with the police in The Hague."

"You mean Nottley or van Aanroy or whatever other alias he might ha' been usin'?" Slooth said, shaking his head. "No, Jack, he was your hired hit man and somebody hit him back, but he didna kill your brother and you know it. When you shove a knife into somebody's aorta, it has a tendency to spread a fair bit o' blood, and Nottley's clothes have proved to be remarkably blood-free. Your own, however, seemed to be somewhat stained, and matched your brother's blood type perfectly. Something of a coincidence don't you think?"

"You haven't got any of my clothes."

"Except for the ones you left in the back of your crashed car. You'd ha' done better to ha' burnt them, but maybe you didna have the time, what with us following you?"

George was too shocked to bluff. His response was instinctive. "It was you was it? On the motorbike?"

Slooth laughed. "Not on your bloody life. It was an associate o' mine. When he found Jack Riley's Jag and no Jack Riley, he guessed you'd managed to get yourself a lift."

George sighed and his shoulders slumped. His bluff was being called and there was nothing he could do about it. The hewn-faced guy seemed to know everything. But how? Had there been a fourth person in the lavatory? Of course not. A hidden camera maybe? How the hell did this guy know that he'd killed his brother? His brain felt as though it was sagging under its own weight, while thoughts whirred around his head like bats without radar.

Meanwhile, the Scottish detective just stared at him, saying nothing. From his previous brushes with the law, George knew that his and Jack's fingerprints were close to being identical. Likewise, he knew that a DNA test would prove nothing. It was the identical twin syndrome working against him again. And anyway, if the police wanted to fit you up, they had ways of concealing evidence that no court would ever be able to discover.

"You're talking bollocks," he said, in a final, weak attempt to bluff himself free.

Slooth held his gaze in silence. George knew now that the game was up. But if nothing else he had to convince this guy that he was George Riley, even if it meant owning up to killing Jack. If he were sent down for all Jack's sins, he'd probably never see the light of day again. They'd bury the key in wet concrete and turn it into a highway bridge. It would keep some of Jack's other victims company.

He sighed again and reluctantly made his decision. His ultimate freedom wasn't worth the risk. Even if he had to serve a long stretch for Jack's death, George Riley could claim self-defence and throw himself at the mercy of the court. If he hadn't learned anything else from years of evading the law, he had learned when to stop playing games and surrender to the inevitable.

"Like you say," he muttered, "it sounds like I'm nicked, but you might as well know that I'm George Riley, not Jack. I'm buggered if I'm going to take the blame for my brother's insanities."

"I ken"

"You what?"

"I ken - I know."

"That I'm George?"

"That you're claiming to be George."

"But I am George."

Slooth humphed like surplus air from a bagpipe. "I'll bet a dollar to a pinch of camel shite that the passport in your pocket says Jack Riley. I'll also bet you a dollar to a pinch of camel shite that the photo and description inside the said passport match the man whose pocket it's in."

George shook his head furiously, like a dog tormented by wasps. "Yeah, but that doesn't make me Jack Riley. I keep telling you, I'm George: Jack's twin brother." His voice had a panicky edge now, and he felt as if someone were pulling a cowl of clammy sweat up his back and over his head.

"Try telling that to the judge," Slooth said. "As far as I'm concerned, I've just nabbed Jack Riley, who's not only responsible for his brother's murder, but also for a string o' disappeared bodies, for grand scale larceny, for smuggling, for extortion, for tax evasion, for perjury, for intimidation, for—"

"You've got the wrong man," George cried, suddenly feeling that he had acquired the ability to shit through the holes of a very fine sieve. "I tell you, I'm George Riley - George bloody Riley."

"Aye, o' course. And I'll bet that not only are your fingerprints all over Jack Riley's car, but that you currently have in your possession Jack Riley's credit card and Jack Riley's wallet. Would I be right now?"

"But—"

"And anyway, George Riley is dead, as the Dutch police can testify, so maybe you can understand how the judge is going to see it."

There was a bleak, cold silence that left each of them holding the other's gaze…

A little way away, Mevrouw Modderkolk cursed silently and crawled out of the shallow water-filled ditch. She was sure her stockings were torn, but she couldn't be sure since her legs were now covered in black mud. God damn this wretched place. Why couldn't they put up streetlights or something? She retrieved her sodden suitcase and straightened her black dress as best she could. She'd not seen Hans for years and he was hardly likely to welcome her with open arms if she arrived looking like a bedraggled hippopotamus. Mind you, it was unlikely he'd welcome her with open arms anyway. Though she'd done her best to make him feel more welcome in their parent's home, she knew she could have tried harder. She could have stopped her brothers picking on him for a start.

Oh well, what was done couldn't be undone. But she needed somewhere to stay now, and Hans was her only option. She prayed he wouldn't be asleep. Hopefully he'd be sitting up watching television. She inadvertently spread mud on her face as she mopped her brow with the back of her hand.

Next to the barn, George glanced over the detective's shoulder for an escape route. If he lunged at the guy, he could probably disable him for a few seconds by using his weight, but what then? Though he had the benefit of size, his bulk had always made him challenged in the speed department.

"There's noo way out," Slooth said, as if reading his thoughts. "What happens now is that you and I do a little deal, George."

"George? You've been calling me Jack for the last five minutes."

"So who would you prefer to be?"

"George. Definitely George." He thought he saw the shine of a tooth through the pipe smoke that surrounded the policeman.

Slooth reached into his pocket. "So if I tell you that I have George Riley's identity here, do you think you'd be prepared to exchange it for all that stuff of Jack Riley's that's on your person?"

George's hand shot straight for his pocket. "Damn right," he said, holding out his brother's passport and wallet.

"I said, all Jack's stuff, George."

"That's all I took off him. That's all he had in his pockets."

"That might be all he had in his pockets, but we both know that there's a bit more than that, don't we. Like the little item you just dug up, perhaps?"

George heaved a sigh and listened as his belly

rumbled in sympathy. Clearly the strange guy in front of him did know everything. He checked his watch: five minutes to midnight. He'd remember this instant for the rest of his life as the moment that Big Jack's wealth slipped out of his grasp. He'd been rich for little more than five minutes.

He reached once more into his pocket and handed the notebook to the Scottish detective.

Slooth exchanged it for George's own passport. "Don't worry," he said, showing another tooth, "there's bound to be some cash. Some of your brother's more legitimate businesses were built on laundered money, and it's unlikely that we'll ever find the laundry. When it's all been sorted out, I don't think you'll starve."

George grunted. "If I ever get out of prison in time to enjoy it. They put you away for a long time when you kill someone, don't they?"

"Only if you killed someone."

George looked at Slooth quizzically, tucking his own documents safely away before the Scotsman could change his mind.

"The Dutch police seem satisfied that they've got their man," Slooth said, "so who am I to tell them any different?"

"But what about the clothes in the car?"

"What clothes?"

George thought for a moment. "Yeah, you're right. What bloody clothes?" I'm wearing the same clothes now as I was when I… as I was when Jack was found. You just bluffed a master bluffer you Scotch git."

Slooth laughed. "Scots, if you don't mind."

A pause as they weighed each other up.

Slooth spoke first. "We both know the truth, George, and I'm sure I could find enough evidence to sink you without trace if I wanted to. But, as far as I'm concerned, justice has been served. Your brother got what was comin' to him and so did his hit man. There's nay point ruining your life when you're just a minor rogue who was on the wrong end o' your brother's vendetta."

George heaved a sigh. "You're not going to turn me in then?"

"Aye, I'm going to turn you in alright. I'm going to turn you in to an honest man. Next time you're of a mind to help yourself to somebody else's belongings, just remember that I'm only one step behind you. History has a habit of catching up with folk, George, and Angus Slooth has a long memory."

"You never thought for a moment that I was Jack, did you."

"Noo."

"And you never had any real proof that I'd killed my brother, did you."

"Noo."

"So why did you trail me here?"

"Because my colleagues at Scotland Yard have been interested in your brother's activities for many a year. We've been keepin' an eye on you ever since you set foot on Manx soil. We thought you might have been tied up in his activities."

"But I wasn't. I went to the Isle of Man to get away from him."

"Aye, we know that now. It became obvious as time passed. In fact, we almost lost interest in you until a few weeks ago when we got word that your brother was unhappy about a certain outstanding sum of money. Then we noticed that you had a late night visitor sent by Jack."

"You mean your blokes just stood by and watched while I was nearly castrated?"

Slooth chuckled to himself, like he was telling himself a joke he'd never heard before. "Worse than that," he said, "we even told your brother where to start looking for you."

"What do you mean?"

"The lorry driver who gave you a lift from Calais to Dordrecht."

"What about him?"

"That was my associate. A man with a grudge, you might say. A petty crook whose best friend had his throat slit by one of Jack's thugs. My associate had been working for us under cover for almost a year, trying to gather enough evidence against Jack to get a good prosecution."

George thought a moment. "But how did he know I'd be on that particular ferry?"

"He didn't," Slooth replied. "You got lucky there. Wally was on a collection run for Jack round Europe, and just happened to be at the docks at Dover. When he saw you dodging around with a nasty looking bruiser a few yards behind, he thought you were Big Jack. He radioed in for instructions and our lot, knowing exactly where your brother was at that precise moment, realised that it must have been you," Slooth chuckled. "Lucky for you, really. Nobby the Knife doesn't usually miss his mark."

"You mean your bloke stopped him?"

Aye, it was Nobby who'd killed Wally's best friend. Wally reversed into him by accident, and then ran over his legs. He should be getting out o' hospital a few years from now. Wally, left him for the harbour police to scrape up, then jumped the queue and got himself on the same ferry as you. He kept an eye on you for the whole crossing and made sure he was close by when you were looking at getting yourself a lift somewhere." Slooth chuckled again. "He reckoned you were a total wreck, George. Kept looking over your shoulder, even when you were in the cab of his lorry. Mind you, he was a bit less smug about the fact that you ate all his cheese sandwiches."

At the mention of food, George impulsively fiddled in his pocket to see if there was a sweet stuck to the lining. There wasn't. "So how come this Wally guy dropped me off," he asked. "How did he know he'd find me again?"

"We sent somebody else to take over his lorry and complete the collection run," Slooth replied. "Wally followed you. He knew exactly where you were within twenty-four hours."

"How?"

"He monitored the line of petty thefts. It's like peeing in the snow and using your own handwriting Wally should know; he's left plenty of trails in the snow himself."

George shrugged his shoulders. His neck moved up to meet his ears. "And your lot have been watching me ever since?"

"Aye. Apart from a couple of days when Wally took his lorry back to London and let Jack know roughly where you were, he's been keeping an eye on you all the time."

George felt the penny drop. "The guy with the green tent?"

"Aye."

"And the big motorbike?"

"Aye."

"I knew I'd seen him somewhere before. I just couldn't puzzle out where. So I was safe all the time?"

"Aye. You were our decoy, George. We had to keep you in one piece." Slooth's shoulders were visibly shaking now. "Wally even negotiated your escape from a clothes shop one night when you were spotted breaking in by a sharp-eyed member of the local constabulary. The Dutch police are willing to ignore the spate of local thefts so long as I get you away from here before you get a chance to totally destroy the local economy."

George choked. "Bloody hell. So the whole thing was a set-up to catch Jack?"

"Aye," Slooth said. He unexpectedly reverted to a more sombre mood. "What we didn't know, George, was that he'd put a contract out on you. We'd tried bugging his phone several times but your brother was a cautious man and had these things checked frequently. He was clearly out to do you some permanent damage and we surmised that he wouldn't waste his energy if it was just a matter of a few quid owed to him, he'd bide his time and give you a damn good hiding when you came back. Obviously you'd severely upset him. That meant that you had to have something of his that was worth a lot more than money. We guessed that you knew too much about his activities and that you had become a danger to him. Would I be right?"

George nodded.

"And would I be right in assuming that this wee notebook contains information that your brother would not have liked the police to know about?"

George nodded again. "You mean you didn't know?"

Another tooth appeared in the darkness and George could smell pipe tobacco as Slooth slid something into his mouth.

"Noo, it was just a gut feeling. I thought it was reasonable to assume that you couldna held any substantial details in your head, so it had to be written down somewhere. I took the liberty of inspecting your hotel room earlier while you and your friends were paying the clerical man a visit. When I couldna find anything, I decided that it had to be hidden here somewhere."

"So you had it all worked out."

Slooth paused to fire up his pipe again, sending showers of burning embers high into the night sky. "Aye," he said, between puffs, "we had most of it worked out. There was one thing that puzzled me though. The knife that killed your brother was definitely one of the collection that the hit man owned, so how did it come into your possession?"

George ran his fingers through his uncooperative sideburns and smiled like a disrespectful schoolboy. He was pleased and relieved that his facial muscles still remembered the drill. "Trade you for my notebook," he said, more in hope than expectation.

"Sod off," said Slooth, blowing smoke at him. "I can assure you that cooperating with me will prove much more beneficial that being obstructive, George. Our wee island home will be much more comfortable for you if you gi' me a bit of help here."

George slid his hands into his pockets and relaxed. It was strangely comforting to be able to wash his conscience: a bit like visiting a psychiatrist or going to confession – not that he'd ever done either of those things. "Okay. You're not going to believe it, though..."

Just 200 metres away, Mevrouw Modderkolk leaned wearily on the hand-painted sign that said 'Welcome to Hans Brinker' in four different languages. Not that she could read it in the dark. Not that she could have read it in daylight either, with the rusty nails and flaking paint. She dropped her dripping suitcase and mopped her brow with a large lace handkerchief that lived in the cuff of her blouse. She peered across the campsite in trepidation and racked her brain to try and remember which caravan Hans lived in. None of them seemed to have any lights on anyway. Though knocking on Hans' door while he was asleep wasn't the most cheerful prospect, it beat spending the night in a field – or worse, a prison cell. She wanted to take a moment, though, to compose herself before making her presence known. She knew she had mud on her hands and face, she could feel it hardening, yet it was important to make a good first impression. She reached down and tried to straighten her dress, but it was soaking wet and slimy.

George coughed and waved the smoke away from his face. "So I go into the bog for a slash, and in walks Jack. He has a grin on his face, like a crocodile with a new baby. He says nothing, not a bloody word, just pulls out a gun. There's me standing there shaking like a Parkinson's sufferer and Jack about to blow out my brains through my posterior orifice when out steps that killer from the crap cubicle, only he isn't dressed as a cleric this time; he's wearing a pair of bleedin' Marigolds and brandishing a knife - and looks like he knows how to use it.

He does a double take of the two of us - identical face, identical hair, identical build, almost identical clothes. He must have thought he was suffering double vision. Then he totally freezes. He just has this stupid stare on his face like he did when he was in his priest outfit a few hours ago. Blank eyes and all that. It was like looking through plate glass into an empty shop. Very unprofessional if you ask me. So anyway, Jack's staring back at him, like what the hell's he doing there, and I grab the moment to whip the knife off the strange guy and stick Jack. Honestly, I didn't expect him to croak, I'm sure he was still breathing when I left. So, after I'd got over the shock of it and saw that the weirdo was still standing there frozen in time, I swapped identity with Jack, nicked his car keys and buggered off quick."

"And what happened to Jack's gun?" Slooth asked.

"Dumped it in the first canal I came across. I don't like guns"

Slooth puffed on his pipe. "Don't worry George, that one was never going to harm anyone. It was one that Wally smuggled over for Jack in his lorry. Our lot got to it first and made sure it would never fire. The worst Jack could have done would have been to have poked you in the ribs with it."

George giggled aloud. It was a nice feeling to know that someone had pulled a fast one on his brother, even if that someone was the law.

"So what did you do after you dumped the gun?" asked Slooth.

George took control of his laughter. "I didn't want to come back here because I knew the police would be watching the roads and probably searching the site, so I hung around on the outskirts of Kinderdijk and slept rough in a hedge. When I spotted Jack's car, I just took off. You know the rest of the story. Car accident - off to The Hague - give the preacher gentleman another surprise, then, as soon as I could get away, came back for the notebook. How long have you been waiting?"

"Too long," Slooth said, clenching his pipe between his teeth as he scratched the back of his hand. "Ruddy mosquitoes have been feeding off me for the last three hours."

A beat.

"But I kept myself amused."

"How do you mean?"

"Well, like you, George, I was curious as to why there were lights on in the barn so, like you, I took a little peek."

"And?"

"And I think my friend, Wally, was so busy keeping an eye on you that he missed the real action."

"Meaning?"

Slooth rearranged his finger in the bowl of his pipe. "What time is it?"

"What?"

"What time is it?"

George checked his watch again. "Couple of

minutes to midnight. Why?"

Slooth sucked air past his finger - noisily. "Because, if your watch is right, George, in two minutes time we're going to either leave here the same shape as when we arrived or there's going to be one almighty bloody bang and we'll both evaporate up our own bottoms."

"Eh?"

"You heard me, George. Two minutes from now, we could both be memories." Slooth scratched his hand again. "When I looked in the barn, I spotted a guy clutching a little device that looked suspiciously like a remote detonator. I saw the tunnel and put one and one together. Apparently I made two because, when I went into the barn uninvited and challenged the guy, he took a swing at my head with a shovel. Good job he missed really, it would have made an awful dent in his shovel. Anyway, while I was taking avoiding action he was swearing and shouting at me. Told me it was too late to do anything to stop it and that the whole bloody world would end at midnight. Then he chased me off with an unpleasant looking pickaxe handle. In the end I had no choice but to disable him."

"How?"

"A little technique I learned when I was in the army. I must have overdone it a bit because he's not bothered breathing since."

"You killed him"

"Aye"

"With your bare hands?"

"Aye"

"Christ. How did you do that?"

"I pushed him."

"You pushed him?"

"Aye. Into the chair. I think he had a heart attack or something."

"A heart attack?"

"Will you stop repeating everything I say, George. I pushed him into the chair and he croaked – just like that. I reckon I did him a favour, he was spitting up some horrible stuff at the time. Talking of which, how is the time?"

"What do you mean? Didn't you disarm the detonator?"

"I couldna see any dials or switches or anything, just a digital display. But I was pretty sure the guy was serious, so I hit it with the pickaxe handle. Trouble is, I'm not sure if I did it enough damage. It was a pretty sturdy bit of German engineering by the look of it. I'd just stepped out of the barn to make a phone call when you turned up. I didna want to scare you off, so I transferred myself into the shadows while you retrieved your wee book."

"Bloody hell, you mean you've been hanging around for the last half hour, knowing that the bloody dyke could disintegrate at any time?"

"Aye"

"You're bloody crazy!"

"So I've heard. I prefer eccentric myself."

"Show me this detonator," George said, reaching into his pocket for the Swiss Army Knife he's used to relieve the French family of their number plates a few weeks earlier.

Slooth marched to the barn, swung open the heavy doors and ran to Hans Brinker's body. "It's here," he said, pointing to the ground at the site owner's feet.

"Oh hell, there's no damn wires."

"I told you it was remote. Anyway, y' didna ask."

George picked up the metal case and turned it over in his hand. The liquid crystal display blinked at him, 00:00:28 then 00:00:27 then 00:00:26.

"Jesus almighty, it's going to blow in twenty six seconds," George shouted.

Slooth puffed out a plume of smoke. "Twenty-five," he corrected as the number blinked again.

George banged the display with his knife. 00:00:24. He banged again. 00:00:23. He looked around. There was a heavy iron bar next to the wheel of the tractor. "Bring me that nail bar, quick."

Slooth reacted with deceptive speed. He was back within five seconds. 00:00:18. George smashed at the remote with the point of the bar. The metal box flew through the air in a graceful arc and landed with a dull thud in a glob of bloody spit. He picked it up and wiped his hand on his trousers. 00:00:15 "Oh no!"

Below the display was a small metal panel, held centrally with a stripped brass screw or rivet. George ripped at it with his beefy fingers and swore as the metal tore into his flesh. 00:00:13

"Unscrew it," said Slooth, taking his pipe out of his mouth.

George fumbled with his knife and opened up the nail file by mistake. There was no time to look for the right blade. He tried to wedge the tip of the file behind the metal cover. 00:00:11. He tried again. 00:00:10

"It's no good," he shouted. "Looks like we're bloody history."

00:00:09

"Could be" Slooth said, replacing the pipe and fingering the glowing bowl.

00:00:08

George threw the detonator to the ground. "Come on!" he screamed. "Run!"

00:00:07

"No point," Slooth said, quietly. "If that thing goes bang, you'd need to be a thousand miles from here not to get caught in the tidal wave."

00:00:05

"What do you mean, if?"

00:00:04

"Forgot to tell you, I went into the tunnel and found a detonator pushed into the explosives. I took it outside and chucked it in the canal."

00:00:02

"Trouble is, I don't know if there were others."

00:00:01

George turned his back to the tunnel. Between the open barn doors, a huge, black, muddy, bat-like creature stood legs apart, glaring at him. Oh my God, he was already dead and gone to hell. He closed his eyes…

CHAPTER FIFTEEN

"What's up?" asked Sandy.

Sean dabbed at his top lip. "I thought the departures board just updated our flight, but it didn't."

Sandy sat down again. "Oh yes, the fearless Sean Legg wetting his knickers over a little aeroplane flight. You never were the best flyer, were you?"

"Just the thought of it makes me break out in a cold sweat. I'd rather walk on water than catch a plane. Why don't we just get a train down to Zeebrugge, catch the boat to Hull, then train to Liverpool? "

"What, take two days to do what we could do in half a day? Anyway it's too late for that. The bags are checked in now."

"Except for that one," Sean said, nodding towards the black leather hold-all that Sandy had refused to let out of her sight. "What's in there that's so important?"

"Oh, just some papers and things," she replied,

looking as comfortable as a fly in a cobweb.

"Well just remember our agreement, Sandy. If you come to live with me permanently, you stop playing Robin Hood. Not that you ever gave any of your ill-gotten gains to the poor. Your Dad's now got the proceeds of this last little escapade in his possession, and I'm sure you'll be making lots of phone calls in the next few days while you arrange to share the loot, but I mean it, Sandy – that's it. No more silly stuff."

"Did I just hear my name taken in vain?" Nick asked, as he placed a plastic tray with three cups of insipid coffee and some curled-edge sandwiches on the table.

"Sean was just reminding me that you still owe me some money," Sandy said, grateful for the reprieve.

"Jesus H, Sand, is that all you're bothered about? Here you are, planning to leave your poor old Dad behind while you fly off to a new life—"

"Can you not mention flying," Sean muttered, dabbing his brow with a large handkerchief.

"—and all you can talk about is money."

"It'll save Sean having to find me any housekeeping for a while," Sandy said with a chuckle. "Anyway, we've always split everything down the middle."

"Yeah?" Nick asked, staring at the hold-all. "I can't help feeling that you're flying off without telling me something."

"For crying out loud, will you not mention flying?"

"We'll talk about it another time," Sandy said.

Nick smiled. "Maybe. But only if I remind you, eh?" He took Sandy's hand gently. "Just get on with your life, Sand. You're a big girl now, and you don't need to be dragging me behind you for the rest of your days."

"I never thought of it that way," Sandy said. "I always felt I'd been holding you back. I mean just look at you. Fifty next month and you don't even have a good woman to take care of you."

"What about Brigitte?" Sean suggested. "Does he fit the bill?"

Sandy giggled. "He's been a good friend and he's got a great pair of legs, but he's not what I would call home-making material. Anyway, I think Dad's tastes are a bit more conventional."

"Well maybe now I've got rid of you, I can take a look and see what's on the market," Nick said. "I always knew that one day some daft egit would take you off my hands and fly off with you into the sunset."

"Who are you calling an egit?" Sean said, "And for God's sake will you stop talking about flying."

"I promise not to mention flying again, if you promise to take care of her for me," Nick said, wiping his eye with the back of his hand. "She's all I've cared about for the last twenty-six years, Sean, and—"

"You going sentimental on me?" Sean asked. "That's not like the Nick Ferris I remember."

Nick stared curiously at the damp patch on the back of his hand, like it hadn't just come from his moist eye. "Bloody mucky airports," he said, tutting. "Dust everywhere." He straightened his bright orange shirt and left Sean and Sandy alone again. "Just going for a leak," he called over his shoulder. "Don't go flying off till I get back."

"You promised not to mention—"

"Leave him be," Sandy said, taking Sean's hand. "He'll be okay in a minute."

Sean clasped her hand in his. "And what about you?"

Sandy stared into her lap. She paused before answering. "Dad and I have been inseparable for a long while," she said, quietly. "But it's time. He needs his life, the same as I need mine." She looked up. "And anyway, I doubt I'll get much chance to turn over a new leaf if I stick around with my father."

"You mean it then, about starting fresh."

"Of course I do, otherwise I wouldn't be here."

Sean's eyes twinkled. "So do you want to make a clean breast of it and tell me what's in the hold-all?"

Sandy flinched, like the spider was sniffing round the cobweb again.

"You must have been expecting me," said a voice attached to a large, podgy hand that grabbed one of the curled up sandwiches. "I'm starving."

Sandy and Sean looked up. "George! To what do we owe the pleasure? And Angus, what are you doing here?"

Angus was joined by a plump-breasted young lady with alabaster-blonde hair, "This is Detective Sergeant Jolanda Duisenberg," Angus said. "And we're trying to get George on a flight back to UK."

Sean groaned. "Will you not mention flying?"

Slooth laughed. "Oh aye, I'd forgotten your little weakness there for a moment." He addressed Sandy. "Did you know that the famous Sean Legg goes weak at the knees when you mention flying?"

"Will you not mention flying!" said Sandy and Sean in unison.

"Good sandwiches," George said, his words muffled between dry bread and synthetic ham.

Slooth, dressed in his more regular casual attire of designer jeans and cotton top, sat down next to Sean and pulled up a seat for Jolanda. "I don't believe we've been introduced," he said, offering his hand to Sandy. "Detective Inspector Angus Slooth at your service. And you'd be Sandy Ferris, wouldn't you?"

Sandy paid no attention to the outstretched palm and reached for the hold-all. "How do you know?"

"I know everything," Slooth said, reaching for his pipe instead.

There was a momentary pause.

"You've got George's ticket organised, have you?" Sean asked, trying to manoeuvre the topic elsewhere.

"Including your possible links to a couple of dead bodies you left behind six months ago," Slooth continued, looking Sandy straight in the eyes.

Another pause.

"But don't worry; Sean talked me into a memory lapse. He reckons you did the community a service. I tend to agree with him."

"Aye, well that'll be enough of that," Sean said.

Slooth kept watching Sandy, but a smile parted his face. "Apart from that, the name Sandy Ferris seems to crop up in the conversation every time Sean and I have a beer together. He never stops talking about you. I'm thinking about finding someone else to drink with."

Sean coloured up. "Cut the crap, Angus, and tell us why you're really here. And don't light that bloody thing, the airport is no-smoking."

Slooth tucked the pipe back in his pocket. "We really are trying to do the same as you," he said. "I made a promise to get George out of the country quick, but it looks like all the seats are booked. What's the delay anyway?"

Sandy still seemed uneasy about sitting so close to a policeman. Nevertheless, she spoke up. "I think there was a bomb alert or something, so all the flights are stacked up."

"There was," George muttered through chewed bread and ham. "Angus nearly got us blown up. Talk about cutting it fine."

"Take no notice of him," Slooth said, "He's delirious. Must be a shortage of food. So what's the score with the flights?"

"Seems as though there was a major country-wide alert in the early hours of this morning," Sandy answered, easing her grip on the hold-all slightly, "I gather it's all clear now, but the backlog hasn't been sorted yet. We've been waiting almost four hours. Sean's getting cold feet – wants us to go back to The Hague and catch a boat tomorrow from Zeebrugge to Hull."

Slooth patted the Irishman on the shoulder. "Good thinking, Sean. You wipe that nasty bead of sweat off your top lip and I'll go and see if George can use one of your tickets. Judging by the state of things here, they probably haven't even loaded your luggage yet. And if they have, you can take George's and you can all swap when you get back to the island."

"I doubt you'll get away with that," Sean said. "They're not into people carrying other folk's luggage."

Slooth nodded to Jolanda. "You'd be amazed what police identification papers can achieve." He shuffled out of the seat closely followed by Jolanda. "You stay here, George. No buggering off where I can't see you."

"No problem," George said. "Bring us back some more sandwiches when you come."

"I'll come with you," Sandy said to Slooth. "If you get it sorted, I'll call the hotel and see if we can get Sean's room back for the day. We can be back in The Hague in less than an hour." She grabbed the black, leather hold-all and hurried to catch up.

Sean smiled to himself. Knowing Sandy's brass, she'd be treating Angus Slooth like an old lost friend before the day was through. He patted the chair next to him, inviting George to sit. "So what's the take on Angus nearly getting you blown up," he asked.

"Long story," George replied. "But if I'm honest with you, I'm getting to quite like Detective Inspector Slooth. I had a little inheritance that nearly slipped away, but Slooth seems to have worked out that I'm still entitled to some."

"So you'll not be coming back to work then?"

"Yeah, sorry Sean, but—"

"Well that'll save me some money."

"Ah come on, Sean. That's not fair."

"Maybe not," Sean laughed, "but it's moderately accurate. Between you, Nick Ferris and a few other scallywags, I couldn't help noticing that my stainless steel reclamation skips never seemed to fill."

"Jesus H. Are you taking my name in vain again?" Nick asked, sitting opposite. "Hi George, what you doing here?"

"Did you get the dust out of your eye?" Sean asked.

"Yeah no problem, when do you fly, fly, fly."

"Bad echo in here," George said.

"Might be going by boat," Sean pronounced, smugly. "George needs to get home quicker than I do. He's just come into some money."

Nick raised his eyebrows. "What's the news then, George?"

"Ah, nothing, nothing," George replied, examining his fingernails. "Sean's a bit inclined to exaggerate."

"You mean you think Nick will wheedle some of it off you," Sean said, laughing aloud. He stood up. "I'll tell you what, I'll go and see how Sandy and Angus are getting on, and you two can swap notes about your inheritances. You know what I mean - you show me yours and I'll show you mine." He made to follow the others. "Better make sure there's no sharp knives lying around, though," he added, with a twinkle in his eye.

UNASHAMEDLY SELLING YOU SOMETHING…

Well that seems to have settled Sandy and Nick Ferris' lives down a little - or has it? And where will Sean Legg and Angus Slooth's lives take them now? I heard a rumour that Sean was thinking of going into politics. But maybe it was only rumour. The only way you'll ever find out is by reading Under the Rock, the third in the 'Manx Connection' series which finds us once more back on Manx soil. But will it stay that way for long?

ABOUT THE AUTHOR

Graham Hamer was born a few years before Queen Elizabeth came to the British throne (the second Queen Elizabeth, that is). One event was televised, one wasn't. His own event happened somewhere between England, Scotland, Ireland and Wales on a funny little island where the cats have no tails and the occasional witch still gets rolled down a steep hill in a spiked barrel. He left the Isle of Man to get a life. He got one. Then he went back. You'll find him there now if you know where to look.

Accountant, pig-herder (briefly), businessman, business analyst, web site builder – hell, writing's more fun.

The following 'Manx Connection' books are also available now or arriving soon...

Chasing Paper - Manx Connection #1

Walking on Water - Manx Connection #2

Under the Rock - Manx Connection #3

Out of the Window - Manx Connection #4

Magic in the Air - Manx Connection #5

China in Her Hand - Manx Connection #6

You can find out more about the author and

'The Manx Connection' books at

http://www.graham-hamer.com